BLOOD AND ROSES

MB PANICHI

2019

Bella Books, Inc.
P.O. Box 10543
Tallahassee, FL 32302

This is a work of fiction. Names, characters, businesses, places, events and incidents are either the products of the author's imagination or used in a fictitious manner. Any resemblance to actual persons, living or dead, or actual events is purely coincidental. The publisher does not have any control over and does not assume any responsibility for author or third-party websites or their content.

Printed in the United States of America on acid-free paper.

First Bella Books Edition 2019

Editor: Ann Roberts
Cover Designer: Sandy Knowles

ISBN: 978-1-64247-076-5

Other Bella Books by MB Panichi

Choosing Love
Running Toward Home
Saving Morgan

Acknowledgments

Thanks, always, to my readers, for giving me a chance to tell you my stories. I sincerely hope you've enjoyed the adventure.

Special thanks to the Minnesota Minions who helped me brainstorm through the initial plotting perils of this book—you guys rock! Also, to Lori, Patty, Linda (Hi, Scout!), and the Colony House retreats for the yearly jumpstart to keep me going, and everyone at GCLS for the inspiration to persevere.

Big huge thanks go out to Linda and Becky and Jessica and everyone at Bella for all their great work and support, and to my editor, Ann Roberts, for asking the right questions and helping me shape the words into a tighter stream.

Also a quick shout out to my buddy Mike who inspired SCE's venerable stage manager. Hugs to you, my friend!

And last, but never, ever least, thanks, love, and hugs to my wife, who puts up with my distraction and obsession. Thank you, Honey Bunny!!! You make my life worth living and bring out my better self. I love you forever!

Peace, Love, and Hugs to all…

About the Author

MB Panichi lives in Richfield, Minnesota in a little house on the corner with her wife and their three dogs. She has three previous books with Bella. In the same series as *Blood and Roses* she has *Saving Morgan* and its sequel, *Running Toward Home*, which are both Sci-Fi/Adventure/Romances. She also has a contemporary romance *Choosing Love*. In real life, MB holds down a day job as a Software QA Analyst to support her writing, drumming, and other obsessions. She's written about imaginary worlds all her life, and is unbelievably honored to be able to share her stories with her readers.

PROLOGUE

Earth Date: September 2453
Nor-Am Continent, near the St. Louis Metroplex

Ari

The music still echoed in my head as I crossed the courtyard between the recording studio and the townhouse where the band was staying. My fingers twitched while I mentally played through the guitar solos I'd recorded, dancing over the fretboard of my favorite guitar, bending the strings, making them scream out the emotions in my heart. I scrutinized the notes I'd immortalized. Should I have held the last one longer? Were the transitions clean enough? Did the bend in the middle work?

After five hours putting down two solos and half a dozen overdubbed tracks, I was physically exhausted and brain fried. I'd listen to the tracks again tomorrow with fresh ears. As my bandmates so often reminded me, I needed to relax and chill.

I trudged along the cobblestone path through the deserted courtyard. A deep quiet had settled over the securely walled compound of Tyrannus Studios. Stars sprinkled across the blue-black sky which held only a hint of the deep, cold blackness of outer space. Growing up in the mineral mining and processing facilities in the Asteroid Belt, I was accustomed to the stars being practically within arm's reach.

I shifted my grip on my guitar case and peered toward the darkened townhouse. Security lights at the door and along the walk lit my way with a soft golden glow. The path rambled through a scruffy lawn of desert grass accented with cacti.

I took the cutoff to the townhouse and climbed the three wide stairs. The front door slid open when I passed my hand over the palm reader beside the doorframe and stepped inside.

The foyer light barely lit the entryway while a dim floor lamp in the corner of the living room pushed shadows around. I leaned my battered guitar case against the couch and headed into the kitchen. Recessed, green-tinted lighting over the sink and back counter provided barely enough light to see, but I didn't need much. All I wanted to do was grab a mug of tea, take it to my room, and crash.

The dark bulk of a bouquet of flowers rested in the center of the dining room table. I wondered if Nori had stolen them from the garden on the other side of the courtyard and if we were going to get bitched at because of it.

With a shake of my head, I chose a mug, set it under the beverage dispenser and tapped in my request for tea. As the machine gurgled and poured, I glanced back at the table. The blinking light from the dispenser skittered off the flowers. The petals, leaves, and the table beneath glistened wetly. Curious, I said, "Lights, bright." I reached for my filled mug and then glanced back toward the table.

Thick red liquid droplets splattered across a bouquet of black roses and dripped down the sides of the crystal vase, puddling on the table. A stained white notecard rested among the roses. My stomach twisted with sick fear, but I couldn't help leaning in to read the handwritten message on the card.

Arienne, my love, if I can't have you, nobody can. Enjoy the flowers, my sweet musician. I am thinking of you. Always. And I will know if you've forsaken me. – Yours, Forever, Celestian

My whole body trembled. My stalker had found me again.

CHAPTER ONE

Earth Date: May 2453 (four months earlier)
Nor-Am Continent, Central Los Angeles Megalopolis

Ari

I picked the plas-sheet letter off the pile of fan mail in front of me and pushed it across the kitchen table toward my best friend and bass player, Nori Beaty. "Check this out. I think this one is nuts."

Nori sipped a cup of caf and read the message out loud in an overly dramatic voice. "Arienne, I would die for you. When you look at the camera, I know you look only at me. Your eyes haunt my every waking moment. I dream of you when I sleep. When you're on stage, I know you play for me alone. Your hands, caressing your guitar, are caressing my body, playing me and making me scream and beg like nobody else can. I am forever yours. Celestian." Nori looked up, making a sour face. "Yup. This one is certifiable."

I tucked a few loose strands of straight brown hair behind my ears. Weird fan mail wasn't unusual. We'd all gotten our fair share of love notes, marriage proposals and declarations of devotion. Our band, Shattered Crystal Enigma, was well known in slam-thrash circles. We'd sold a lot of recordings, regularly filled concert venues and had a solid following. We had plenty of freak fans.

But this Celestian pushed the limits. I said, "This is the fifth or sixth message I've gotten in the last couple months. It's starting to seriously creep me out."

"Did you tell Wayne?"

"No." I didn't want to whine to our manager about some bizarre fan. Over the years, I'd gotten love notes from prison inmates and lonely soldiers, and scathing fire-and-brimstone lectures and threats from angry religious zealots. This one felt different though, if only because of the persistence. "I saved the last few letters, just in case."

"Go with your gut. If it feels weird, then pass it on to Wayne. It's his job to deal with this kind of crap."

I sighed. "Not like a bunch of stupid messages are going to hurt me, you know? It's only words. If all they do is send me a bunch of creepy love notes, it's not a big deal."

Nori stood and refilled her thermal mug. "It's a little like the guy who was sending crap to Toni last year from his prison cell. He was a maniac. But at least we knew he was behind bars for life." She tapped a finger on the message. "You don't know anything about this one."

A sick feeling twisted my guts. "True."

"So, send them to Wayne and let him worry about it."

"Yeah. I will." It was the safest route, and if it turned out to be nothing, I was no worse off.

"Where the hell is everyone? I thought we were rehearsing this afternoon?" Nori glanced at the chron on the wall.

"Toni and Dia are on their way but got held up in traffic. They were at Guitar Emporium because Dia heard they released a new sound module for her amp."

Nori laughed. "Ten to one she comes home with a new toy."

"She's such a gear hound." Unlike my bandmates, I didn't buy a lot of equipment anymore. I had tried and true sounds that defined my style and worked for me. If I updated my sound or my amps, it was because the music called for it or something was broken beyond repair.

I hadn't bought a new guitar in years. A few scratches marred my favorite's deep blue surface and some of the wood-grain finish was worn, but she sang under my fingers and felt good in my hands. Our sponsors gave us guitars to try from time to time when new models came out. I used them for vids and as backups on stage, but when it came down to it, I reached for my baby.

The front door opened and Dia and Toni strode into the living room of the open-design house.

"Honey, we're home!" Dia may have stood at barely a meter sixty-two, but she was a little powerhouse. Her wild black hair was tied back with colorful scarves and she wore a skimpy, multicolored silk blouse knotted just under her breasts, a short black skirt, and high-heeled, calf-height black boots.

Lead singer Toni Catone loomed over Dia at nearly two meters tall, even wearing low work boots. Dark skinned with liquid chocolate eyes and multicolored dreads hanging nearly to her waist, Toni intimidated in a skintight black tank and loose-cut black cargo shorts.

Nori said, "What'd you buy, Dee?"

Dia dumped a box and a bag on the coffee table in front of the sofa, smugly polishing her fingernails over her shirt as she crossed to the kitchen. "Custom programmable Jo Scarrel Sound Module, V21A, with multiphase inputs and triplex output. It's totally sweet. I want to use it for the studio. Ric's gonna swoon." She took a glass from the cupboard, set it under the beverage dispenser and tapped in her request.

"All we need is the engineers drooling all over the sound board." Toni draped her long body into the kitchen chair next to mine.

Nori looked at me. "Told ya she'd come home with toys."

Dia flipped me a petulant glare. "At least all the cool kids love me."

Toni snickered. "Get me an ale, Dia?" She glanced around. "Stacy's not here yet?"

I hated to be the bearer of bad news, and I wanted to think the best of our erstwhile drummer, but it was getting harder and harder to excuse her increasingly destructive behavior. "I reminded her we were rehearsing, but she went out with a couple of her friends. Didn't sound like she'd be back tonight."

"Not if she was going to Central LA," Dia said.

Toni took a couple swallows of the ale Dia put in front of her. "We're recording in two weeks. We can't afford to waste time in the studio working stuff out. She better not be fucking hungover tomorrow if she doesn't show tonight."

Nori muttered, "I'm getting tired of her crap."

"She's a great drummer," I said.

Nori scowled. "Doesn't do us any good if she's too fucked up to play."

"She's getting worse," Toni added. "Used to be only once in a while. Now, every couple weeks she's partying and too out of it to practice. We're finally getting somewhere, getting some real recognition. We need her with us one hundred percent."

Nori nodded emphatically. "We're all working our asses off. She needs to do the same and quit coasting."

I had to agree. The music we wrote continued to become more complex. "I feel like we're losing her, but I don't understand why."

Nori stood up and snapped impatiently, "She's got a problem with intoxicants. We've been watching it happen for months and pretending it will go away. But it won't unless we confront her and she takes responsibility for it."

I knew Nori spoke from personal experience. She'd been sober for over a decade, but I remembered all too well when she'd hit rock bottom after we graduated out of basics school. I'd stood by her through rehab and the rocky, difficult years afterward, when we started to dream of this band. We were an item for a while, but eventually realized we made better friends than lovers.

"Are you talking about doing an intervention?" Dia asked.

Toni said, "She's gonna freak if we confront her as a group."

"It's going to keep getting worse unless we do," Nori pointed out. "It sucks. But if we want this, and we want her with us, she needs to get her shit under control."

I dreaded the confrontation, but said, "I think Nori's right."

"When?" Toni asked.

Nori said, "Tomorrow, at rehearsal."

"Are you sure?" Dia asked.

"Yes. Let me start it. Follow my lead."

Toni chewed her bottom lip. "You've been thinking about this for a while."

"I have. A lot."

"Do you think it will work?" Dia asked.

"I don't know. I hope so."

Toni asked, "What happens when she freaks out?"

"I don't know."

Toni rubbed the back of her neck. "Do we want to risk it this close to studio time? We can't afford to lose her right now, issues or no issues."

Toni had a point. She was practical, as always. I wanted to do the right thing for Stacy, but whether it was right for the band at this point was another question. Stacy's destructive behavior was escalating, but we couldn't afford to screw up this studio session. Professionally we needed the new release to be mind-blowing. And when we finished recording, the tour had to be equally amazing. Trying to find a new drummer right now was potentially disastrous.

"I think I'm with Toni on this one," Dia said. "I'd hate for her to freak out and quit or self-destruct right now. Let's get the album recorded before we confront her."

Nori focused her stare on me, raising a dark brow. I ran my fingers back through my hair, twisting a few strands idly as I considered our options. What was the best thing to do? This band was my dream and I didn't want to throw it away when we were so close. "I think we need to wait," I said finally, knowing it wasn't the answer Nori wanted to hear. Nori felt strongly about confronting Stacy, but for the immediate future, keeping the band in one piece seemed more important.

The following afternoon I sat on the edge of my chair in our rehearsal space, running warm-up scales on my guitar. I was alone in the soundproofed room at the back of the house. The floor-to-ceiling windows looked out on a small yard surrounded by high fencing. Short, thick grass surrounded the patio and a rectangular swimming pool. The sun glinted off the still, blue-green water and light flooded the quiet rehearsal space. I hadn't powered up my amps or the wireless connection from my guitar. I preferred doing warm-ups without amplification. Nori called it my Zen time, when I relaxed into the space, warming up my fingers and focusing my brain on playing.

I generally wrote and learned my parts separate from the band, ironing out solos and cleaning up tricky transitions outside rehearsals. I hated wasting everyone else's time. Rehearsal was for putting all the pieces together, especially with recording sessions scheduled in a couple weeks. Studio time cost big money and the more time we spent preparing, the less money the record label needed to spend on studio time. The money we saved laying tracks would cover post-production that could make or break the release.

The studio door opened and Nori and Toni strolled in. Toni turned on the PA, checked her mic and organized plas-sheets of lyrics on her music stand.

Nori grabbed her bass and powered up her amp. "Dia's right behind us. Stacy just got home. I imagine she'll be down soon."

I let the last bit of news flow past me. Stacy hadn't made it home last night, so whether she was in any state to rehearse was yet to be seen. I hoped she wasn't too hungover. I sucked in a long breath and let it out slowly, deciding not to get angry about something I couldn't fix. I flipped on my amps, feeling the low buzz in my chest as the dual heads powered up. I killed the volume on my guitar and continued running warm-up scales and exercises.

A few minutes later, Dia strode in and headed straight for her guitars with a "Hey guys," tossed in greeting. Three of her favorite guitars were lined up in a multi-stand. She grabbed one and flipped the power switch on her amp, pausing to watch the lights across the front flash from red to green before she sat on the folding chair to the right of her speaker stack.

Stacy wandered in about five minutes later, silently glancing around as she slipped behind her drums. Dark circles stained the skin under her eyes. Her hair was pulled back into a messy tail and her clothes rumpled. On the upside, she didn't appear to be either stoned out of her mind or falling down intoxicated as she switched on the pre-amp that pushed her drums' signal to the main PA.

Her kit was made up of electronic pads for the drums and cymbals. She had a ton of top-of-the-line sound mods programmed. Only the richest of the rich could afford to use real acoustic drums anymore, and the electronics were easier to mix into the band's overall sound. Stacy tapped out a few beats as her power came up, flipping through the sound controls until she found what she wanted. She rattled off a quick riff around the twenty or so pads mounted on adjustable arms extending from a tubular rack. Her feet danced in sync on six footpads laid out on the floor. The solid thunk of bass drums rumbled through my chest. No doubt about it, Stacy had some serious chops. She made it look effortless as her drumsticks traveled across the matte-black surfaces of the trigger pads while her feet moved in tandem.

It only reminded me more forcefully why we needed her right now, despite her flaws.

Toni cleared her throat into the mic. "Okay, let's start at the top of the set list and work our way down. Stop if you hear something that's not working so we can clean it up. Stacy, count us off."

Stacy slashed at the hi-hat pad for a four-count and we launched into the first tune. I plucked out the intricate opening riff, and then tapped a couple foot pedals, changing my tones as I joined Dia on the chord progression for the verse while Toni's growling voice blasted through the PA. We transitioned smoothly from the verse to the chorus and back again, but when we hit the odd time signature in the bridge, Stacy blundered the transition and the rhythm stuttered and hesitated for a couple beats before dropping into place.

Toni signaled a stop.

Into the resulting quiet, Stacy muttered, "Sorry. I got it."

Nori slid Stacy an irritated frown. "Start again at the chorus."

Stacy counted off and we picked up and played through the transition without any issues. We'd worked on it before and I knew Stacy could play it. I tried to focus on my own playing, but Nori's annoyed energy grated against me.

Fortunately, the tensions between Nori, Toni, and Stacy evened out. We cleaned up some changes we'd been working on, played through the set list, and after about three hours called it done. I flipped off my amps and took my time wiping down my guitar. The deep royal blue woodgrain body was scuffed, the finish worn and dulled where my arm rested across her angular top, the pick board scratched and the smooth wood of the fretboard stained by oils from my fingers. Her electronics had been updated over the years, but the way she played, the way she felt, hadn't changed. She fit perfectly in my hands, comfortable and reassuring.

Nori was wiping down her bass with a soft cloth when Stacy stopped in front of her, waiting until Nori looked up.

Stacy's expression was challenging. "If you have something to say to me, say it."

Nori's expression remained bland. "Your use of intoxicants concerns me."

"Great. Thanks for caring. My use of intoxicants is none of your fucking business."

"It is if it affects your playing."

"My playing is fine. Get over yourself, Nori. Just because you have a problem using doesn't mean we all do."

Everyone in the room stopped. I held my breath.

Nori's jaw clenched. "At least I deal with my problem. I know I'm an addict. You, on the other hand, need to start dealing with yours before it destroys you."

"Fuck you. I don't have a problem, so stay out of my life."

Stacy stomped away, brushing roughly past Toni to get out the door.

Dia said, "Well, that was fun."

Nori glanced at us with an irritated frown. "I told you. She's a powder keg waiting to explode."

Toni said, "We need to get through this recording session."

I kept my silence. I saw both sides. Either way, it wasn't good and a sick feeling twisted my stomach. I gently secured my guitar into her worn but well-padded touring case.

Dia said, "I'll talk to her and explain we're worried about the sessions going smoothly."

"Let her cool down first," Toni advised.

"Sure. I'm gonna go get something to eat." Dia left the room and Toni followed her.

I considered Nori, who still sat with her bass in her hands, glaring at the floor. "You okay, Nor?"

"This is not going to get any better, whether Dia talks to her or not."

I had no good answer to that, and I felt the threads of our band's fabric starting to unravel. "It'll all work out, one way or another." Maybe I was hoping to make myself feel better.

We scattered to our own rooms after rehearsal. Stacy took off again without talking to anyone or saying when she'd be back. Not that we were her keepers, but my uneasiness increased, worrying that one of these times she simply wouldn't return, whether it was because she overdosed, decided to leave the band, or got into trouble she couldn't handle. The implications rattled in the back of my head.

After stowing my guitar in my room, I shucked my clothes and pulled a thigh-length, long-sleeve cover-up over my head. Grabbing my comp pad from the nightstand and a beach towel from the closet, I wandered through the living room and out the sliding glass door into the backyard.

The relentless Los Angeles sun baked the patio and pool. It was early evening, and the heat index was well over thirty-eight degrees Celsius. The glassteel awning fully covering the backyard was set to a clear but blurring opacity, letting in most of the sun's heat and light while keeping out curious eyes. The panel slid out on runners extending from the roof of the two-story house, high enough over the full-story fencing to let in a breeze.

I was glad for the extra privacy, since we tended to nudity around the pool if we didn't have guests. It was one of the highlights of living in a house with only women.

Dia was the only one who brought any guys around, and she was always careful to warn us. Stacy never brought anyone home, though it was common knowledge she hooked up outside the house often enough. And if Nori, Toni, or I ever brought home a date, it was another woman, so not a problem.

I stepped onto the concrete patio, burned the bottoms of my bare feet, and jumped over to the thick, coarse grass.

Dia floated on her back in the pool and lifted a hand to acknowledge me. Her long black hair fanned out in the water. Nori lay face down on a lounge chair at the edge of the pool, leaning on her elbows to read her comp pad. Her smooth latte-colored skin showed no tan lines. She looked up and grinned. "Hey, Ari, you made *Hard Core Guitar* magazine again."

"Yeah? What's it say?" I made my way across the grass toward the pool, leaving my comp pad and towel on a lounge chair and stripping off my cover-up.

Nori said, "Jo Lupine's going on and on about the show at Mystique last week. Did she corner you there again?"

I rolled my eyes. Jo Lupine was a pain-in-the-ass fan and reporter who had a thing for me and made no attempt to hide it. She was obnoxious and rude and I avoided her as much as I could. Unfortunately, she was persistent. "Yeah. She was grilling me about the new songs and when we were going to be in the studio, and trying to get free show tickets, which I didn't offer. I practically had to slap her hands off me."

Dia said, "Good goddess."

Nori continued reading. "She's going on about how you're this magnetic force on stage. Ha! And then she writes, and I quote, 'But does this amazing specimen of hard-core perfection have a special someone she's hiding? Her heart-rending lyrics would suggest it, but Ari Walker insists there is nobody in her life but her beloved guitar, and her focus is solely on her music. Sorry, ladies, this hot rocker is not on the market!'"

I groaned. "Ugh."

"Glad she's not obsessed with me," Nori said.

"Lucky you."

I stepped to the edge of the pool and dove in, reveling in the feel of the cool water enveloping my bare skin. I swam to the surface, stretched out and lazily breaststroked the length of the pool. The water sluiced over my skin, exhilarating, cooling and calming all at the same time. It reminded me of the weightlessness of space, one of the few things I missed from my childhood.

The patio door opened, releasing the heavy strains of slam-thrash music along with the aroma of spicy cooking.

Toni poked her nose out. "Hey, anyone want some stir-fry?"

Nori said, "If you're cooking, absolutely!"

"I'm in." Dia swam for the pool's ladder.

My stomach growled and I rolled over in the water. "Save some for me."

I did a few more laps then climbed out. I padded across the hot cement to the chair and picked up the towel, drying my hair and wrapping it around my body as I entered the air-conditioned living room.

Tunes were cranked up. I recognized the latest demo release from a group of guys we'd played with locally a few times. Toni pushed a bowl of stir-fry across the counter toward me as I settled on the stool beside Nori, who gleefully spoke through a mouthful of food, "You rock, Tone. This is great."

Toni leaned against the opposite side of the breakfast bar with her own bowl. "I'm sure you guys would starve without me." The door buzzer sounded over the music.

"Expecting anyone?" Toni asked. We all shook our heads. Toni ran an appraising eye over us. Nori was stark naked. Dia and I had short towels wrapped around our bodies. "Guess since I'm the only one dressed, I'll check the door."

She slipped from the kitchen and crossed the living room, keying the security screen at the side of the door, "Hello?"

I watched as I chewed, knowing multiple camera views would be scrolling across the palm-sized screen above the control panel.

Nori asked, "Who is it?"

"Whoever it was is gone."

Dia grumbled, "Damned neighbor kids doing ring and runs."

I pushed away from the breakfast bar and joined Toni at the door. She flipped through the camera views and stopped on the overhead camera in front of the door. A red envelope rested on the doorstep. "Looks like someone got fan mail," she said.

I stepped back and Toni palmed the lock. As soon as the door slid partially open, she grabbed the envelope and shut and locked the door again. She turned it over. "It's for you, Ari."

My stomach clenched sickly and I wished I hadn't eaten. I was still getting weird net mail from Celestian. Attempts to send cease and desist notices had bounced back, address unknown. I sucked in a steadying breath and took the envelope from Toni, tearing the plastic strip to open it. My fingers shook as I removed a red, folded plas-sheet and saw the cursive silver handwriting.

My sweet Arienne; I miss you. You haven't been out in a while. Are you hiding from me? You are the light in my life. I ache and I burn for you. You have such a beautiful body. I long to touch you, to run my hands over your gentle curves. I wish I were the water in your swimming pool, able to consume you whole and caress every centimeter of your skin. Forever and Always Yours, Celestian.

The plas-sheet and envelope slipped from my grip, fluttering to the floor. I wrapped my arms around myself, feeling horribly exposed and vulnerable. I needed to find my clothes. I needed a blanket and my bedroom, and no windows to the outside world.

Toni picked up the letter, her eyes widening as she read. Dia and Nori joined us.

Nori scanned the plas-sheet. "What a freak."

Dia said, "I'm checking the security vids to see if anyone shows up." She stalked to the desk in the corner and logged into the main house computer. The vid screen on the living room wall duplicated the monitor on the desk with several feeds from the video security system, showing views around the outside of the property.

Dia let the previous quarter hour play back. We stared at the monitor. Toni leaned over Dia's shoulder and Nori rubbed my back. I leaned into her, needing the comfort and the warmth.

"There!" Dia stopped the feed from the front door camera, bringing it forward and enlarging the window. She backed it up a few seconds and then let it play again in slow motion. A few seconds in, the red envelope appeared out of thin air and floated slowly down to rest on the concrete of the entryway. It didn't fall. It didn't flutter. The movement seemed deliberate. The envelope was suspended in midair and set on the stoop as if by magic.

"What the hell?"

"Look really close." Dia paused the feed. She stepped forward and traced her finger along the vid screen. "Look. It's kind of wavery, like an outline."

"But an outline of what?" Toni squinted and moved closer to the monitor.

Dia said, "A person. In a chameleon suit. I've seen it on spy shows. It bends light around so whoever is wearing it is virtually invisible against any background."

"I really, really don't like this." I shuddered and swallowed hard in an attempt not to throw up. How long had this person been hiding, watching us? Seeing me swim naked? Looking in our windows? I heard what sounded very much like a whimper, and realized it was me.

Nori pulled me into a tight embrace. "We need to call the police and then call Wayne and let him know what's going on."

Toni said, "Save the vids. But, honestly, I doubt the police will do anything."

CHAPTER TWO

Earth Date: June 2453
Moon Base Domed City

Rhynn

Drummer Rhynn Knight leaned against the matte black wall of the music club, swirling the dark green liquid in her glass. Heavy, throbbing rhythms and crunching guitar riffs assaulted her ears and reverberated in her chest. She rested one elbow on a high-top table, letting the tensions of a long workday ease out of her shoulders as the music rolled through her chest and the alcohol pumped through her veins.

Nightwalker was her favorite local slam-thrash band. Club Tranquility was her favorite hangout, as well as the best concert venue on Moon Base. She loved the driving music, the lights, and the boisterous fans. In a little while she'd join the gang slamming in the two-story high zero gravity cube to the side of the dance floor. But for the time being, she was content to watch her friends' band and absorb the frenetic energy.

On the dance floor in front of the stage, her girlfriend Britt danced by herself and flirted with everyone. Her long red hair whipped around her head as she spun. Rhynn supposed Britt's constant flirting with other women should have bothered her, but the only emotion she managed to dredge up was a slight irritation.

Britt sang lead in a slam-thrash band, though not Rhynn's, and her brash aggression on stage usually crossed into her offstage life as well. Rhynn accepted Britt's attitude, took it in stride. They'd been dating for nearly a year.

"You're gonna lose her, Rhynny."

Rhynn glanced across the table at the tall blonde glaring at the dance floor. Her roommate and bandmate Leigh downed the last of her drink and slammed the glass on the tabletop. "Your girlfriend is a bitch."

Rhynn shrugged. She knew at some point Britt would get tired of her. Someone else would be sexier, more interesting, more doting. Britt wanted Rhynn because she was the available rock star of the hour. Rhynn's band, Black Plague, was riding a wave of popularity in the slam-thrash community and she was friends with the guys in Nightwalker, so she had some clout.

She didn't pretend to be in love with Britt and she knew Britt wasn't in love with her. The sex was good. They got along. She was willing to leave well enough alone. Leigh reminded her constantly that she could do better, but it wasn't like there was a wealth of prospects in the limited population of Moon Base.

Leigh waved down a waitress and ordered refills. Nightwalker finished their second set, and a theater-size vid screen dropped in front of the stage and announced the upcoming concert by Shattered Crystal Enigma, an all-female slam-thrash band—Rhynn's favorite band of all time. SCE would be coming to Moon Base in a few months and Nightwalker was slated to be the opening band—the lucky bastards.

Rhynn almost cheered when one of SCE's live concert videos started. The camera locked in on the lead guitarist and Rhynn felt her heart race. Ari Walker was so intense, so focused. Her fingers moved up and down the fretboard with careless ease. She was an accomplished guitarist and songwriter.

The band's other guitarist, Dia Caban, jogged crossed the stage, and she and Ari played a riff together. Ari broke into a huge smile and the camera captured her joy as she and Dia leaned together to fire off an intricate run of notes.

Rhynn fixated on the vid screen, completely captured. Ari was breathtaking. Straight brown hair hung past her shoulders as she stalked toward center stage, casually handling her guitar until she stopped, head down, shredding like a master, her fingers a blur on the screen. Some people fell in love with movie stars. Rhynn had fallen in love with Ari Walker.

Leigh bumped her shoulder. "You're drooling!"

"I got my tickets for the show so I can drool in person."

"They are so going to rock this place."

"No doubt."

* * *

"Another day, another slice of the salary pie, huh, Rhynn?"

Rhynn looked away from the monitor on her desk to watch her workmate Krys fold his long, skinny body into the chair at the desk next to her own. "Something like that. You're late."

He snorted. "Things got a little crazy last night. Hell, you were at the club too. Weren't you drinking?"

"Apparently not as much as you. Besides, this is second shift. What the hell time did you get home?"

"About an hour ago. The after-party was at Luke's."

"You're a dumbass."

He laughed as he logged into his terminal.

Rhynn glanced around the room full of low cubicles and desks to see if anyone else had noticed Krys straggle in, but everyone had their heads buried in their own work. Sighing, she returned her focus to the bland drudgery of verifying account entries. Krys may not be worried about getting laid off or fired, but she couldn't afford to be so nonchalant. She was too practical to push her luck with the whims of upper management. Lately there'd been rumors about budget cuts and "re-orgs." She'd gotten caught in that bullshit enough times to know to keep her head down and hope for the best.

Krys was an idiot to flout his lack of responsibility, but he was a decent enough guy. They had mutual friends; it was hard not to in a place like Moon Base. Transients came and went, but regulars who'd lived and worked there for more than a couple years, ended up knowing each other, at least in passing. She'd grown up here. Krys had been on Moon Base a year or so. She didn't think he'd stay much longer. Most people didn't.

She'd considered moving Earthside and trying something new, but she never got around to it. She had a comfortable life. Her mom lived here. She had a decent job, a band, friends. Moving to Earth would be more hassle than she needed.

Rhynn glanced down at her personal comp pad as it blinked awake on her desk. The room hummed with the click of keyboards and muted conversations. Leigh's avatar popped up on the comp pad's screen. The cartoonish and over-exaggerated image of a female thrash-metal fan waved silently, trying to get Rhynn's attention. She was drawn with heavy black eye shadow and short spiked hair. Heavy chains draped around her neck and waist.

Rhynn scanned the office. Nobody was paying her any attention, so she tapped out a quick text reply. "At work. What's up?"

Leigh's avatar rolled its eyes. Text scrolled across the screen. "This is HUGE! You want a gig on October thirty-first?"

Rhynn typed, "No way. SCE show."

"You wanna open for SCE and Nightwalker?"

Excitement surged and Rhynn nearly jumped up from her seat. Her fingers danced on the pad screen's keyboard. *R u shitting me? Seriously? SCE?*

YES!

Holy fuck!

I know! Jose from Tranquility called to book the gig. I said yes! Leigh's avatar twirled around waving her hands. *Gotta go, I'm at work too! Later!*

Rhynn stared at the screen as Leigh's avatar grayed out and disappeared. Holy lunar hells! Opening for SCE? For real? Her heart pounded practically out of her chest. And then she wondered if Leigh was scamming her.

Another avatar popped up, this one a black wolf with glittering ice-blue eyes. The text scrolled in bright blue block letters.

SCE!!! Can u believe it?

Rhynn recognized her lead singer Vicki's avatar and knew Leigh wasn't playing jokes, because Vicki would literally kick Leigh's ass over a joke like this. Rhynn typed back, *Insane!*

Krys muttered under his breath, "What's going on? Tone down the silent excitement, man. Colter's back."

Rhynn blanked the comp pad screen with a flick of her finger and forced herself to appear calm and focused on her work. She didn't dare gooseneck to see where their department head, Orren Colter, was standing. She imagined him hovering in the back of the room, arms crossed, beady eyes staring daggers into the backs of anyone who didn't look busy. If he caught her communicating with her friends on work time, he'd dock her pay and write her up. If she didn't get her accounts cleared by the end of the day, he'd either dump more work into her queue or read her the riot act about time-sensitive data, the company's bottom line, shareholder value, blah, blah, blah. Three concurrent abuses and she'd be looking for a new job.

The spreadsheet data blurred on the monitor as her mind wandered. She thought about the video of SCE she'd seen the night before. She couldn't believe her band was going to open for Shattered Crystal Enigma. She wondered if they'd get to meet the band. She could admit to herself it was all about Ari Walker. She'd probably faint on the spot if the woman even looked at her. Lunar hells, this was going to be unbelievable.

CHAPTER THREE

Earth Date: August 2453
Nor-Am Continent, Central Los Angeles Megalopolis

Ari

I remained in our rehearsal space long after Nori, Dia, and Toni had given up and left. The pall of their anger and frustration remained behind. Stacy hadn't shown up for practice and tonight was our last chance for rehearsal before we left for Tyrannus Studios. We had finally moved up far enough in the ranks of thrash bands to be able to record with Ric Orrechek, one of the industry's most notable producers. He'd spawned more hit songs and album releases than any other producer in the hard core and slam metal genres. We couldn't afford to throw away this opportunity or show up unprepared.

A perfectionist, I shoved aside my lingering ill will toward Stacy and worked on my guitar solos. I jacked my pad into the mixer and played a rehearsal recording of "Lullaby for Nikita" over the PA. Chording under the verse, I weaved my lead lines into the mesh of the arrangement. Melody and countermelody wound around Toni's vocals and Dia's chord progressions until I launched into the solo. All the pain of Nikita's emotional abuse poured from my fingers to make my guitar cry out her anguish, ending the song with a scream of feedback that faded into the plaintive wail of a bending chord.

Letting a long breath out into the silence after the chord faded, I killed the volume on my guitar. Catching a hint of movement to my left, I glanced toward the door. Stacy stood just inside, leaning against the frame.

She raised a tentative hand. "Hey."

I took in her dilated pupils and slightly panicked expression. "Hey, yourself. Rehearsal was a couple hours ago. Everyone else is gone."

"I lost track of time."

"Your timing kinda sucks, Stace."

"I'm really sorry."

I slouched back on my chair, suddenly very tired. "Everyone's pretty pissed off at you right now."

"Are they home?"

"Toni might be. Dia and Nori were making a food run."

"Okay." Stacy shifted on her feet, gave me an apologetic look and left.

I sat in silence, pondering how recording would go if Stacy remained on her downhill slide. Maybe her behavior would even out until we'd finished the release. While we recorded, we would be sequestered at the Tyrannus Studios compound, in the middle of nowhere, far from the city and Stacy's partying friends. That might keep her in line, but how would she handle the tour afterward?

The desire to play slipped away. I turned off my amp and the PA, wiped down my guitar, put her in her case, and left the studio. Trudging down the hallway, I stepped into the living room and kitchen area. Recessed lights lit the kitchen and living room with a dull yellow blush. Beyond the patio doors, the low flames of scattered tiki lights shimmered in the pool, but nobody was outside.

I retrieved a thermal bottle from the cupboard and got a fizzy cola. I paused to look at the pool and shivered. The water was enticing, but as much as I wanted a swim, no way was I going outside, in the dark—alone—even in my own backyard.

Celestian, whoever the hell he or she was, was still out there. Still watching me. I'd gotten another email a couple days ago. They declared their love with the familiar hint of a threat in the words. The message came from a public com unit with a spoofed net address and an anonymous guest account. I didn't even know if Celestian was male or female.

I hadn't gone to the clubs and hadn't been out to the pool unless I was wearing shorts and a swim shirt. I wanted to say fuck it and do my thing, but the thought of being on display made me nauseous and anxious. I left my bedroom window shaded day and night and avoided passing too close to the patio doors if I was home alone.

After the letter had been left on our front porch, the police had taken our statements and collected the envelope and letter as evidence. Nothing identifying showed on our security videos. The vague outline they were able to discern suggested a small man or a woman, but they didn't find any forensic material on the front entryway or the envelope and note. My case remained open. There were a few more patrols in our neighborhood. It didn't make me feel any safer. I retreated to my room with my cola. I needed to finish packing for our two-week stay at the Tyrannus studio compound. In the morning, we would load the trailer and pile into our air-van for the ten-hour journey across the Southwest desert and the arid lower Midwest plains.

I stepped into the bedroom I shared with Nori and closed the door. The lights came up automatically. Dim lamps under each of the two lofted beds lit the room with a soft glow. Under my bed I fit a narrow dresser, a student desk piled with music notebooks, and a stand for my guitars. An open suitcase rested on the floor, surrounded by the clothes and personal items that would eventually be packed inside.

I considered the array of stuff, trying to decide what else I needed. Next to the suitcase, my hard-sided backpack was already filled with song notes and lyric sheets. I'd need to add my comp pad and an extra set of earbuds.

A knock on the door startled me. I spun around, heart pounding.

Toni's dreadlocked head popped in. "Hey."

I closed my eyes and took a shaky breath, willing the panic to subside. "Shit, you scared me."

"Sorry. I talked to Stacy."

"She stopped in the rehearsal space when I was there."

Toni flopped into the worn memory-form chair under Nori's loft. The soft cushions hugged her long, rangy body. "What'd she tell you?"

"Not much. Said she was sorry she was late. I wasn't going to argue."

Toni said flatly, "She's still stoned."

I nodded my agreement but held my silence; I didn't feel like initiating a pointless venting session.

"I told her she'd better fucking well be on top of her game in the studio. She said she knew that and not to worry about it." Toni twisted one of her waist-length dreads around her fingers. "I think we need to start thinking very seriously about replacing her."

I plucked my favorite hoodie from a drawer and added it to my suitcase. "I don't want to think about it until after the recording."

"I don't know anyone I want to work with, anyway. And I don't want a guy in the band."

I agreed on the last part, for sure. I liked the dynamic of an all-female group. "Shirry Lorel is okay."

Toni wrinkled her nose. "Key word—okay. She thinks she's a lot better than she is."

"True."

"Wayne's gonna push for a guy because that'd make it a lot easier to find someone, and he's going to want a quick replacement if we fire Stacy."

"Wayne can stick it up his ass."

Toni laughed. "Damn, I love you, girl." She stood. "You hungry? I was gonna make some dinner if you're interested."

"Sure."

"Great." She grabbed me by the hand and pulled me out the door. "In that case, you can cut up veggies."

CHAPTER FOUR

Earth Date: September 2453
Nor-Am Continent, Mid-Continental Desert, Tyrannus Studios Compound
Studio day 3

Ari

The plan was to spend the first week in the studio laying down all the basic tracks and making changes based on Ric's input. He had a ton of great ideas and a well-defined overall vision for how he wanted to produce our work. It was a vision we were ecstatic about, creating an album both heavier and darker than our previous releases, but with more nuance and subtlety.

Being in the studio is no vacation. It's grueling both physically and mentally to be on top of your game all the time. Time is money, and even if Wayne thought we were the next up-and-coming "big thing," the record label wasn't willing to give us carte blanche to take all the time we wanted, so we had a tight schedule.

On the third day, we ended our recording session earlier in the evening than planned because Wayne had set up an interview with one of our favorite fanzine reporters, J'Nell Inagayl.

J'Nell wrote for a major music fanzine posted on the net, and her byline was often re-posted by the smaller fan sites. I knew

J'Nell when we were kids. Her family had lived for a while at the same asteroid mining facility as my mom and me. Her dad was ex-Earth Guard military and had taken a position in Security with Mann-Maru. It had been her first time living in one of the cramped mining colonies that combined ore mining and processing along with workers' living facilities into one ugly sprawling structure.

J'Nell and I had bonded quickly over a mutual love of music. I'd taken her under my wing, glad to have another girl my age to hang out with. J'Nell had been relieved to find a friend at another of her dad's transitory postings. There weren't that many kids at the facility, and most were either much younger than me, or just didn't get my obsession with music and my guitar. J'Nell had seemed to understand, and I'd been grateful to have a real friend even though it wasn't long before her family moved to a different facility.

We kept in touch off and on over the years. She'd gotten into journalism, at first working for military news sites through her father's contacts at Earth Guard, then shifting to general entertainment reporting after a job featuring how Earth Guard's Service Organization provided entertainment to the scattered troops of the Guard.

We met again in person when Shattered Crystal Enigma had just gotten together. I ran into her at a club where she was reviewing the bands for a slam-thrash show we were playing. We renewed our friendship and she became one of our staunchest supporters.

At the band house at Tyrannus Studios, everyone spread out on the worn faux-leather couch and a couple mismatched lounge chairs. Toni passed out bottles of beer and collapsed onto the sofa next to me. I slouched into the form-molding cushions and took a long swallow of the cold liquid. "Thanks, T."

She slammed half of hers. "Ahhhhhh. That's good."

"Great job today, you guys," Nori said. "We got a ton done, and it's sounding great."

Toni said, "I need to give my voice a break. Might not have too much to say when J'Nell calls."

I heard the rawness in her throat. She'd been taking it easy, knowing the initial vocals were scratch tracks, but that much singing still took its toll.

Dia crossed the room to the house com system, flipping on the vid monitor which took up a good portion of the wall facing the sitting area. It came up to a world news channel with the audio set low. She glanced over her shoulder. "Wayne gave J'Nell a one-time call code," she said. "He was bitching because Ric's security routes all the calls through the main guardhouse, so any time he wants to contact us, he has to go through them."

Nori grinned. "Yeah, keeps him from driving us nuts in the studio. I think it's great. Kind of sucks our personal coms are blocked, but honestly, it's nice not worrying about the outside world."

I shrugged. "Nobody calls me anyway." Except for my mom, who had the guardhouse number for emergencies.

The house com beeped, and Dia opened the connection to the main vid monitor. "Hey, J'Nell."

J'Nell relaxed behind a delicate white desk. Fine-boned with long blond hair and pale skin, she wore a flowery one-piece jumpsuit snugged to her body, unzipped at the neck to expose a hint of cleavage. Nestled just above her full breasts, a rough quartz crystal shot through with gold hung from a thin gold chain. She greeted us with a wide smile. "Good evening, ladies!"

We returned the greeting and she took the reins. "I know you've had a long day, so I'll try to keep this short."

Nori said, "We know you better than that."

We all laughed. Our interviews with J'Nell generally ended up deep and involved and often went off on tangents. She was good at drawing us out, even Stacy, who rarely had much to add.

"So, tell me about the studio. How are things going so far? How is working with the famous Ric Orrechek?"

We discussed the upcoming release and how we were working with Ric and reminded her of our upcoming tour dates to promote the new album. In turn, J'Nell related the latest gossip from the slam-thrash scene and which shows she'd seen. Finally, though, she realized our energy was waning. Stacy and Nori looked like they were falling asleep. J'Nell made us promise to keep her up to date and ended the call.

Stacy stood and yawned. "I'm gonna go shower and crash." She shuffled out of the room, tossing her beer bottle in the trash regenerator on her way past the kitchen.

When her bedroom door shut, Nori said quietly, "Going better than I expected with her."

Dia said, "We're all focused right now. Let's hope it stays that way."

I was glad Stacy was doing her part. I wanted to believe she'd turned a page, but I knew people didn't change overnight. She'd fall apart again. It was inevitable. But if we kept her focused, we had a better chance of getting through this recording session without losing her.

I pushed to my feet. "I'm going to get some sleep." I set the lock on the front door and made sure the kitchen entry was locked as well. "If anyone goes out, please make sure to re-lock the doors, okay?"

They promised and I stumped upstairs. After a quick stop in the bathroom to brush my teeth and do my business, I flipped on the light and scanned the bedroom, locking the door behind me. Paranoid? Sure I was. I liked the idea of having my own space but being alone made me uneasy.

Nori always volunteered to room with me because she could sleep through a hurricane, and I tended to talk in my sleep and thrash around when I dreamed. My mom said I used to scare the hell out of her when I was a kid. My animated sleep also had annoyed the crap out of girlfriends who happened to spend the night. Generally speaking, I was a love 'em and leave 'em kinda gal because of it. Of course, girlfriends and hookups were few and far between. I was married to my music, and my guitar was my wife.

Sadly, my guitars didn't keep me safe from Celestian.

Four days later, I discovered a bloody bouquet of black roses on the kitchen table.

CHAPTER FIVE

Earth Date: September 2453
Moon Base Domed City

Rhynn

"I need the following people to accompany me to conference room 212 immediately."

Rhynn's stomach dropped to her feet and she looked over her monitor. Her supervisor, Colter, marched to the front of the workroom. Over his standard-issue black jumpsuit he wore a formal, short-collared jacket emblazoned with the corporate logo. He looked down at the comp pad in his hand and read off the names of most of the twenty people in the room, hers included. When he looked up, his expression was empty. "Take your coats and bags but leave all other items on your desks."

"What about the rest of our stuff?"

The young woman sitting to Rhynn's left flinched under Colter's callous gaze.

"You'll get your belongings." He pointed toward the door. "If you were named, let's go. If you weren't called, I'm sure you have work to do."

He strutted around the edge of the room and out the door. Two corporate security guards stepped inside.

Rhynn swallowed. Damn. This had not been in her plan for the day. She was glad she'd never bothered to put any personal items on her desk. She shoved her comp pad into her backpack and shouldered it.

Beside her, Krys muttered, "Bastards."

She joined the queue shuffling out the door, following Colter down the hallway.

A serious woman in a gray jacket stopped her as she reached the door to the conference room. "Your name, please?"

"Rhynn Knight."

The woman handed her an envelope with her name typed on the front. The woman's expression remained neutral, but Rhynn fancied she saw a sympathetic light in her pale eyes. "Please take a seat."

The chill of nervous sweat gathered under the plain forest-green jumpsuit Rhynn wore. She knew what was coming. She took an open seat at the rectangular table, sitting stiffly with her hands in her lap.

Colter stood at the far end of the table, waited for everyone to find a chair and then paused an extra few seconds to extend the anxious discomfort permeating the air. Rhynn truly disliked the man. He was the kind of arrogant asshole she'd have liked to have taken into a slam-thrash cube and flipped around in zero-g until he puked his guts out, then slung him back and forth across the circle until he was scared shitless someone would smash his head into the glassteel walls just to see the blood.

"You should each have an envelope. In the envelope is a receipt for your final paycheck deposit. There is also information regarding signing up for unemployment. Your termination is immediate. You need to leave the building without delay. Any personal items from your desks will be collected for you and will be available at the security desk at the front entry within the next hour. Are there any questions?"

Rhynn clamped her jaw shut on the desire to demand to know why they were being laid off. She wanted to ask how many employees further up the ladder had been let go. Did the pompous bastards in upper management compete to get the biggest raise for trashing the most lives?

"Mann-Maru Universal Industries wants to thank you for your hard work. The company's need to reorganize and downsize is not to be taken personally. You are welcome to apply for any currently open positions for which you qualify. Please feel free to call the personnel department with any questions. You may now leave the building. Please leave your access passes at the registration desk."

For a few seconds, nobody moved. Rhynn looked down at the envelope on her lap.

Fuck.

The woman beside her stood up, starting a wave of motion. Rhynn followed suit, picking up her bag as she did so. She had no loyalty to Mann-Maru, but she still felt betrayed. And ticked off.

Of course, she'd half expected the layoffs. Rumors had been running rampant because of profit losses last quarter. It'd been all over the net news. Two major accidents in the asteroid mines had wreaked havoc on capacity and output. Instead of sucking it up for a couple of quarters, Mann-Maru simply laid off a bunch of low-level workers to offset their losses. Pathetic, but not surprising.

Rhynn dropped her security pass into the lock box at the front desk as she walked out. She was tempted to throw it at the guard's chest, but she figured the young, uncomfortable-looking kid wasn't much happier than she was about the current situation.

She paused as she stepped onto the sidewalk, glancing up and down the narrow street. The three-story Mann-Maru corporate office building butted against a row of several similar nondescript buildings. Krys stopped beside her and said, "I'm going to get a drink. You wanna come?"

Rhynn considered it. Getting wasted wasn't such a bad idea. On the other hand, it wasn't going to change anything. And drinking oneself into oblivion cost money. Which she was no longer making.

"Naw. Think I'll head home. Guess I need to start checking the job boards."

He laughed. "I'll take advantage of unemployment payments. Figure they owe me, you know?"

"Sure. Take it easy, Krys." With a small wave, she trudged down the sidewalk toward the housing units on the opposite side of the dome. She walked the familiar path through the corporate district and past a cluster of restaurants and bars. Familiar aromas of ethnic foods assailed her. Today she didn't feel hungry or tempted.

She crossed the central park, which lent a bit of green space to the harsh utilitarian atmosphere of Moon Base Dome. The sidewalk cut through a lawn of short, dense grass dotted with potted shrubs and dwarf trees that required minimal watering. Brightly colored flower beds, carefully and lovingly tended by volunteers, lined the walk.

On the far side of the park, rows of minimalist condos and apartments took up several blocks—three-story buildings painted in dull grays and beiges, with the occasional faded green thrown in for variety. She shared a single-bedroom unit with Leigh. They'd been roommates for almost five years.

Rhynn palmed the door lock on the second rowhouse and headed up to the third-floor apartment she called home. She pushed open the manual door to apartment 317 when the lock released. Stepping inside, the first thing she noticed was a loud action movie playing on the vid-screen. She frowned when she saw Britt lounging on the sofa in the cramped living room.

Her girlfriend looked up in surprise, immediately using the remote to mute the volume.

"Wow, you're home early," Britt said.

Rhynn shut the door and trudged through to the single bedroom. Two lofted beds split the room, with wardrobes under each, and fold-up desks built into alcoves in the walls. She dropped her backpack onto the worn memory-form chair in front of her desk and took a few long breaths to settle herself before dealing with Britt. She didn't want to talk to anyone right now. She needed to process her options and figure out her finances.

She hooked an arm through a rung on the ladder to her loft and rested her forehead against the cool plastic molding curving along the bottom of the bed frame. Exhaustion washed over her, as though she'd been holding herself under control for hours. Now, in her safe place, she could let go. She heard Britt shifting around in the living room. What she wanted to do was climb up and close her eyes. Instead, she blew out a long sigh and left the bedroom. In the cramped kitchenette, she made a mug of tea and added a long squirt of honey.

Dropping heavily into a kitchen chair, she rested her elbow on the plastic kitchen table and her head in her hand and stared blankly into the steam rising from her mug.

"Why don't you come sit over here on the couch, baby?"

Because I want to be by myself. Because I lost my job and need to think and wallow in my misery for a while, not play games with you.

She heard Britt get up and cross the room. The strawberry blonde sat across from her. "Come on, Rhynny. It can't be that bad. Are you sick or something?"

Rhynn finally lifted her head. "I got re-orged from work." At Britt's blank look, she clarified. "Laid off."

"Oh. Well, when is your last day?"

Could the woman be any denser? Rhynn studied Britt's eyes to see if she was wasted on something, but her green irises were bright and clear. She said, "An hour ago." Lifting her head from her hand, she sipped the fragrant tea, savoring the strong flavor and warmth as it slid down her throat. The familiar taste calmed her nerves.

Britt said, "You can live off the unemployment for a while, so you may as well enjoy it. Take a break, you know?"

Rhynn stared at her girlfriend for a long time. "I'll probably hit the job boards tomorrow."

"Why? You deserve a vacation."

"I don't need a vacation. I need a job." Rhynn focused on the amber liquid in her mug and took another long swallow. It would be easy to put off her job search. She could manage for while on the unemployment stipend and what little savings she had put away. She could be a bum and sleep late, be a lazy musician.

The thought was enticing, and she allowed herself the luxury of considering it as she drank her tea. But she needed to be working. To be useful and productive. She'd always had a job separate from her drumming and the bands she'd played with.

Her mom was a single parent. There hadn't been much extra income when she was a kid. As she got older, when she wanted new drum equipment or spending money, she made her own earnings. As soon as she'd finished her basic school courses, she took technical training courses, got her mechanic's certifications and worked as a spacer. She'd held jobs on the cargo docks as part of a building maintenance crew and in construction at the Moon Base space dry docks. Five years ago, a major construction accident took the lives of half her crew and nearly hers as well.

Once she'd recovered, the next job she took was a desk job. Now that job was over. She supposed she could go back to the docks or try to get on another construction crew. She'd kept her certifications current. At the very least, she could sling cargo.

Britt sighed loudly. "Well, you're not going to go job hunting today, are you?"

"No. All I want to do right now is take a nap." Her limbs felt heavy as she pushed to her feet.

Britt stood with her, circling Rhynn's wrist with long fingers. "Then I'll hold you while you sleep."

Rhynn was pretty sure that Britt's concerned green eyes were meant to assure her she would be in good hands. Shrugging, she let Britt lead her to the bedroom. Britt stripped her of her work jumpsuit and then removed her own shirt and pants while Rhynn clambered up onto the loft. Britt shimmied in behind her and pulled the blankets over them.

Rhynn relaxed into the warmth of Britt's body, already half asleep. Britt wrapped a possessive arm around her middle, her breath feathered against Rhynn's bare shoulder, and she felt the soft pressure of a kiss on her skin.

"I've got you," Britt said.

Rhynn didn't know why Britt was being so sweet. She was more accustomed to Britt's sly sexiness and aggressive passion. But for once, she was content to be held and glad Britt wasn't pushing.

She gave in to her exhaustion. She would deal with it all later.

CHAPTER SIX

Earth Date: September 2453
Nor-Am Continent, Mid-Continental Desert,
Tyrannus Studios Compound Studio, evening, day 7

Ari

Toni and I stood at the entrance to the kitchen. I tried not to look at the bloody bouquet of roses on the table, but my eyes kept sliding back and reinforcing the fear twisting my stomach. Ric Orrechek and Neil, the guard who'd been on duty at the security gate, stepped carefully around the kitchen, trying not to touch anything as they studied my latest "gift."

Toni's arm rested protectively over my shoulders. I wanted to run, but my feet remained rooted to the floor. Questions raced through my brain. Had Celestian been in the house? Had someone else delivered the flowers? Did they know I'd been in the studio or that Toni was sleeping upstairs? Had Celestian been hiding in the shadows, watching me cross the courtyard? Were they still here?

My hands shook even though I'd stuffed them deep into the pockets of my loose workout pants.

Ric said, "Neil, did you let the flowers in?"

"No, sir. No deliveries at all today and no visitors. Maybe the other ladies put them here? For a joke or something?"

Ric glared. "Don't be a fucking idiot. Get back to the guardhouse. Call Todd and Adam and start going through the footage for the last five hours. Go."

"Yes, sir." Neil rushed out the front door.

Ric said, "Toni, can you get a hold of the other women and get them back here?"

"Sure. Let me get my pad and I'll message them."

I had to stop myself from pulling her back when Toni walked away from me. I said, "They wouldn't have done this."

"I know. I want all of you here so I know where you are."

I swallowed.

The flowers still dripped with thick red liquid I suspected wasn't real blood. Resting against the vase, the notecard taunted me.

Arienne, my love, if I can't have you, nobody can. Enjoy the flowers, my sweet musician. I am thinking of you. Always. I will know if you've forsaken me. - Celestian

What did they want? How could I forsake someone I didn't even know? Why did they think I would enjoy black roses dripping with fake blood? If they loved me so much, why send me bloody roses and scare me half to death? How did Celestian get past Ric's security? How did they get into the house? Were they invisible again? How in the hell could anyone protect me from someone they couldn't even see?

Fifteen minutes later, the local police showed up. Ric greeted two uniformed officers and two plainclothes detectives. The lead detective, Jules Redding, was a tall woman with shoulder-length red hair pulled back into a tight tail at her neck. She introduced her partner as Detective Boyston, a stocky dark-skinned man with a shiny bald pate and a no-nonsense demeanor.

Boyston walked around taking video with his comp pad.

Redding said, "You're sure nobody touched the flowers or the card?" She pulled on gloves.

I shook my head. "No, we didn't."

Redding leaned in close to the flowers. I watched as she and Boyston exchanged glances, the silent communication of partners, hers questioning, his nod confirming whatever she was asking with her eyes. She read the note card, straightened and pointed to me. "You're Arienne, right?"

"Yes."

Redding said, "You have a history with this person? You know him?"

I swallowed. "History, yes. But no, I don't know them."

Toni said, "This isn't the first note Ari's gotten from this freak."

"Do you have the other notes?"

I said, "We keep all the weird ones. Our manager has them. We've all gotten creepy mail from time to time."

"How many from this person?"

"I don't know. Maybe ten."

Toni said, "There was an incident, a few months ago. They left a threatening card on the doorstep at our house. There's a police report. They think the person was wearing a chameleon suit so they wouldn't appear on the vid cameras around the property."

Boyston scribbled furiously with a stylus on his comp pad.

Redding's dark eyes flicked toward Ric. "I'm leaving a squad here. Do you have heat-detecting scanners on site?"

"Yes, though generally they aren't used. I'll make sure they're on going forward."

"We need all your security data from the last day, any incoming/outgoing delivery and visitor logs, and I'll need to interview your staff."

"No problem."

"None of the band members leave this house alone, even to go across the plaza to the studio. Has anyone checked out the rest of the house?"

"No. We've only been from the entryway to here. Let me make a call and have my guys pull together the data and an employee list." Ric stepped into the living room and keyed his com.

Toni said, "I was in my room sleeping until Ari woke me up. We've been right here since then."

I said, "I was at the studio. When I got here, I crossed the living room, put my guitar on the sofa, and then I went into the kitchen and saw the roses. I yelled Toni's name and woke her up, but I didn't go anywhere else."

Redding jotted a couple notes into her pad. "Would you know if anything was disturbed in your room?"

"Depends."

Redding's smile was a wry twist of her lips, as if she was thinking, *Well, you're rock musicians. Of course the place is a pigsty.* "Let's go take a look. Don't touch anything. Don't go past the doorframe into the room. I may need to have forensics go through it."

I led the way up the stairs and down the hallway, stopping at the open second door on the right. Someone turned on the hall light. I peered inside the mostly dark room. A shaft of dull illumination crossed the floor to the writing desk against the far wall.

Through the dimness, I could see the sweatshirt draped haphazardly over the back of the desk chair, and the suitcase laying open on the floor beside the closet. The double bed was rumpled and unmade.

I said, "Looks like how I left it."

Redding said, "Lights, on." She stepped past me. "I don't imagine you left black rose petals on your pillows?"

Suddenly lightheaded, I backed away from the door. Toni caught me from behind and I leaned into her, barely able to breathe. Shudders ran through me, making my knees weak.

Celestian had been in my room. In my space. Watching. My eyes darted toward the closet.

For all I knew she was still here.

Redding spoke sharply into her com, "Boyston, get a scanner in this house right now. Heat, motion, infrared, everything. Keep all nonessential personnel in the living room."

Panic rose in my throat, my heart pounded painfully in my chest, and I couldn't get enough air.

Toni murmured, "Come on, let's go sit down."

She guided me back to the living room and pulled me down beside her on the sofa, keeping an arm around my shoulders. I was too overwhelmed to resist. I peered anxiously into the dark corners of the dimly lit room and whispered, "Can you turn up the lights?"

Toni did, and the brightness made me blink. But at least there were no more shadows.

Ric remained by the doorway, talking into his comp pad. Redding, Boyston and the two other officers searched the rest of the house with scanners. Someone put crime scene tape across my bedroom door and the entrance to the kitchen.

I said, "I can't stay here."

Ric looked up. "I got you guys a hotel."

The front door opened and Nori, Dia, and Stacy stormed through the entryway.

Nori pulled me into a tight hug. "Oh, honey, are you okay?"

I managed a nod.

Dia muttered a string of expletives in at least two languages as she walked across the room to stand at the neon yellow tape, peering into the kitchen. "Holy shit, you guys. I can't believe this."

Stacy stood in the middle of the living room, her expression somewhere between freaked out and angry, arms crossed.

"There were rose petals in Ari's room, too, on her bed," Toni said.

Dia turned back to the living room, crossing herself. "This is fuckin' creepy."

Nori asked, "Toni, are you all right?"

"Just a little shaken up. I mean, fuck, I was here sleeping for chrissake."

I squeezed Toni's hand and wondered how long it would take me to feel safe anywhere.

CHAPTER SEVEN

Earth Date: September 2453
Nor-Am Continent, Mid-Continental Desert
Terrace Regency Hotel

Ari

Ric had gotten us a suite of rooms at the Terrace Regency on the outskirts of Kansas City, about an hour from Tyrannus Studios. The sun glared into floor-to-ceiling windows that looked across the city toward the surrounding brown and gold expanse of desert and scrub grass. Sliding glass doors opened to a broad patio where most of my bandmates lay soaking up the heat. Past the patio, other skyscraper hotels faced our own.

Once upon a time, scientists and history books said we'd have been gazing into a vista of wheat fields and farm country. Severe man-made climate change and the resulting famine and wars had forever marked this land, and the Mid-Continent looked very different than it had four hundred years before.

I curled up in the corner of the sofa, as far away from the windows as possible and eyed the sunny patio with both suspicion and a wistful desire to be out in the warmth. Instead, I shivered in the climate-controlled coolness with my knees pulled up to my chest, covered with my oversized hoodie, wondering if anyone was spying into the windows and if they could see me hiding in the corner.

Dia and Toni lounged in the sun, wearing shorts and cut-off T-shirts. Stacy was in her bedroom. Nori sprawled on a low recliner in the sunlight near the patio doors, reading on her comp pad. I caught her glancing at me from time to time, and it was easy to read the concern in my best friend's dark gaze.

I didn't blame her or the others for being worried about me. Over the four days since the roses had shown up at the band house, I had become withdrawn, silent and moody, glancing over my shoulder constantly. We'd packed up all our stuff that night and moved into the hotel. Of course, I hadn't been able to take most of my things. I had finally gotten my comp pad and clothes back from the forensics lab yesterday. Thank the Goddess my guitar had been with me and not in my room.

Toni and Nori bought me a couple changes of clothes the first night, including the huge black hoodie I wore like a security blanket.

A knock at the door sent a pulse of fear and adrenaline through my veins. I almost bolted for the back bedroom, even though I knew Ric had two security guys posted in the hallway with scanners and guns.

Nori unfolded from the recliner and marched to the door. She keyed the controls to see the video feed from outside. "It's Wayne and Nelda with the stage designer they told us about last week."

Wayne Neutron strolled into the room. His dark hair was slicked back against his head, and he wore a skintight silver ship suit unbuttoned halfway down his chest. "Hey, girls."

Nelda Tremain, Public Relations Specialist, followed him sedately, dressed in her conservative best. A young woman entered the room a step behind her. She had bright blue eyes and wildly curly blond hair. Her obvious excitement rolled off her in waves. She hung back near the door, smiling widely as she looked around the room, nodding to me and Nori.

Wayne opened the patio door and called the others inside, then looked around. "Where's Stacy?"

Nori said, "I'll get her."

"Good."

When we were all present, Wayne started the impromptu band meeting. His gaze focused on me first. "Are you doing okay?"

"Yeah, I'm fine." Not like I'd have said anything else. I liked Wayne okay, but I wasn't going to bare my soul to him.

Toni said, "Ric's been leaving two of his security people here twenty-four-seven."

Wayne said, "Ari you shouldn't go anywhere without at least one of Ric's people."

I sent him an annoyed glance. Like I would even think about going anywhere alone.

Nelda added, "We'd also prefer none of you talk to the press about what's happening. If anyone calls, refer them to me."

Nori asked, "What happens after we're done in the studio and we don't have Ric's security?"

"I'm working on it," Wayne assured us. "I'll let you know."

Stacy stood abruptly from the stool at the breakfast bar. "This is crap, Wayne. It's like we're in fucking prison. The only one this freak wants is Ari. She can hide in here, but I'm not going to."

Toni snapped, "Don't be an idiot."

Stacy ignored her. "We aren't children. We don't need to be treated like we are. I can take care of myself."

"The security is for your own safety. We don't know what this person is liable to do," Wayne said.

Stacy scowled. "It's all just stupid threats. Nothing's going to happen."

Nelda said, "Hopefully the police will track this person down and things will get back to normal."

Dia rolled her eyes. "Like the police are going to spend any time and effort on the likes of us."

Nori shot her a look and Dia shrugged. "We don't have enough money or power for them to care."

Toni said, "Dia, you're so negative."

"It's true."

Wayne held up his hands to stop the argument. "On to the next thing." He gestured toward the young woman by the door and waved her toward him. "Come here, honey, and meet the band. Girls, this is Friday McKiern. She's going to be designing and managing your stage sets, lighting, and live video. She'll also do the artwork for the new album. I wanted you to meet her in person since she'll be joining you on tour. She'll work with Mykal Izak, your favorite stage manager, to run all the on-stage video and direct the light show."

Toni said, "It's great to meet you, Friday."

"Thanks, it's great to meet you guys too. This is such an amazing opportunity. I'll do my best to make it all perfect."

Nori grinned. "You're sure jumping into the fire, coming on tour with us and working with big Myk."

"I'm looking forward to it."

Stacy said, "Yeah, you can be in prison with the rest of us."

Friday pressed her lips together, then said, "Umm, I know it's not my place to say anything, but, well, if you're looking for tour security, my foster parents have a specialized security business. I bet they could do security for the tour, and Morgan loves slam-thrash."

Wayne raised a brow. "What's your dad's security company? Maybe I've heard of them."

Friday giggled. "My moms, actually. Both of them. Shaine Wendt and Morgan Rahn. They own Wendt-Rahn Private Special Forces, and they do a lot of work for Mann-Maru Industries and for government ambassadors and officials."

Nelda frowned, then said, "Mann-Maru? Wait, isn't that the Rahn woman—the one from Moon Base—who turned out to be a relation of Tarm Maruchek?"

"Yeah, Morgan. Shaine was in Earth Guard special forces. I met them on Mars. They were heading up security at the Mann-Maru mining site there. They saved my life."

Toni stared at her. "I want to hear that story."

Friday smiled shyly. "Sure."

I almost snickered to watch them goggling at each other.

Wayne said to Friday, "Give me a number to call so I can talk to them. With any luck, though, the police will deal with this before the tour kicks off and we can use standard concert security."

Nelda said, "Friday, why don't you show the band the stage design you're working on? I think they're going to love it."

CHAPTER EIGHT

Earth Date: September 2453
Nor-Am Continent, Central Los Angeles Megalopolis

Ari

The security guard of the day was a woman named Panther, one of several provided by our record label. She was serious, dark-skinned, with hair braided tight against her head and falling in short beaded tails almost to her shoulders. She had a solid, muscular build and a no-nonsense attitude. She told us she'd done a short stint in Earth Guard, but it made me wonder how short it had been because she wore her military bearing like a dangerous shroud. Her presence was reassuring. She exuded a sense of competence and control without being overbearing or obnoxious. She was completely professional, though she admitted to being a big fan of slam-thrash music and having all of our recordings.

She spent most of her time at the comp terminal in the corner of the living room, watching our newly updated security monitors and sipping a mug of caf. She walked the perimeter of the house at least once an hour and used a handheld scanner to check for heat signatures and the elusive Celestian. So far all she'd found were neighborhood kids and a couple stray cats.

I curled up on the sofa with a book on my comp pad, glad to have a quiet day to relax. Toni and Dia were out by the pool. Stacy had disappeared again. Likely she would show up in two or three days, wearing the same clothes and looking like she hadn't slept or showered, and then she'd crash for another day and a half. Nori sprawled on pillows on the floor, earbuds in, playing games on her comp pad.

Today we didn't have much going on other than a call from J'Nell Inagayl for a group interview. We'd talk up the new release and the upcoming tour. We'd been back from the studio for almost two weeks, and we'd leave on tour in another three.

When the com call came, we put J'Nell's vid feed on the main house screen. Her wide smile broadcast her bubbly personality. She wore a bright pink ship suit today, her blond hair pulled back under a jaunty brimmed cap.

She was calling from an air-car. I recognized the light tan ceiling of the vehicle and heard the occasional background noise of other cars passing. I supposed she was on the road between appointments. "Good afternoon, ladies! How are you? Ari, it's good to see you again. How's your mom?"

"Hi, J'Nell. Mom is good. She told me to let you know she really liked the Archangels interview you did."

"Your mom is the best. Tell her hello from me."

Dia, Toni, Nori, and I gathered on the sofa with the vid camera focused on us. Panther stayed out of sight at the breakfast counter, monitoring security camera feeds pushed to her comp pad. We weren't publicizing anything about my stalker or the incident at the studio. Wayne wanted to keep it under wraps. I simply didn't want to talk about it, so I pretended I wasn't completely freaked out and afraid to leave the safety of our house.

After a few more pleasantries, J'Nell launched into the interview. "Let's talk about the new release. Compare it to the last one. Are you going in a new direction? How is this collection different from the others?"

Toni jumped in. "The new release isn't a new direction, though we amped up the intensity, and it's a bit darker. We're pushing our boundaries musically and lyrically."

Nori said, "The arrangements are deeper, more complex and driving. Everyone has stepped up their musicianship. We can't wait to play the songs live."

"Tell me more about the tour. What can we expect this time around?"

Toni's face lit up, and she leaned forward, elbows on her knees. "The stage show is going to be excellent. We've got a new stage and lighting designer, Friday McKiern, and she's phenomenal. She's put together some wild video for the playlist we're working on, and the light show is going to be crazy."

Dia said, "We'll play a lot of the new songs, but we'll make sure to bring back old favorites too. We're starting with a couple Earthside dates to get warmed up and see how fans react to the new material, then a show on Moon Base before the 'Hammer Down Cruise' starts."

As usual, Toni, Nori, and Dia did most of the talking. They were better at schmoozing about the band than me. While they laughed and bantered with J'Nell, and the reporter drilled them with questions, I wondered how I was going to deal with being in front of a crowd, because right now I was barely able to be in my own backyard without my heart beating out of my chest and constantly feeling watched.

"What about you, Ari?"

I blinked. "I'm sorry, I missed that?"

J'Nell's smile widened. "I asked if you were looking forward to the big cruise?"

The standard answer came out automatically. "Sure. It's going to be a lot of fun. Performing live is always a rush." Being on a space cruiser—a party barge—with hundreds of fans would likely be a disconcerting and terrifying experience. Too many people in close proximity, and likely limited downtime. As a band, partying with our fans every night was out of the question if we planned on performing well at shows. A drink maybe, and hanging out, but we couldn't afford drunken binges. How Stacy handled the easily accessible intoxicants was yet to be seen. Given her track record lately, it worried the hell out of the rest of us. But that wasn't anything we wanted to share.

J'Nell wrapped up the interview, thanked us, then signed off the call. She hoped to be able to connect with us at some point on the tour and join us for a few days. We could do a lot worse than having J'Nell Inagayl covering some shows.

Toni and Nori wandered to the kitchen. Nori called, "Anyone want something to drink?"

When they joined us again, Nori handed me a hot tea. I cautiously sipped from the non-spill container and set it on the floor beside me.

From her place at the breakfast counter, Panther asked, "Do you guys do a lot of interviews?"

Dia said, "We do some here and there. More often when we've got a new release or a tour."

"I gotta say, I thought this job was going to be a lot different than it's been," Panther said.

Toni snorted. "You figured this was gonna be a party house? Crazy drunken, oversexed thrash musicians?"

Panther flushed. "Something like that, yeah."

I laughed. "We're pretty tame compared to some."

"I think I like tame better," Panther said. "I'm going to do a quick perimeter check."

She unclipped her scanner, her demeanor shifting from casual to serious. Even her posture changed before she opened the front door and stepped outside. As the front door shut behind her, I felt a little wave a relief knowing she was doing her job.

Nori said, "I want to start running sets as soon as Stacy gets back."

"I wouldn't put money on when that's going to be," Dia said. "She has a new boyfriend."

Toni rolled her eyes. "Boyfriend or fuck-buddy?"

Dia shrugged. "She didn't say."

"This doesn't bode well, does it?"

"Depends on how hung up on him she gets, or how good his drugs are," Nori muttered.

"She knows we're leaving on tour soon. She's not going to get that involved," I said, hoping that if I said it, it would be true.

Nori made a face. "Yeah. Right."

The front door opened and Panther stepped in, holding a red plas-sheet by its edges in her gloved hand. "This note was lying in front of the door when I came back around the house. It's got your name on it, Ari."

My stomach plunged and bile rose up the back of my throat.

Toni jumped to her feet. "What the fuck? I thought you were here to stop this shit!"

Panther glared at her. "There has been nothing on the feeds. But that doesn't keep someone from watching from a distance, does it? They probably waited until I went around back and then dropped the note."

"This is crap," Toni growled, crossing the room and reaching for the note. "What does it say?"

Panther pulled her hand back and shook her head. "Find me a bag to put this in. We need to give it to the authorities."

Dia jogged to the kitchen while Toni stood scowling at Panther, purposely encroaching her personal space.

I clutched my shaking hands between my knees. Celestian was here again. My gaze flicked to the patio doors and I sprang to my feet, bounding across the room to slap the controls on the wall. The glass turned instantly opaque. Weak-kneed, I slid down the wall, pulled my knees up and wrapped my arms around them. What did Celestian want from me? Why wouldn't they leave me alone? I wanted to cry but swallowed back the tears.

Nori sat on the floor beside me and I leaned gratefully into her embrace.

Panther carefully slid the plas-sheet into the clear plastic bag and then thumbed her com and faced away. I was vaguely aware of her low, confident voice.

Toni stomped to the computer. "Maybe we can see something on the vid stream during the time you were in back. This is seriously pissing me off."

Panther said, "Detective Greene is on his way with a forensic team."

I couldn't tear my gaze away from the plas-sheet she still held. "What does it say?"

Panther read the words in an even, calm voice. "Arienne, my love, please, do not fear me. I would never hurt you. You are the light in my life. I dream of you. I listen to you play and my heart soars. But you never come out any more and I miss you. Please don't hide from me. Yours, always, Celestian."

I fought down the ever-present fear. How could I hide from a ghost?

"Panther, look at this!" Toni leaned toward the monitor.

Panther peered over Toni's shoulder. "Back that up, slow. Shit, I think that's a woman."

Toni nodded, excited. “Look at the heat signature, here, and that vague outline. Boobs.”

“We’ll need experts to confirm,” Panther cautioned.

So, Celestian was a woman. I swallowed. That eliminated half the population of the world. But it didn’t make me feel any better. She was still out there.

CHAPTER NINE

Earth Date: October 2453
Moon Base Domed City

Rhynn

Rhynn hurried into the busy cafeteria in the Mann-Maru corporate building, searching the sea of faces for her mother. She spotted Cassandra Knight's familiar visage in the back corner. Her mom wore her hair short and neat with a colorful poncho over her plain gray ship suit.

Rhynn picked her way through the tables, dropping into the chair opposite an older version of herself. They shared the same wide dark eyes in an angular face, but where her mom's hair was plain brown and reasonably conservative, Rhynn's long bangs flopped over her face in a magenta flash. The sides of her head were shaved close over her ears and at her neckline, leaving a slash of long hair pulled up in a top knot of alternating neon green and electric blue streaks that hung past her shoulders. "Hey, Mom."

Cassandra pushed a bowl in front of her daughter. "I got you the vegetable stew."

"Thanks." Rhynn leaned forward and breathed in the savory aroma. She picked up a spoon and dipped it into the thick combination of gravy and vegetables. She took a bite, chewing slowly and enjoying the rich, slightly spicy flavor. "I swear this is the only thing they never screw up."

Cassandra leaned back in her chair, nursing a cup of caf. She and Rhynn met for lunch once a week, every week, and had for years. For Rhynn, it was simply a habit and a way to stay connected since she'd moved into her own place. Both she and her mom had busy lives, friends, hobbies, and relationships, and it was hard to get together in the evenings. They'd started having lunch instead. Rhynn swallowed and paused with her fork in the air. "How's your day going?" she asked.

"Oh, busy as always. Project coordination is like herding sheep, always someone to track down and get back on schedule. It keeps me on my toes. At least today I have time for lunch." Cassandra smiled and Rhynn marveled for the millionth time at how well her mom handled the stress of her job. Had it been her, she'd have been throwing people through walls by now.

"How's the job hunt going, Rhynny?"

She shot her mom an annoyed look at the diminutive name. "I picked up a couple day jobs last week, shuffling cargo down at the docks. I put in for a couple construction openings. Keeping my fingers crossed. Helps that I've worked the scaffolding before."

"Are you okay for rent and food?"

Rhynn rolled her eyes. "I'm fine. I've got my unemployment stipend, and I've put emergency money away. As long as I find something full time in the next few weeks I'll be okay."

Her mom studied her. "Britt stay last night?" she asked pointedly.

Rhynn scowled. "What? Is it written on my forehead or something?"

"You have bags under your eyes."

"I might have been up late reading a good book."

Cassandra snorted.

Rhynn dug into her stew, hoping her mother would move onto a different subject.

"That woman is nothing but trouble," Cassandra said. "You deserve a hell of a lot better than her."

Rhynn didn't bother to argue. It was true. And at some point, she'd end things with Britt. "I've been focused on finding a job and the gig coming up."

"Maybe you were up practicing last night?"

"Nice. I should have been. I can't believe we're going to open for Shattered Crystal Enigma. Absolutely crazy. Vicki and Harris want to do a couple of their covers. I'm not so sure."

Cassandra sipped her caf. "If you've got a chance to show off a little, why not do it?"

"As long as we don't screw it up."

"I have faith in you. And I know that band of yours is good, even if the noise you call music is not my cup of tea. You're damned talented, daughter of mine, but your talent is wasted out here on the moon."

"I like it here." Rhynn recognized the expression on Cassandra's face. Proud of her, but also a little disappointed. She knew Cassandra wanted more for her. She'd encouraged her to go to university, so Rhynn took classes over the net, but only finished enough to be able to get a decent job.

As so many musicians put it, she worked to support her band habit. The gigs brought in a little additional money, most of which she ended up putting back into rehearsal space and equipment.

She knew Cassandra would love to see her get a degree—any degree—and leave Moon Base, get a job that paid more than a basic salary, settle down with a decent woman who also had a good job, have kids, and live happily ever after.

Rhynn didn't see it as a path for herself. Ideally, she would become a famous thrash musician and never again work a menial day job, but that was, truly, only for the lucky chosen few. She was perfectly happy being a big fish in her relatively small pond, playing the music she liked with friends she enjoyed.

Cassandra said, "So, tell me more about this big gig. You haven't said much about it."

Rhynn grinned. "Don't want to jinx it. It's going to be crazy wild. We'll open first, then Nightwalker, then Shattered Crystal Enigma goes on. We have backstage privileges. I'm sure we'll meet the band. From what I've read, they're pretty accessible."

"Are you nervous?"

"Hell, yes. I'm trying not to think about it. I mean, chances are they're not even going to be there to hear us play, you know? Leigh and I were talking about it, and we decided what we need to do is go out there and do our show and treat it like any other show."

Cassandra patted her arm. "I'm sure you'll do fine, honey."

"Thanks for the confidence. I figure as long as I don't completely choke, it'll be great." She finished the last of her stew and pushed the bowl away. "What about you? Been seeing much of your new boyfriend lately?"

Cassandra blushed. "We're going to dinner tonight. He's very nice. I think you'll like him."

"You think he's the one?"

"Oh, I don't know, but we get along well, and he doesn't push, so that's in his favor."

"You'll have to set up dinner so I can meet him and give you my stamp of approval."

"Always, daughter mine, always."

CHAPTER TEN

Earth Date: October 2453
Nor-Am Continent, New York City Megalopolis
Tour venue: Louie's

Ari

Before we headed to Moon Base to kick off the out-system cruise portion of our tour, we had a final Earthside show. Louie's Lizard Lounge was a crazy-as-shit thrash club in the New York City megalopolis that sprawled along half the Eastern seaboard. Anyone who was anyone played Louie's. Tickets were almost impossible to get. Concerts were always standing room only and we were psyched as hell to be able to play there.

After ten shows in two weeks, we had settled into the usual tour routine. Play, load out, drive and sleep, load in, play, load out, drive and sleep, and do it all again.

The fans loved the new songs and were already learning the lyrics thanks to illegally shared recordings. You couldn't get around the pirating, so we used it to our advantage. The more people shared, the more people showed up at the shows and legal recording sales were still good.

Best of all, there'd been no sign of Celestian. No new notes. No flowers. Nothing. I hoped she'd given up and found someone else to stalk, though I knew it was unlikely. Our tour dates were well publicized, so if someone wanted to follow us around, they wouldn't have any trouble doing so. We certainly had fans who followed us from show to show. In any case, the police had no leads on the previous incidents.

Tonight's gig was a full-blown concert setup with all three vid screens displaying live camera footage as well as Friday's vid compilations. The light rigging was set up and we'd run the full concert set. All our stage and lighting techs had joined us, directed by Friday and Mykal.

We gathered in the dressing room backstage before the show. Stacy stood at the makeup counter, warming up on a silicone drum pad. Nori, Dia, Toni, and I sprawled on the couches. Dia and I ran scales on our guitars, keeping our fingers limber.

Stacy said, "Did you get a look at the crowd? It's wall to wall out there."

Toni grinned. "Damn, I hope this goes well."

"It's gonna be great," Nori said.

Mykal poked his head through the door. "Three minutes, ladies!"

Performance nerves tickled my stomach. Toni stood. "Huddle!"

We gathered in the middle of the room for a group hug, arms looped over each other's shoulders. Toni asked, "We ready?"

Dia whooped. "You know it, baby."

Mykal opened the door again. "Let's head to the stage."

He led us down the short hallway, then up the back stairs to the wings of the darkened stage where our techs waited for us.

Each tech wore night-vision goggles and we put our hands on their shoulders like blind people as they guided us to our places on the blacked-out stage. The rowdy crowd was losing their collective minds. Cameras flashed, and I could make out the dim glow of the bar way in the back.

My guitar tech squeezed my arm. "You good to go?"

"Yeah. Good. Thanks, Gavin."

I checked the dimly lit settings on my amps, verified the power lights were on and flicked on the power to my guitar. I swear I felt her humming in my hands. The energy of the crowd was almost a live thing, making my blood rush and my heart pound with adrenaline.

I heard Stacy count us off through my in-ear monitor and we slammed out the opening power chord as the lights came up and pyrotechnic explosions flashed at the front sides of the stage.

Toni paced the center, growling out the lyrics to "Dark Room."

Fans packed the dance floor shoulder to shoulder, fists in the air, hollering the lyrics back to us. Crunching out the rhythm line in tandem with Dia, I strode closer to Toni.

That's when I saw it.

A single black rose with bleeding red edges, lying on the stage a few feet in front of me.

I almost stopped playing.

My fingers stuttered across the guitar strings before muscle memory kicked in; my hands knew what to do, even if my brain was in shock.

The world narrowed down to the rose glistening in the stage lighting.

Suddenly Nori was at my side and I blinked back into focus, aware again of my fingers moving over the fretboard. Facing away from the audience, she mouthed, "Are you okay?"

I nodded, even as I scanned the front rows of fist-pumping thrashers who were more focused on Toni than on me. I stumbled back toward my amps.

I saw Mykal hovering on the side of the stage, his expression worried as he bellowed furiously into his headset. I flashed him a tight smile and a barely perceptible nod, indicating I was okay.

But I wasn't okay. Or anywhere near it. I was unsettled and scared. Celestian was back. I stayed away from the edge of the stage, hovering by my amps or the drum riser. Everyone in the crowd was a threat. Was the rose thrown onto the stage or had Celestian gotten backstage? Was she in the dressing room? In the bus? Was she hiding in the dark in the wings right at this moment? Watching me? I knew Panther and a couple others were regularly using their heat scanners on hotel rooms, backstage areas, and our tour buses, but I also knew they were fallible.

I scanned what I could see of the crowd. I didn't know who I was looking for. The police agreed that the heat scans and the video we'd gotten suggested that Celestian was a woman, and for some instinctive reason I had to agree. But my two-week reprieve was over.

Dia and Nori drifted closer than usual, one or the other sticking near my side. With my friends circling me, I managed to push the fear away and force myself to focus on the music, concentrating on the feel of the strings under my fingers, the physical sensation of bass and drum riffs driving through my body.

Toni ground out, "I will not fear! I will not surrender! I am the beast you created!"

I fired off the chord progression, tight, staccato, driving, then dropped into the solo, ending in a screaming feedback and segueing into the next verse.

When I looked back to center stage, the rose was gone.

Fear and panic rushed back as we hustled off stage, my thoughts quickly turning into a jumble of worry. What would I find backstage addressed to me? My nerves jangled alongside the adrenaline of the gig. The background roar of an appreciative crowd demanded more as I followed my bandmates toward the dressing room. Panther stood guard at the door. She gave us all high fives as we passed through.

Wayne stood in the center of the dim room, preening like a proud father. "You gals were great! Phenomenal!"

He patted Dia on the back and gave Toni a quick one-armed hug. I almost laughed when Nori expertly sidestepped him. Almost. I hung back, scanning the room, clutching my guitar in my arms for something to hold onto while the others congratulated each other.

Mykal pushed into the room. "If you're gonna do an encore, and I think you should, you're on in three."

One of the other stage techs shoved water bottles into our hands. I drank mine without comment, slamming down the cold liquid with gratitude. Panther moved to my side, speaking quietly. "Myk told me about the flower. Someone must have thrown it onto the stage. The room is clear. Nobody came in and I never left my post. I did a scan before you all finished and verified nobody's hiding in here."

"Thanks, Panther, I appreciate that."

She gave my arm a quick squeeze and returned to her post by the door.

A minute later Myk was back. “Let’s go, let’s go! Encore in one minute! Stage lights are coming up as I speak!”

We filed back out, running onto the stage. I watched the floor as I jogged to my place, cranking up the power on my guitar, relieved to see no flowers waiting for me.

Perhaps, if I were lucky, Celestian wouldn’t follow us to Moon Base.

CHAPTER ELEVEN

Earth Date: October 2453
Moon Base Domed City

Rhynn

Rhynn lay on her back catching her breath. Her body shuddered with aftershocks. Britt lay on top of her, nuzzling her neck, sucking and nipping, her fingers still flicking between Rhynn's legs as Rhynn came down from Britt's not-so-gentle ministrations. When she finally opened her eyes, Britt grinned at her. "How was it, baby?"

"You know it's always good," she said. And it was. The sex was pretty much the only good thing about their relationship. Even when it was surprise wake-up sex before Britt had to be at work in the morning.

Britt rolled off and rested on her side, head propped on her hand. Her expression sobered as she studied Rhynn with narrowed green eyes. "Are you ready for the big gig tonight?"

Rhynn sensed a mood shift. "Sure. As ready as I'm going to be."

Britt's smile didn't reach her eyes. "I hope Vicki's not going to try to sing any SCE covers."

"We haven't written the set list yet."

"You know she can't handle the vocals."

Rhynn closed her eyes. She hated this conversation and she hated Britt's jealousy of Black Plague. They were the only local band who covered SCE's songs, because Vicki rocked the vocals. Britt's band had tried but Britt couldn't pull it off, not that she would ever admit it.

Britt shimmied off the loft bed, down the ladder and started dressing. Rhynn watched her, not feeling anything as Britt bent over to pick up her clothes. Her rail-thin body had few curves and little muscle. Rhynn wondered when she'd last eaten.

Britt pulled on a form-fitting jumpsuit in shimmering jade and stepped into ankle-high boots. She glanced over her shoulder. "You know, just because you got the opening spot doesn't mean anything. You're not anywhere near their league."

It always amazed Rhynn how Britt could turn on her so quickly. In a heartbeat, she went from fucking her silly to telling her she wasn't good enough. She didn't bother to respond to the verbal jab.

Britt huffed and stalked from the bedroom. Rhynn heard the soft bleep as the apartment door locked behind her. Fucking girlfriends.

* * *

"That everything?"

Nightwalker's drummer, Erik, shoved the last case into the back of his beat-up air-van. It was a repurposed delivery truck painted flat black with Nightwalker stenciled across the sides in block lettering.

Rhynn studied the packed array of equipment cases and stands. "Should be. Thanks again for the transport."

"No worries." He slammed the hatch shut with a hollow clang. They both cringed at the sound. Rhynn hoped the dilapidated van would make the short trip to the club as she settled into the passenger seat. Erik jammed the van into gear and the hover jets kicked in with a stuttering growl, the van jerking up and forward.

When they reached the loading dock at the back of Club Tranquility, Rhynn stepped out of the van and swung open the rear hatch while Erik climbed onto the loading platform and rang the stage door alarm. After a minute or two, the smaller side door opened. One of the regular stagehands, Zeke, snaked his head out.

"Hey! And you're even on time!" He ducked back inside and the garage-size loading door rose with an ugly grinding.

"Go ahead and set up on the side drum platforms. You can decide who gets the right and who gets the left. Shattered Crystal Enigma gets the main drum riser. I'll jack you into the boards and make sure I'm getting a good signal when you're set up."

Erik gave him a thumbs-up. "Works for us."

"I'll leave ya to it, then." Zeke headed offstage and toward the sound booth at the center of the room.

Rhynn started lifting equipment cases out of the van and onto the dock while Erik hauled them into the backstage loading area. She claimed the stage left drum riser, leaving Erik the platform on stage right, and hummed to herself as she uncrated her equipment, falling into the Zen state of setting up her drums. She configured the three-sided blue chrome frame, attaching the drum and cymbal pads and electronics. Her amplifier ran a stereo pair of two-meter-high speaker cabinets, one on each side of the drum riser.

Perched on the padded swivel throne, she hung her stick bag between the tom pads on her right. She fussed with the placement of the two bass drums and their foot pedals, the hi-hat pedal, and a bank of sound-effect pedals she used to trigger rapid changes in the controller and kick off a handful of pre-recorded sequences. Everything needed to be exactly where she expected it. Muscle memory was key. If any of the pads or foot-pedal triggers were out of place by even a centimeter, she would have to think a hell of a lot harder.

She powered up her amps and the controller brain. With a sigh of satisfaction, she started to play, checking all the pads and tweaking the placement. The mesh drum surfaces and the hard silicon of the cymbal pads responded as she rapped out the beats, sensitive to pressure and to where on the pad she hit. She knew she could make her drums sing, and she smiled as effortless rhythms blasted through the speakers.

On the riser on the opposite side of the stage, Erik completed his own set up. He had a few more pads and triggers than she did, and his controller, amps, and speakers were more powerful than hers. Rhynn sighed when he started to play, drooling a little over his drum kit. Even though they considered each other equals, there was always that "mine is bigger than yours" game musicians played, and Rhynn was as guilty as anyone.

After Zeke ran quick drum checks, she and Erik left to drop his van off so the rest of Nightwalker and Black Plague could use it. Then he and Rhynn decided to grab some food at the Afterburner Grill to kill some time before the main sound checks started.

A couple of hours later, Rhynn opened Club Tranquility's backstage door to a cacophony of guitar riffs and bass notes. Her bandmates were on stage setting up. She wound through the maze of empty equipment cases and paused at the side of the stage.

Leigh waved a hand, beaming as Rhynn approached. "Hey, girl, you excited?"

"Fucking freaking out. You guys about ready? Are we sound-checking soon?"

"Zeke is waiting on the rest of his crew. Probably fifteen, twenty minutes or so."

Their lead singer Vicki met them at center stage. "What do you want to sound check with?"

Leigh slung her bass strap over her shoulder. "What do the guys wanna play through?"

Harris, their rhythm guitarist, wandered over. "Let's do 'Cracked Earth.'"

Rhynn sent him a dubious look. "An SCE cover? To sound check? Seriously?"

He smirked. "I love that tune. Besides, they're not here yet and it's a good mix for us."

Vicki said, "Good vocal for sound check too." She sauntered over to let their lead guitarist, Rod, know.

Rhynn hopped up onto the drum platform.

Fifteen minutes later, they kicked off their sound check. Zeke ran through the drum checks first, then bass, guitars and vocals.

Finally, Rhynn clicked off "Cracked Earth," and they launched into the intricate rhythms, offset by the haunting melody of the chorus.

Vicki was in prime form. In one breath she was growling and in the next her voice rang clear, belting out the melody. Harris and Leigh crunched out the bass and rhythm guitar parts, and Rod took the solo, fingers flying over strings and fretboard in a flurry of notes and scales.

Rhynn drove the band hard and fast, her hands and feet working in synchronous coordination, whipping out rapid-fire fills under the guitar lines. This was what she loved—when the beats she heard in her head flowed out through her limbs, and her body existed in harmony with the music.

When they finished the tune, Vicki asked for a little more vocal and rhythm guitar in the center monitor mix, and Rhynn asked Zeke to pull some of the vocals out of the drum monitor. Then Black Plague cleared the stage, leaving it for Nightwalker to take over and do their sound check.

Rhynn leaned against the bar at the back of the club, sipping a fizzy drink and watching Shattered Crystal Enigma's road crew unpack and set up. A young woman with wildly curly blond hair directed them as they raised two vid screens, one on each side of the drum riser.

Rhynn wished she could go up and take a closer look at the drummer's sound mods and amps, though she knew she'd probably drool all over the state-of-the-art drum kit and custom tiered rack. She'd read the specs on Stacy Rowe's equipment, but she really wanted to see it up close and personal.

The members of SCE hadn't arrived, but Rhynn overheard their stage manager, a bear-sized man with a short beard, bald head, and tattooed arms, tell Zeke the band was on their way. She also heard something about additional security before the two men had walked out of earshot.

She glanced at the time on her comp pad. The club wouldn't open for another four hours. She had time to go home but told herself she didn't need to waste energy crossing the Dome and then coming all the way back. She laughed at herself. What she really wanted was to see Ari Walker when SCE finally arrived.

The club staff was starting to drift in, stocking the bar, cleaning up and getting ready for the concert. Part of the road crew for SCE set up a merchandising table near the main entrance, selling T-shirts, holo vids, and trinkets with the band's name and logo.

Rhynn glanced around. Her guitarists played vid games with two of the Nightwalker guys. Vicki sat at one of the tables near the stage with Sully from Nightwalker, watching SCE's road crew and talking. Leigh sat beside her at the bar, texting on her comp pad.

A flurry of voices and motion announced the arrival of Shattered Crystal Enigma. Rhynn watched as the women wandered onto the stage. They interacted good-naturedly with their techs and the local stagehands. The band appeared to be at ease; as though this was just another gig.

Rhynn recognized Toni Catone immediately. The singer's waist-length dreadlocks hung down her back. Her dark chocolate-toned skin glowed in the warm tones of the working stage lighting. The curly-haired blond stage tech who'd been directing the light riggers jogged across to Toni's side, and Toni's mouth widened into a full smile as she slid an arm around the other woman's shoulders. The two stood close as they talked.

Thoroughly intrigued by the humanity of seeing the band in their natural environment, Rhynn couldn't pull her gaze away from the stage.

She identified Dia Caban and Nori Beaty and found herself staring as Ari Walker ambled toward a stack of guitar amps and speakers where she stood with one of the techs, gesturing toward the equipment, nodding seriously as they conversed. Ari was taller than Rhynn thought she'd be—at least, taller than her tech. Her straight brown hair hung loose around her shoulders and she wore an open, dark-colored shirt over a tank top and tight pants tucked into low boots. Her legs went on forever.

Rhynn wished she were closer to the stage.

The drummer, Stacy Rowe, jumped off the drum riser and marched purposefully across the stage, jogging down the side stairs and stalking across the dance floor. She flipped her red hair behind her shoulders as she approached the bar, ignoring Rhynn and Leigh, her attention solely on the bartender.

Willy stopped what he was doing and greeted her with a smile. "Hey, welcome. What can I get you?"

"Stassers. Double," she said flatly, without returning either his smile or his greeting. Her pixy-like face was carved into a cold, hard expression.

"Sure." He stepped away and poured her drink.

Stacy said, "Run me a tab. It's going to be a long night." She took her glass and walked away.

Willy frowned and shook his head before returning to his work.

Leigh muttered, "What a bitch."

"No doubt." Rhynn hoped the whole band didn't have the same lousy attitude. Stacy disappeared backstage without talking to her bandmates. Toni and Dia continued to talk with the curly-haired blonde. Ari had left the stage. Rhynn sighed and felt a little silly. She was too old to be starstruck, but she hoped she'd at least get to meet SCE's lead guitarist.

Leigh bumped Rhynn's arm. "Well, fuck. Look who showed up."

Rhynn shifted to look in the direction Leigh indicated. Her girlfriend Britt, in her dressed-to-the-nines glory, crossed the back of the room with one of the club staff, hanging all over the tall brunette, their heads together as they talked.

Rhynn's heart pounded against her chest. What the fuck? The two stopped near the Employees Only door and kissed passionately before the brunette slipped through the door.

Rhynn's stomach lurched and fell toward her feet. Memories of Britt fucking her this morning flashed through her brain. *Guess that meant exactly nothing.* What a phenomenal way to find out your girlfriend was sleeping around on you.

"That fucking bitch," Leigh hissed.

Rhynn swallowed, not sure if she was angry, relieved, or hurt. She felt mostly numb as she watched Britt's new girlfriend return. They crossed to the bar where Rhynn and Leigh sat. The new girlfriend slipped behind the bar and greeted Willy. Britt was about to take a seat on the end when her eyes met Rhynn's.

Rhynn caught a flash of surprise and then something akin to embarrassment flash over Britt's face before the emotion faded and she sauntered over.

"Hello, Rhynn, Leigh."

It took Rhynn a couple seconds to find her voice. "Hey, Britt. What are you doing here?"

Britt smiled innocently at Rhynn. "Kellyanne got me in for the show. Are you excited to play?"

Leigh stood and took an intimidating step toward Britt. "Is Kellyanne the one you were making out with?"

Rhynn felt a flash of appreciation for her best friend's obvious defense of her as she struggled to find her equilibrium.

Britt's smile faltered. "About that—"

"Maybe you have something to tell your *girlfriend*?"

Britt had the grace to blush as she met Rhynn's stoic gaze. "I'm really sorry, Rhynny. But you know it wasn't working out."

"A little heads-up would have been nice." Rhynn's voice sounded emotionless to her own ears.

"Yeah, I know. I just—you know. I didn't want to hurt you."

"That didn't work out so well."

"I'm sorry, Rhynn."

"Yeah, me too."

Britt gave Rhynn one last, apologetic look before turning away.

Leigh said, "I'll beat the shit out of her if you want me to."

Rhynn watched Britt walk away. "Wouldn't be worth it," she muttered.

CHAPTER TWELVE

Earth Date: 31 October 2453
Moon Base Domed City
Club Tranquility

Ari

I followed my bandmates onto an expansive club stage. The two opening bands had already set up, leaving more than enough room for us. A dance floor spread out in front of the stage with a zero-g dance cube to the left, probably the largest I'd ever seen. Wayne had promised they liked their slam-thrash bands up here. Seeing the two-story high cube, I believed him.

I squinted out into the dimly lit club. A handful of staff and others, whom I assumed were musicians for the opening bands, milled around or sat in small groups. Friday turned from the techs she was directing and greeted Toni. I laughed when Toni's face lit up with a happy grin. Yeah, she was definitely smitten with Friday. And they made a cute couple, a contrast in light and dark.

I crossed the stage to check in with my guitar tech Gavin.

"Hey, Ari. Everything's under control. The stage manager knows his stuff. Had everything ready for us."

"Good. What time are we sound-checking?"

"Maybe another half hour or so."

We chatted for a couple more minutes and I decided to check out the dressing room. As I walked off stage, Stacy brushed past me, headed into the club. I jogged down the cement staircase to the green room below the stage. Panther stood watch at the door.

"Hey, ladies. All quiet here."

"Thanks, Panther."

The dressing room was reasonably well lit and set up with several couches and tables. A heavy black curtain closed off a changing area. Three makeup tables with lighted mirrors lined the back wall.

At the center of the room, two tables were piled with finger food and sandwiches as well as water and fizzy drinks in buckets of ice. Our guitars rested in stands, lined up beside a couple of mini amps. Stacy's practice pad and sticks waited on the table in front of one of the couches.

Standing by the food tables, Nori popped open a fizzy drink and handed one to me. "Cheers."

I raised the bottle toward her. "Back at'cha."

"You wanna check out the club? I'm feeling restless."

"Sure."

We went back upstairs and wove our way through the stage right area, cluttered with empty crates and open equipment cabinets. A short set of stairs at the edge of the right side of the stage led down into the club. As we approached, Stacy stepped around us, holding a full glass.

Nori's dark eyes narrowed as she saw the drink in Stacy's hand. "Starting a little early, aren't you?"

I groaned inwardly, wishing Nori would leave well enough alone.

Stacy glowered at her. "Don't even go there. Why are we even playing this backwater bar?"

I said, "This isn't the backwater. I grew up out-system."

"And you left pretty quick when you had the chance."

I wasn't sure why I needed to defend either the bar, Moon Base, or the tour, but the words flowed out of my mouth anyway. "Touring is touring and exposure is exposure. We'll be back on Earth in a month for the second leg."

"Yeah, well, not soon enough for me."

Nori said, "If you were so against this leg of the tour, why didn't you say something when we first started talking about it?"

"Like it would have done any good. Not like Wayne listens to anyone but himself and whatever the record label tells him to do."

I said, "What the fuck, Stace? Where is this coming from?"

"Maybe I'm getting tired of the bullshit. You and your stalker, all the fucking security, having to be out here in the middle of fucking nowhere."

"Especially when your new boyfriend is back on Earth," Nori said.

"Fuck you, Nori. Maybe I miss him, but what do you care?"

"I care because it's the human thing to do, Stace. And whether you believe it or not, I do care about you, and everyone else in this band."

"Right."

I opened my mouth to reply but was rescued by a call from on stage. "Hey, Ari, you wanna check out your system?"

Relieved, I jogged over to my stacked amps and speaker cabinets. Gavin handed me a guitar, and I ran through the settings on my pedal board. I tweaked a couple sound mods as I played a few scales and chord progressions. As always, Gavin's setup up was impeccable. I powered off my guitar and handed it back to him.

On the other side of the stage, Dia checked her rig. The crunch of rhythm guitar riffs filled the room. At the same time, Stacy's drum tech made his own checks. Punctuated accents cracked out of the drum monitors as he tapped through the drum pads. Toni stood with Friday in the sound booth in the middle of the club, where they leaned over the lighting and stage effects boards.

Mykal shouted into a mic over the noise, "Full sound check in half an hour."

Suddenly overwhelmed by the cacophony of conflicting sounds, I wanted to be outside. Not that a person could technically be "outside" on Moon Base. I crossed the stage and threaded my way through the loading area. The guard who should have been at the backstage doors wasn't there. Maybe he'd been called away or was taking a bathroom break.

I hesitated. When was the last time I'd gone anywhere unguarded? I chewed my lip, my fears battling against the need for some space. Being on tour was hard on introverts, always being with people, rarely having the time to decompress. I was in need of alone time, but I'd seen Nori head back toward the dressing room, and there was nowhere else to sit quietly.

I palmed the lock for the door to the cement loading dock and pushed it open. The sour odor of refuse from the narrow alleyway assaulted my senses—stale beer, rancid food, grease, urine. Not fresh air, but at least when the door shut, the alley was quiet.

The gray duracrete loading dock extended about four meters out from the building and ran along the back. I sat against the wall between the side door and the loading door and wrapped my arms around my knees.

Rubbish bins, empty cargo flats, and boxes lined the buildings on the other side of the alley. Floodlights pooled dirty golden light onto the duracrete road surface. A light strip above me bathed the loading dock in cool white light.

I felt better for having the light, but continually searched the shadows. Thoughts of Celestian pricked at my thoughts. Still, I wasn't as anxious as I expected to be. Maybe it was because we were so far from Earth. Maybe it was because there would always be a part of me that felt more comfortable away from Earth, more like I was wrapped in the safety of my childhood. Looking up through the slightly hazy glass of the Dome, space extended endlessly, spritzed with the bright pinpoints of stars. This was the familiar vista of my youth—blackness and diamonds. It was cold and endless, but also weirdly reassuring.

My thoughts turned to Stacy. Over the past few weeks and months she'd drifted further and further, separating herself from us both physically and emotionally. I wasn't sure if it was because of the intoxicants or if she simply wasn't happy being in the band anymore. Nori was convinced the drugs were a big part of it.

Nori would know. She'd been there. But sometimes instead of being understanding, she egged Stacy on, which annoyed me. I think Stacy reminded Nori too much of herself, and she didn't want Stacy to have to go through the same bottoming out and recovery she'd experienced. Or she didn't want to be part of the process all over again. Nori's insecurities tended to come out sideways. I worried that the band was unraveling before we even got started on this tour. Resting my head against the wall, I reminded myself it would be what it would be. All I could do was push forward and do my best. The Universe would take care of the rest.

The side door opened with a grating squeal, and a woman stomped through. "Fucking stupid bitch," she ground out and kicked an empty drink bottle lying on the dock. It spun across the alley and shattered against the building.

I flinched. I may also have squeaked.

"Oh!" She stopped short and held up her hands. "Sorry, I didn't know anyone was out here." Her hair was shaved close, except for a white-bleached topknot hanging to the side and a splash of flourescent pink bangs falling over her eyes.

"Just me," I said. "Pull up some cement if you want. Plenty of room."

The door shut behind her with a heavy clunk. She wasn't tall but had a wiry build. Pale, almost translucent skin suggested she had grown up in space. She held two long-necked containers of beer in one hand.

She swallowed as she recognized me, and I realized she was likely a musician from one of the other bands. Her glance was uneasy, but she slid down the wall to sit beside me and offered up one of the beers. "Two for one, and I sure don't need two, so you're welcome to it."

It didn't sound like a bad idea, and I accepted.

"I'm Rhynn. Rhynn Knight. Drummer for Black Plague. The first opening band."

I heard apology in her voice. I said, "Good to meet you, Rhynn. I'm Ari Walker."

"Yeah." She blushed a deep red. "Wild to actually meet you."

I held up my bottle. "Thanks."

"Sure. I mean, I usually don't drink like this. It's been a day of revelations."

The cool liquid felt good going down. "I know what you mean."

Rhynn played with the bottle, turning it slowly between long fingers before finally taking a deep swallow. "My girlfriend just showed up with another woman and dumped my ass." She looked away, down the alley, like she was embarrassed to have said too much, and to have been dumped. "Sorry. I also don't usually spill my guts to strangers."

"I think I'd be having a drink too. I'm sorry about your girlfriend."

"Thanks."

We sat quietly. I stole a couple glances at her. She was pretty. Her colorful bangs and the topknot was tomboyish. I wanted to see her eyes, but they were hidden from me as she looked down. She wore knee-length shorts with cargo pockets and zippers, a black concert T-shirt from a band I didn't know and worn ankle-high exercise shoes with thick rubber soles.

I almost never start a conversation, so I was surprised when I said, "Tell me about your band."

Rhynn's head snapped up, as though startled. "We're local, all of us. We do about half and half covers and originals, all slam-thrash. We've been together a while now, gigging mostly here at Moon Base, though we got a couple opening shows in Luna City. The Jupiter there does a three-day slam-thrash festival every year, and we've gotten to be part of that." She shrugged. "Not much else to tell. I love to play, even if it's only up here with my friends."

"Everyone starts locally. Some of us get lucky and get to make a living out of it."

Rhynn's lips curved into a crooked smile. "And the rest of us are jealous."

"Some days, it's not all it's cracked up to be."

"It's gotta be better than working a day job to support your music habit."

"I can't argue that."

"So, you think, maybe later, you could autograph a tour photo for me?"

"Anytime. I'd be happy to."

"Does it get old, people asking for autographs and telling you how incredible you are?"

I laughed. I heard no animosity in her tone, only simple interest and honesty. "The attention can be intrusive sometimes, but it never hurts to have someone tell you they appreciate what you do. We work hard and being on the road can be grueling. But it's worth it to know what you've created might have made a difference."

"I get that."

We settled into an oddly comfortable silence. I finished my beer and set the bottle aside. I didn't feel the need to fill the quiet between us, and for whatever reason, Rhynn Knight didn't need to either. Very seldom did I meet a fan who was content to hang out without asking a hundred questions or telling me seven different ways how much they loved this song or that song or how I played some riff. I decided I very much wanted to see her band and hear Rhynn play.

The side door slammed open and we both jumped.

"Ari!" Nori pinned me with a furious glare. "Damn it, I've been worried sick looking all over the fucking place for you!"

I sighed. "I needed a break."

"You shouldn't be out here alone!"

I gestured to Rhynn, who sat wide-eyed and obviously wondering what was going on. "Do I look like I'm alone?"

After a couple seconds Nori's shoulders dropped. "Fine. Just don't do it again, okay? You scared the piss out of me, and Panther ripped the security guy a new one because he left his post and didn't see you leave."

"I'm sorry, Nor. I needed to get away."

"You're forgiven. Also, FYI, the special tour security people are supposed to be here in a little while. Sound check in five." She aimed an intense gaze on Rhynn and snapped, "Don't let her out of your sight." Then she spun on her heel, palmed the door and disappeared inside.

Rhynn studied me thoughtfully for a couple beats and finally said, "Should I ask?"

I really didn't want to talk about it. The words tumbled out of my mouth anyway. "I've had someone stalking me for the last few months. They've left creepy, threatening love notes and flowers with fake blood on them. They've gotten past security to leave things. It's unnerving not knowing when and if I'm being watched."

Rhynn frowned. "Wow. That's scary."

I nodded. Sure, I was scared, but whining wasn't going to change anything. I didn't want to talk about waking up shaking and panicking because of dreams with faceless eyes looking in my windows, or running from a shadowy pursuer, terrified that if I stopped, she'd catch me. And Rhynn Knight didn't want to hear about the great Ari Walker having bad dreams.

Rhynn said. "I hope the authorities get whoever it is. Meanwhile, I guess you're safe enough with me." She wrinkled her nose and smirked, shaking her bangs from her face. "I'll smack 'em silly with my drumsticks if they get too close."

Her bravado made me smile and put a warm feeling in my chest. "I'll hold you to that."

CHAPTER THIRTEEN

Earth Date: 31 October 2453
Moon Base Domed City
Club Tranquility

Rhynn

Rhynn followed Ari back into the club where a dissonant thunder of riffs, tuning scales, and drumbeats blasted out of the PA. As the door closed behind them, Ari rested a warm hand on Rhynn's arm. "Thank you, for the beer and the conversation."

Her low, mellow voice flowed over Rhynn, and she lost herself in Ari's hazel-green gaze. Her skin tingled from the casual touch. "You're welcome. It was good to meet you."

Ari started to reply, but someone called her name over the PA, and she gave Rhynn a smile and joined her bandmates for their sound check.

Rhynn stood rooted to the floor, staring for a few seconds before she managed to force her feet to move. She weaved through the equipment cases to the short stairway at the edge of the stage and crossed the dance floor, angling toward the high tables in front of the sound booth where her band and Nightwalker had gathered to watch SCE's sound check. She grabbed a low-backed stool beside Leigh and hopped up, letting her feet swing.

"Where you been?" Leigh asked.

"Out on the loading dock with Ari Walker, having a beer."

The deadpan statement got the expected reaction and Leigh's jaw dropped comically. "You were hanging out with Ari Walker? Fucking seriously?"

Rhynn laughed. "Yeah. Seriously. She's super nice. And I only made a little fool of myself being a stupid fangirl."

Leigh punched her in the arm. "I want details."

The soundman's voice boomed across the main PA. "Anytime you're ready."

SCE's drummer clicked off and they launched into one of Rhynn's favorites, "Ignorance is Bliss."

Rhynn wanted to cheer but managed to curb the urge. Instead she focused on Ari, who stood by her amps, occasionally fiddling with a control, then walking back and forth across the stage. The mix balance between the instruments shifted slightly through the song. Toni's vocal mellowed as the painful high-end pitches were removed and the instrument balances fell into place. By the end of the song, it was almost like listening to the original recording.

The band ran through a few more tunes, including a couple Rhynn assumed were from the new release. She was entranced to hear SCE live. They were every bit as talented as she imagined. The drummer was rock solid. Even if she acted like a bitch, she played well. Rhynn had learned the drum parts for every song. She'd learned them all because she loved the music and because she loved the challenge. The forceful energy of SCE's songs and their lyrical messages spoke to her, made her feel stronger, braver, more in control. Maybe because they were all women. Maybe because they were just that good.

Ari Walker was, of course, mind-blowing. She was so confident. She made it look effortless as she cranked out her riffs and solos while moving casually around the stage, interacting with the rest of the band.

Rhynn thought about her conversation with Ari, as well as the heated but concerned words Ari'd had with her bass player. Rhynn wondered about the stalker and if it was weird that she felt a deep sense of concern for Ari, or that she'd truly meant it when she promised to protect her. She knew if she saw anyone even remotely threatening Ari, she'd be all over them in a hot minute.

Ari seemed so straightforward, not holier than thou, arrogant, or looking down her nose at a peon musician from Moon Base. Rhynn wondered how much was real, how much was put on, or her own personal bias and expectations. She wanted to believe Ari was the person she thought she saw.

She understood she'd never know. Her band would play this gig tonight, and she'd never see Ari Walker again. She wanted to memorize today for what it was, write the video in her head and hold it safe. These were her personal fifteen minutes of fame.

Even though Britt the bitch had dumped her ass, it was going to be a good night.

CHAPTER FOURTEEN

Earth Date: 31 October 2453
Moon Base Domed City
Club Tranquility

Morgan Rahn

Morgan Rahn, former Senior Ship Systems Mechanic, walked the familiar roadway past the Aldrin Hotel and toward Club Tranquility. Her wife, Shaine Wendt, sauntered alongside, tall and confident in black cargo pants and tunic with the "WR Private Special Forces" logo on the shoulder. Shaine was the epitome of a security specialist, Morgan thought, openly admiring her partner. Morgan wore the same black uniform, but it simply wasn't as impressive on her. She was much too thin and wiry to be outwardly threatening, not to mention a head shorter than Shaine.

Still, she was learning to be as dangerous as anyone in their company. She and Shaine had been training hard since she'd left her home here on Moon Base a year ago. Under Shaine's exacting tutelage she studied hand-to-hand combat, mixed martial arts, and self-defense. She'd beaten guys three times her weight during Shaine's training sessions in their security company's workout facility.

Several of the personnel from their stint at the Mann-Maru mining facility on Mars had joined WR. Dark-skinned Del Marin and the albino Gohste Rock were part of the command staff.

Shaine's military and corporate contacts allowed them to compete for jobs protecting local and System politicians who needed escorts. They had taken courier jobs delivering confidential packages and worked as bodyguards for prominent government and entertainment figures. Shaine had also agreed to a couple of security jobs for corporate allies of Morgan's birth father, Tarm Maruchek, head of the ubiquitous corporate conglomerate that was Mann-Maru Universal Industries.

And now this opportunity had come through their foster daughter Friday, of all people. It hadn't taken Friday long to convince them to provide additional concert and personal security to an up-and-coming slam-thrash band on the fast track to fame.

Shaine had thought it was a joke at first, but after talking to the band's manager and PR consultant, the guitarist's threatening stalker seemed serious. Besides, Friday wanted them to take the job, and both she and Shaine were inclined to trust Friday's instincts. Morgan was especially intrigued because they would be joining the tour on her home turf at Moon Base, where her good friends' band Nightwalker was opening, and of course, because slam-thrash was her favorite music, and she'd heard enough of SCE's recordings to be psyched to work with them.

As she and Shaine approached Club Tranquility, Shaine nodded toward the alley. "I want to walk the perimeter."

Morgan focused on the job at hand. Given the history they'd received, Shaine was sure the stalker would show up along the tour route. There'd already been an incident in New York.

Morgan scanned the flat, windowless backs of the buildings along the alley. Light pooled around the back entrances, leaving dark shadows between rubbish bins and piles of packing flats. They passed Tranquility's loading dock made of worn duracrete. Nothing there to hide behind.

Refuse bins opened their odiferous maws to the alley, and Morgan scrunched her nose against the cloying stench. She'd forgotten how close the air got under the dome. Shaine ran a flashlight over the bins and between them while Morgan held a comp pad searching for heat signatures and movement. They were alone in the alley, other than what appeared to be a couple of rats.

They walked to the club's front entrance, where a line of eager fans waited to get into the show. Earning catcalls and shouts of frustration for jumping the line, Morgan smirked as they walked past everyone and into Club Tranquility. She had been a member of that queue more times than she could count.

Unsurprisingly, nothing had changed. Same club. Same decor. Same smells. Slightly sticky flooring. Walls painted dark red and black. The back part of the main floor, behind the bar, had pool tables and vid-game centers with virtual reality booths. The bar was rectangular with a couple mirrored walls up to the ceiling, between which were open spaces to allow the bar staff to move easily between the front and the back. To one side of the entryway, stairs led to the club's second level, usually saved for VIP guests or private gatherings. She followed Shaine to the bar.

Shaine asked, "Is Rand Bohler here? We need to speak with him."

The young woman paused as she stacked some glasses. "Um, yeah, I think so. I'll see if he's in back. Who should I tell him is here?"

"Shaine Wendt of WR Security."

"Okay." She slipped around the bar and hurried toward a red door marked Staff Only.

Shaine raised a questioning brow and Morgan shrugged. She didn't recognize the girl, but it'd been more than a year since she'd been here. Her comp pad beeped from its clip on her belt and she grabbed it, quickly opening the connection when she recognized the call sign. A minute later, she killed the call and said to Shaine, "Del's on her way from backstage."

Rand Bohler sauntered across the floor toward them. His slightly overweight form bulged out of tight pants, and he wore a blood-red shirt zipped down to reveal too much of his pale, hairy chest. Heavy titanium and gold chains hung around his thick neck and wide rings adorned his stubby fingers. His dishwater blond hair was combed over the top. Morgan pushed down a shudder as his gaze ran up and down her body, and she knew he was trying to figure out if he recognized her. She let him stew over it.

Shaine held out a hand. "Mr. Bohler. Shaine Wendt, WR Security. I wanted to check in before I got my people into place. Do you have any additional questions?"

Bohler shook her hand. Morgan was amused that he had to look up to meet Shaine's gaze. "No, no questions. Your people are directing security. My staff has been informed to take orders from you and to bring any issues to you and let you handle it." He paused and added, "Though I'm not sure why the band is so worried about security. I run a tight ship here."

Shaine said, "I'm sure you do, Mr. Bohler, however there are some extenuating circumstances requiring additional precautions."

He waited for more, but when it wasn't forthcoming, he said, "Right, well, if that's all, I have business to attend to."

"Of course. Thank you."

Morgan held back the urge to snicker as she watched him try to decide whether or not he should be saluting. Finally, his head bobbed a couple times and he hastened back through the red staff door. Bohler had always been full of himself, and not against cheating the bands he hired if shows didn't pull in as much business as he wanted, especially if they were locals. Musicians bitched, but Tranquility was the only show in town, so they dealt with it.

Del Marin joined them as they walked to the front of the club. Short dreadlocks erupted from her head in a storm of black curls and her muscular arms extended from a tight, sleeveless black tunic. "Hey, Boss. Morg."

"Tell me what you've got," Shaine said.

"The record label people have things well in hand, except one guy, and I sent his ass home. The bouncers for the club seem pretty good. I told them to do their jobs the way they always do. I've got our people on the doors and covering the stage. Gohste is going to stay in the sound booth watching in-house video surveillance and we're setting up infrared and heat-sensing scanners. The band has a gal named Panther. She's on top of things, and she's posted at the dressing room with Mitch. I think we're in good shape."

"Thanks, Del."

The former Marine dropped Shaine a quick salute. "Right, Boss." She shook her dreads back off her face. "Hey, did ya see Fri yet? I talked to her. She's looking good, excited to see you guys. And she has someone she wants you to meet."

Morgan grinned. "Her last message kept dropping Toni Catone's name."

Del laughed. "Yeah. They make a cute couple. Don't give her too much shit, huh?"

Shaine rolled her eyes. "As long as Toni Catone treats her well, we've got nothing to say. Come on, I want to see the backstage setup and meet the stage crew. Then we can visit the kid and meet her friends."

CHAPTER FIFTEEN

Earth Date: 31 October 2453
Moon Base Domed City
Club Tranquility

Rhynn

Rhynn hung out in the club with her bandmates while eager concertgoers filled the venue. She shifted from foot to foot, unable to sit still, fingers tapping restlessly to the music blaring over the house PA. She watched a few spacers floating and flipping around in the zero-gravity cube to the right of the stage and thought maybe she'd jump in when Nightwalker was playing.

She knew when she was done playing she'd have adrenaline to spare, and joining the intricate patterns with the slammers in the cube was always a blast. Slamming was a spacer thing. Most Earthers didn't understand the thrill of zero gravity or play grav-ball in zero-grav arenas or learn how to whip each other around to the wicked beats of slam-thrash bands. But she had grown up out here. She'd learned the patterns, the intricate rules of the cube. To outsiders it looked like a free-for-all, but not to her or her friends. She wondered if Ari Walker indulged in the slammer's cube. She'd never read that in any of her interviews, though. It'd sure be crazy to have the chance to slam with her if she did. The thought of flying through the cube with Ari put a dopey grin on her face.

She sipped on the beer Leigh had put in front of her, trying to slow her heart rate and calm down enough to play. Her band would go backstage in a few minutes. She shook out her hands. Fuck. She needed to get her shit together. She wasn't usually so uptight before a show. Excited sure. But this was different. Tonight they were opening for Nightwalker and SCE.

Even if the headliners didn't watch their show, it was the opportunity of a lifetime to open for a band like Shattered Crystal Enigma. She didn't want to fuck it up or make a fool of herself or her band. The show was sold out. All their friends were here, hovering around them, fueling the excitement. It was impossible not to get drawn into the energy.

Rhynn used the enthusiasm to push away her underlying angst about not having a permanent job and being tossed aside for a hot bartender. Fuck it all, she was opening for the coolest slam-thrash band in the system. She'd had a beer with Ari Walker, and for once the Universe was moving forward on her behalf.

Now if she could only chill out enough to play.

Her two guitarists, Rod and Harris laughed at her. "Don't be so fuckin' nervous!" Rod teased.

She flipped him off. "Fuck you. Like you're not."

Harris snickered. "Rhynn's all worried 'cause she's got a hard-on for the lead guitarist."

Rhynn glared at him, feeling the heat on her face. She backhanded him below the belt. "At least mine's not obvious."

Rod and Leigh laughed uproariously. Harris flushed and slammed back the rest of his beer.

"Come on, you guys, let's get backstage." Leigh led the way through the thrashers already standing in front of the stage. They flashed their passes at the burly security guards and were allowed up the side stairs and into the wings. Stage security brought them down into the dressing room they shared with the other bands.

The room was empty because SCE hadn't arrived from their hotel and the Nightwalker guys were still out in the club. Black Plague's bags and guitar cases were piled in the far corner. Rhynn picked up the drumsticks she'd left with her backpack and wandered over to one of the worn couches. She stood behind the couch and warmed up, using the back cushion as a drum pad.

"You guys are on in fifteen minutes!"

Rhynn looked up. SCE's stage manager, Myk Izak, a beefy, bald, bearded guy, leaned in through the open door. He'd introduced himself earlier and said he was in charge and they'd better not be late. And when they were done, they needed to clear the stage quickly. He didn't seem to be the kind of guy to argue with.

Vicki acknowledged the hail while the guys and Leigh tuned their guitars.

Adrenaline flooded Rhynn's body with crazy nervous anticipation. Fuck. Maybe she should have had another beer to take the edge off. Too bad drinking and drumming didn't mix. Rhynn preferred her sticks to stay in her hands.

When it was time, the crew ushered them up to the stage like they were a headliner band. Under the cover of darkness, guided by a roadie's flashlight, Rhynn stepped onto the drum riser and sat behind her drums. Out front, under a single spotlight, one of the local DJ's was kicking off the show with a bunch of bullshit hype. She checked the power on her amps and the sound mod controller, flipped everything from stand-by into live mode and adjusted her in-ear monitors.

She pulled a pair of sticks from the bag on her right. Her feet settled onto her primary bass drum pedals without triggering them, then touched each of the other pedals. All set. Her body thrummed with energy.

The DJ was still hyping his net music channel and making rude jokes.

Get the fuck on with it so we can play!

Finally, he introduced them.

Rhynn took a breath to set the tempo in her head and played them in with four slashes to her hi-hat cymbals. The song started with a blast of guitars. The stage lights flashed on and Vicki and Harris wailed out the dual vocals.

She felt the pressure of the music, heard the shouting crowd over the monitors. She couldn't see into the dark past the first few rows of fans pressed against the stage, yelling the lyrics back at them with raised fists and bobbing heads.

She relaxed as the music took over her senses. Watching her bandmates, listening, taking cues, pushing the songs forward, she ripped through the set list. Her hands and feet moved in sync and the rhythms flowed through her body. Her feet pumped the pedals in fast staccato while hands whipped drumsticks around the pads. The complex patterns fell into place instinctively, a combination of machine-gun speed and delicate finesse.

She followed the set list taped to the floor at her feet. The songs flowed one into another, spinning the crowd up and sucking their energy back to the band.

Vicki launched into one of the SCE covers. Leigh skipped back toward the drum riser, long fingers spidering over the frets of her bass guitar. Rhynn exchanged triumphant grins with her as they nailed a tricky passage between the verse and chorus. Then Rod wailed away up front, and Rhynn kicked back into a driving beat, feeling damn good. The notes flowed from her sticks in a flurry of beats designed to make even the unlearned take notice.

A flash of motion in the wings caught the edge of her vision, and she glanced over to see Ari Walker standing there, watching and grinning.

Holy fuck!

Rhynn nearly missed a cymbal hit as her heart skipped. Panicking, she forced her attention back to the music.

Forget her. Play. Just play.

Fucking breathe!

She didn't get her equilibrium back until they returned to their original songs again and Ari Walker was no longer in her line of sight.

Fuck. Fuck. Fuck.

And they still had another SCE song in the list.

They finished their set with a spot-on cover of SCE's "Ignorance is Bliss" and were rushed off the stage as the lights went down and the crowd yelled their appreciation. Rhynn was as close to heaven as she ever expected to be.

A few seconds later, the stage crew pushed her drum riser and their guitar amps and speaker cabinets to the far back of the stage, behind SCE's vid screens. Her hands shook with adrenaline as she shut down her power and unplugged the cables. Fuck. What a rush. What a crazy fucking rush. She clenched her fists and took a couple calming breaths, and then went back to wrapping cords and putting them into a gear bag. She had a system. Packing up her equipment was a methodical ritual to help ensure she didn't forget anything. Besides, the sooner she finished, the sooner she could watch the rest of the show.

"Hey, Rhynn, great show! You guys rocked!"

Her head snapped around so fast she nearly gave herself whiplash. Ari Walker stood to the side of her drum riser, hands in the pockets of her pants. Beside her, Nori Beaty raised a hand in greeting.

Rhynn stuttered, "Uh, wow, thanks."

"You have some serious chops, girlfriend," Ari said.

Nori snickered. "Scared the shit out of Stacy."

Ari shot her bass player a look.

Rhynn tried to think of something to say.

Ari said, "We'll leave you to your tear down, but I wanted to tell you it was a great set. We got to see most of it. Thanks for being part of the show."

Rhynn felt her face flush and knew she was probably beet red. "Thanks. Wow. Can't wait to see you guys play."

Ari gave her a wink and a smile and Nori grabbed the guitarist's arm, pulling her back into the wings.

Rhynn stared blankly for a few seconds. Holy fuck. Ari Walker said she had chops. Said thank you. Talked to her. *Ari Walker winked at me! Holy fuck!*

She grinned like an idiot as she disconnected the drum pads and mounting hardware from the rack's tubular frame. *Hot fuckin' damn.*

CHAPTER SIXTEEN

Earth Date: 31 October 2453
Moon Base Domed City
Club Tranquility

Ari

Loud, rowdy slam-thrashers packed Club Tranquility to capacity and the crowd was super hyped by the time Panther and the stage techs ushered us to the stage. Hundreds chanted and cheered, filling the dance floor. Flying bodies flipped and twisted around each other in the zero-gravity cube. Black Plague and Nightwalker had played phenomenal sets and it was obvious the crowd loved them and knew them well.

And Rhynn Knight. Damn, that girl could play. She covered all of Stacy's riffs with ease. Through the rest of their set list, both covers and originals, Rhynn kept whipping out licks that blew me away. Watching her play, I was unaccountably pleased to know she was such a wicked good drummer.

Before the end of our first song, we had the fans eating out of our proverbial hands. A few songs in, during "Broken Hearts, Beaten Minds," I crossed to center stage at the end of the second verse, sharing the front with Toni, both of us leaning forward with a boot up on the center floor monitor. I loved this song, and as she finished the verse lyric, I launched into the solo. I needed it to sound like my heart was being ripped from my chest while I watched helplessly through the unbearable pain of it. I focused on the emotions, on the feel of the strings bending under my fingertips, on the aching pain I pushed into the notes.

The spotlights focused on me and their heat burned the top of my head. On the vid screens, close-ups of my fingers flying along the guitar's fret board were interspersed with haunting images of war-torn cities and beaten-down refugees. On the final note, I threw back my head and held the vibrato, upping my gain into painful feedback before I let it go and backed away into my space to the right of the drum riser.

That's when it happened.

As the lights flickered and refocused on Toni for the final chorus, red and black rose petals wafted down from the rigging, drifting like snow and leaving wet red stains on my arms. On my guitar.

No, not here! Not again! My heart stuttered in my chest. I couldn't breathe. I faltered, but somehow, mechanically, I kept playing.

Until Stacy screamed. Jumping up, dropping her sticks, she frantically tried to brush away the petals. Her face a visage of pure terror, she slapped at her arms, at her body, her hair. Her tech, Jax, ran up to the riser, and the rest of us turned to watch as the song fizzled out. Stacy didn't have a mic, but I heard her screaming, "Get them off me! Off! Off!"

She spun past Jax, stumbling from the riser and running off the stage, screaming hysterically. Nori and Dia bolted off the stage after her.

Toni stopped to turn toward the audience. "Um, sorry folks. Give us a second. This wasn't planned."

I was vaguely aware of the rumble of voices from the fans, of the yells from the stage techs. I got backstage to see Panther catch Stacy just before she ran out the back door. Holding Stacy in front of her, she managed to guide her down into the dressing room. By the time I got there, Panther held a thrashing Stacy from behind in a basket-hold restraint and was doing her best not to get knocked in the chin by Stacy's head. I stayed to the side with Toni and Nori, trying to stay out of the way.

Dia tried to rub Stacy's arms and spoke in a soothing tone. "Stace, honey, it's okay. You're okay. Just breathe."

Morgan Rahn burst into the room. "Everything is locked down. Is Stacy all right?"

"She's higher than a fucking skyscraper," Nori muttered.

Morgan tapped her com transceiver earpiece. "Shaine. We need anti-tox for the drummer. Send someone down with Del's med bag and call for emergency medical. Panther, what can I do to help?"

Stacy wriggled wildly, crying and shouting, "Let me go! Let me out of here!"

Panther said calmly, "Nothing to do until she calms down. I've got her."

Morgan's sharp gaze shot around the room. "Is everyone else okay? Ari, are you all right?"

"I'm not hurt," I said.

Toni asked, "How the fuck did Celestian get past everyone again?"

I stared down at my hands, smeared with the red substance from the petals. I knew it wasn't blood because the color and the consistency were wrong. A red sticky gel remained when I tried to rub it away. I swallowed hard.

One of the new security people came in, a broad, husky dark-haired guy who looked very earnest. He held up a small soft-sided pack. "Med bag. Emergency medics on the way."

Morgan grabbed the pack and picked through its contents until she had an injector. She primed it. "Ben, help Panther hold her still. Keep her from kicking me in the head, okay?"

He knelt, wrapping arms as thick as small trees around Stacy's knees. Morgan pressed the injector against Stacy's thigh until it beeped. A few seconds later, her eyes rolled back and closed as she relaxed in their hold.

Morgan said, "Bring her to the couch. Find a blanket and cover her. She's in shock."

I knew there weren't any blankets backstage, but I went over to my guitar rack where I had a packing blanket I used to cushion the cases. I brought it over and Panther tucked it around Stacy. Her face was sickly pale, her breathing fast and shallow.

Nori, Dia, and Toni clustered at the end of the sofa, and I joined them. I wanted to be furious with Stacy but seeing her so vulnerable only made me feel sad. How could she have gotten so fucked up? Is there something we could have done to stop this?

Toni asked, "What do we do about the show?"

I wanted to yell at her, to tell her that the show didn't matter, that we had to help Stacy. But I knew there was nothing we could do for her. Panic, adrenaline, and agitation made my whole body shake inside. Rose petals had fallen on the stage. Celestian was here. Stacy lay semi-conscious on the couch, and I didn't know what to do.

"We can't play without a drummer," Dia said.

Nori turned toward me. "What about the drummer from the first band? She was fantastic. Maybe she could play so we could finish out the night. I mean, they did great covers of two of our songs."

I couldn't quite process thinking past what had just happened. Bloody rose petals stuck to my arms and clothes. How in the hell was I going to go back on the fucking stage? I needed to wash the red goo off my skin and out of my hair. Where was Celestian? Was she in the club? Was she hiding among us even now? No. I'd seen Panther with the ever-present scanner. I searched the empty surfaces in the room for a note. Celestian always left a note. How did she get flower petals in the rigging? My brain raced.

Toni stared at me, waiting expectantly. "The drummer? From the opening band?"

I blinked, but it took another few seconds to realize what she was asking. "Oh. Rhynn. The drummer's name is Rhynn."

CHAPTER SEVENTEEN

Earth Date: 31 October 2453
Moon Base Domed City
Club Tranquility

Rhynn

Rhynn saw the red and black confetti fall from the rigging and thought it was odd timing, given the darkness of the song. She watched Ari Walker look up, her expression turning to what appeared to Rhynn to be both surprise and fear. Then SCE's drummer jumped to her feet, screaming, trying to brush the confetti off herself with panicky, sharp movements. The music skittered to a stop as Stacy stumbled, still screaming, off the drum riser and ran off the stage.

"What the fuck is going on?" Leigh shouted over the crowd noise.

"I don't know," Rhynn yelled back.

Lead singer Toni Catone lifted her mic and faced the audience. "Um, sorry folks. Give us a second. This wasn't planned."

The band raced off the stage after their drummer.

Rhynn slipped off her stool, realizing she wanted to see if Ari was all right. Security surrounded the stage and the main houselights came on. Background music came up on the house PA.

Rhynn listened to her friends and others around her speculate about what was going on. Ari had mentioned she had a stalker. Rhynn wondered if whatever happened on stage was related. She opened her mouth to tell Leigh but snapped her jaw shut. What Ari had told her was probably not something she wanted the world to know.

She hopped back onto her stool. A group of security personnel collected some of the confetti into a clear container before the band's techs started cleaning off the stage. Med techs pushed through the crowd and rushed backstage with a gurney. Rhynn waited impatiently to find out what was happening. The bar seemed to quiet down, an undercurrent of concern rolling over the crowd as everyone watched the empty stage.

A few minutes later, one of the uniformed security guards jogged toward Rhynn and her friends.

Ben from Nightwalker raised a hand as the slight, wiry-framed woman double-timed it to them. "Hey, Morgan, what's going on?"

Rhynn realized the woman seemed vaguely familiar.

"Nothing good," Morgan responded. "SCE's drummer is being taken to the med center." She turned to Rhynn. "Ari Walker asked if you would come backstage. The band wants to talk to you."

"Me? Why?"

Morgan said, "It's nothing bad. Please, can you come with me?"

Leigh gave Rhynn a push. "Go on, girl."

Why in the hell did SCE want to talk to her? Why would Ari ask for her? Rhynn followed Morgan through the crowd, past the security barrier, and down to the dressing room. The band huddled with a couple of the stage techs, including their stage manager.

Medics surrounded SCE's drummer on an air-gurney near the couch. Rhynn didn't want to stare, but she got the impression Stacy was either unconscious or sedated, because she didn't seem to be responding to her caretakers as they finished what they were doing and hurried the gurney out the door.

Ari stepped away from her bandmates. "Rhynn, thanks for coming."

Rhynn nodded warily as she felt everyone's eyes aimed at her.

Ari said, "Guys, this is Rhynn Knight."

Rhynn managed a weak hello.

The lead singer, Toni, rested a hand on Ari's shoulder as she stepped forward. "Hi, Rhynn. Look, this is crazy. Obviously, Stace can't finish out the night, but we were wondering, in the interest of not disappointing the audience too much, if you'd be willing to sit in and finish out the set with us?"

Rhynn blinked. *What?* She stammered, "Uh, you mean, as in play?"

Ari said, "Yeah. I mean, if you want to? You did a couple of our songs in your set and you're good. No pressure, and we'll help you through the tunes, but we want to be able to finish out the night, you know?"

Rhynn felt the blood rushing to her head and wondered if she should sit before her knees gave out.

The bass player, Nori, said, "I'll count everything off, we can start the tunes, and you can jump in when you get the riff. We'll call it a jam session, and since everyone out there knows you, hopefully they'll be cool with it."

"Maybe we should ask if she knows any of our other songs," Dia said.

Rhynn felt like she was in a soccer match with the ball flying back and forth around her. Ari rested a hand on Rhynn's upper arm. Her fingers were warm. "Maybe you'd better breathe," she said, waving her other hand at her bandmates to quiet them. "Give the woman a chance to think, you guys."

Rhynn gulped air. They wanted her to sit in. Her. With them. On stage. In front of all these people. Ari's hand sent tingles through her body and it didn't help her think. She focused on Ari's open gaze. "I know most of your songs from playing along with the recordings, but not playing them live or anything. You really want me to sit in?"

Ari nodded. "We do. Will you play?"

Holy fuck. An ocean of emotions crashed over her: fear, excitement, terror, even something like pride. SCE wanted her to play with them. Ari wanted her to play. For Ari, she'd do about anything. "I'll do it. I hope I don't fuck up too badly."

Ari squeezed her shoulders. "You won't. We'll have fun, right? And if things crash and burn from time to time, we'll start over. No issues."

Toni Catone punched a fist into the air and whooped. "Rockin'. You'll do fine, Rhynn."

The stage manager came forward. Rhynn shook his hand, almost twice the size of her own. "What do you need? We'll use Stacy's kit since it's all hooked up. Go with Jax and you can shift stuff around to make it more comfortable if you need to. Do you want to use your own sticks?"

"Um, yeah, my stick bag is with my stuff, over by the loading doors."

"Great. Let's go."

Rhynn sat behind Stacy Rowe's top-of-the-line drum kit. This was not the way she'd imagined being able to check out Stacy's gear. *Holy lunar fucking hells!* With shaking fingers, she settled the earbud monitors and moved her feet between the bass drum and hi-hat pedals, shifting them to a more comfortable distance. A couple additional triggers were set up, but she didn't know what they were for and didn't have time to experiment. She moved some of the drum pads and cymbals closer to where she would expect them to be and raised the throne.

The stage lights went up as Shattered Crystal Enigma took the stage.

Rhynn wiped sweating hands on her thighs. Her heart pounded wildly. Nori Beaty and Ari Walker stood at the edge of her drum riser. Ari gave her a thumbs-up and Nori mouthed, "You're gonna be fine!"

Toni Catone stood at center stage with Dia and greeted the crowd. "All right, you guys! Are you ready to finish this?"

The audience roared.

"Stacy isn't able to finish the show, but we recruited one of your own to help us out! Everyone give a huge welcome to Rhynn Knight, who's going to sit in with us for the rest of the set!"

The cheering response from the crowd nearly knocked Rhynn off her seat. She lifted a stick and waved.

"We're gonna coach Rhynn through the tunes a little bit, so bear with us and let's have some fun!"

Nori counted off the first song. Rhynn managed to jump in right away since her band had covered it in their own set.

Buried behind Stacy's drum kit, with more drums and everything set up just a little differently than she was used to, Rhynn had a lot to contend with besides playing. Fortunately the monitor system was great, and she was able to hear all the instruments and the vocals clearly while still keeping a close eye on Nori and Ari for cues.

The music expanded around her, lifting her with it. As they progressed through the set list, Rhynn lost herself in the energy of the audience and the encouraging and appreciative smiles from Ari, who stayed close to the drum riser, cueing her with a lift of her guitar neck, a nod of her head, or mouthed warnings of what was coming up.

Rhynn was painfully aware of every time she stumbled over parts or missed a transition, or didn't quite get an ending right, but overall, the set was a huge success. The band made her take a bow with them after the encore. The audience screamed their approval, and even though her muscles were weak as wet noodles when she stepped off the drum riser, she felt like she could have taken on the world.

Jax, the drum tech, kept patting her on the back as they were ushered off stage to the dressing room. "That rocked, man! You did great!" He handed her a bottle of beer. "You deserve this!"

Overwhelmed, she stood in the middle of the dressing room, not knowing quite what to do or say. Everyone hugged her and thanked her and exclaimed over her performance. But the only hug that mattered was when Ari held her tightly for an extra couple of beats, murmuring in her ear, "You were fantastic."

CHAPTER EIGHTEEN

Earth Date: 31 October 2453
Moon Base Domed City
Aldrin Hotel

Ari

The meet and greet after the show felt weird, as though it was wrong to celebrate and mingle after what had happened with Stacy, knowing she recovered in the hospital while we moved on without her. As the adrenaline of the gig wore off, I felt more and more uneasy. I wanted to know how Celestian had gotten to me yet again amidst a club full of fans and security. I wondered if she was in the crowd during the after-party, gloating over having scared the piss out of me and Stacy.

I stuck close to my bandmates throughout the gathering. Panther had attached herself to me like a dangerous shadow. Between the WR and club security, the room crawled with guards. Del Marin and Morgan Rahn escorted us back to the hotel.

We were a subdued group of women when the elevator opened into the short hallway to our VIP suite. A beefy guard in a WR Security uniform stood in front of the door. He said, "Been a quiet night up here. A couple guests coming and going. I let room service in and watched while they put out some hot food and snacks."

"Thanks." Del slipped past him and made us wait outside with Morgan while she did a sweep of the rooms. She returned to the hallway, holding a red plas-sheet in a clear bag. She stopped in front of Adam and held it up, glowering. "Did you see this?"

The young guard blinked. "No, ma'am. All the servers left was the food, on the bar at the kitchenette."

Del said, "This was on the pillow in one of the bedrooms. I bagged it for forensics."

Morgan jabbed a finger at him. "Go find out who brought up the food. I want names, and I want to talk to them in five minutes. Del, re-sweep the rooms with both the heat and bio-scans before I bring the band inside."

My stomach clenched and I closed my eyes, swallowing down bile.

Dia asked, "What does the note say?"

I wasn't sure I wanted to know.

Morgan read, "Sweet Arienne, I am so sorry my rose petals distressed your drummer so badly. I had only meant to surprise you with flowers from the heavens because you are my sweet angel. I saw you in the alley, talking to the local drummer. You should be careful of overzealous fans. They don't care for you as much as I do. Love to you always, Celestian."

I felt an arm around me, opened my eyes as Nori said, "It'll be okay."

I shuddered. I hadn't been alone in the alley behind the club. Celestian had seen me talking to Rhynn. Goddess. Was Rhynn all right? Celestian wouldn't go after Rhynn for talking to me, would she?

Morgan said, "Shaine has connections with Mann-Maru security. We'll use their lab and see what we can get off the note."

Del Marin returned. "Rooms are clean, Boss."

"Thanks, Del. Give Shaine a call and let her know what's going on while I get the band settled. And have someone track down Rhynn Knight, make sure she's all right." Morgan turned her attention to me. "Just a precaution. I'm sure Rhynn's fine and celebrating with her friends."

Morgan led us into our suite. As hotels went, this one was small, but that was the way of things on Moon Base. Limited space within the dome meant no room for sprawling skyscraper hotels. We had a cramped three-room suite with a common room and kitchenette. The bedrooms were barely large enough for beds and a dresser.

One thing I knew for sure. I was not sleeping in the room Celestian had invaded. In fact, someone else could get my stuff for me. "I'm sleeping on the couch."

Nori hugged me. "I'll sleep out here with you," she offered.

Dia said, "Why don't you guys crash in Stacy's room? At least you'll have a bed."

I was too tired to argue.

Nori disappeared into the back bedroom. I sat on the couch, wrapping my arms around myself. Even in a hotel swarming with guards, Celestian had gotten to me.

CHAPTER NINETEEN

Earth Date: 1 November 2453
Moon Base Domed City
Rhynn's apartment

Rhynn

Rhynn slowly became aware of the incessant beeping of a call coming through on her comp pad. She swam up through the fog of sleep, struggling for clarity. Where the fuck was her pad? Why the fuck was she still dressed? Her head pounded as she shifted on her bed and fumbled in her shorts' pocket for the comp pad.

She swiped her thumb to connect the call.

The vid link filled the palm-size screen with her ex's smiling face, way too awake and cheerful. "Hi, Rhynn! You were so amazing last night!"

Rhynn groaned and fell back into her pillow. "Fuck."

"Did I wake you?"

What the fuck do you think?

Rhynn grunted and tried to clear her throat. Her mouth felt full of cotton, tasted terrible, and she squinted blearily at the screen. "Uh, yeah."

Britt's lilting laughter grated and annoyed the crap out of her. "Boy, you look like hell, Rhynny."

No fucking kidding. "What do you want?"

"I feel so bad about yesterday. I made a huge mistake with Kellyanne. I want to talk to you. Maybe we can get together later?"

Rhynn would have laughed if she didn't feel like she'd been run over by an air car. Twice. "No, we can't. Don't call me again."

"But, sweetie—"

"Go away, Britt. Go fuck someone else over."

"That's not—"

She disconnected the call and let the comp pad drop onto the bed. Fucking bitch, sucking up to her because she played with SCE last night. And now that she was awake, she had to pee. She dragged herself off the bed, down the ladder and into the living room.

Leigh sprawled on the sofa, looking as though she'd already showered, reading something on her comp pad. "Hey, master drummer."

Rhynn scrunched up her face. "Right." She trudged into the cramped bathroom.

A few minutes later the hot steam of the sonic shower vented around her and she used a bit of soap as she ran her hands through her hair, ducking in front of the misting jets to rinse. The sonic waves did most of the cleaning; water wasn't technically necessary, but the damp heat felt good on her aching muscles, helped get the sleep out of her eyes and sluiced off the dirt and cell layer the sonic shower loosened.

Feeling clean and more alive after dressing, she joined Leigh, who was kind enough to hand her a hot mug of caf after she dropped onto the sofa.

"Thanks."

"So, how does it feel to be famous?"

"Ugh. Tired. And hungover. What the fuck was I drinking last night?"

"Pretty much a little of everything."

"Feels like it. Man, what an experience. I hope someone got it on vid."

"What, the party and you stumbling drunk?"

"No, asshole. The show. My sixty minutes of fame."

"I think we all got clips. But I bet if you were to check with SCE, they probably had vid running."

Rhynn had no intention of bugging SCE for video. The gig had been a once-in-a-lifetime opportunity. Tomorrow, she'd be back in the job lines, hoping for a steady income. Still, she didn't mind staying in the afterglow for a little while.

CHAPTER TWENTY

Earth Date: 1 November 2453
Moon Base Domed City
Aldrin Hotel

Ari

The common room in the suite had become too full for my liking. After a fitful night of sleep, I was not a happy person. I woke up twice with nightmares and both times Nori held me until I stopped shaking and crying. I was seriously messed up.

It was late in the morning. We sat in on a call with Wayne Neutron. He leaned on the front edge of his desk, trying to look tough and important in a forest-green ship suit, wearing flashy gold and silver necklaces, his hair slicked back. Shaine Wendt, Morgan Rahn, and Del Marin stood in the room with us. They shared what they learned about how the flower petals had been released over the stage and how Celestian had gotten a love letter into our hotel room.

Shaine said, "We've contracted with the local Mann-Maru security forensics team to go over the club, but I doubt they're going to be able to tell us much."

"Why didn't the local authorities handle that?" Wayne asked.

Shaine said, "Because nobody was hurt and there's no one to press charges against. Because half a dozen people were up in the rigging over the course of the night, and it's not a clean crime scene."

"That's ridiculous."

"I don't disagree with you, sir, but it is what it is. If there's anything to find, Mann-Maru will find it."

"But how did she get the flower petals up there?" I asked. I didn't care about the legal details. I needed to understand how in the fuck Celestian was getting to me.

Morgan looked at me with understanding in her eyes. "The fake flower petals were in containers covered with chameleon mesh and attached under the club's light rigging. Anyone doing standard light setup would have totally missed them because they were between the lights, tucked up underneath the beams. Each container had a remote that triggered the container to open and release the petals. Whoever did it could have set it up days ago."

Toni said, "Our tour dates are posted. Everyone knew where we'd be."

That did not make me feel any safer.

Wayne cleared his throat, folded his arms. "How do we keep this from happening again, Ms. Wendt? I can't have my girls under constant threat of attack."

I was impressed with the way he stood up for us, straightening his shoulders and doing his best to seem intimidating. Judging by the smirk on Morgan's lips, though, his posturing wasn't taken very seriously.

Toni said, "The incidents are escalating."

Shaine said, "On the cruise ship, we'll be in the same venue for all the shows except for the two shows you're doing at the 'Belt mining facilities and then at Luna City at the end of the tour. The plan will be to go through the venues with a fine-tooth comb and do everything in our power to keep it secure. I'm passing out scanners to all our people, so we can sweep for anyone wearing a chameleon suit and set up scanner alarms in the band's living spaces. And we will keep close watch on the band at all times."

"We'll utilize and work with the cruise line's security resources as well," Morgan added. "They'll be able to make recommendations based on their familiarity with the ship."

"That will have to do for now." Wayne frowned. "Be sure I get regular reports."

Shaine said, "We'll do our best."

"Has anyone talked to Stacy this morning?" he asked.

"I talked to her nurse," Dia said. "She said Stace was resting and it'll take a couple days to get all the toxins out of her system and get her body chemistry back to normal. She was in the trauma bay most of the night because her heart rate was erratic from the drugs and the anti-tox serum. But she's doing better now and we can see her any time today."

"Let her know we're all concerned."

"We will."

"Good. I'll leave you girls to it. Keep in touch."

When we got to the hospital a couple hours later, Stacy looked like death warmed over. Her long red hair was greasy and tangled, her skin sallow and her eyes sunken. She clutched the hospital blankets to her chest and glared at us through reddened eyes.

Dia sat beside her on the edge of the bed, gently rubbing her arm. I stood on the other side, wishing I could think of something to say other than asking how she was feeling. It was obvious she wasn't well. Nori stood a half step behind me, and Toni stood behind Dia, with one hand on Dia's shoulder.

Stacy didn't want to talk to us. She blew off our concerns about her health and demanded that we call Wayne on the vid screen in the room. Then she announced she was quitting the band. We all tried to talk her out of it, but she remained adamant.

"No, I'm done. I quit, and that's it."

Wayne held up his hands, his voice going up a notch. "Stacy, you're under contract, you can't just quit."

"I don't give a fuck. I've had enough. I'm going home."

"You can't walk out on a tour!"

"So, sue me, Wayne." Stacy closed her eyes. The heart-rate monitor beeped a warning as the beats per minute spiked. Whatever drugs she'd taken were still kicking the hell out of her system.

A med tech charged into the room and tapped frantically on the IV monitor, trying to even out the chemicals still wreaking havoc in Stacy's body. He said curtly, "The call's over. She needs to rest. I need you to clear this room."

Wayne snapped, "Call me back," and the vid screen went blank.

We filed out of Stacy's room and back to the sitting area where Del Marin waited for us.

"We should go back to the hotel and talk to Wayne," Toni said.

I thought of how fragile Stacy looked and how alone she must feel. "Someone should stay here with Stace."

Dia said, "You guys go on back. I'll stay."

"But what are we going to do?" Nori asked. "If she's quitting, we need a drummer or we're going to have to cancel the tour."

Toni said, "I'm sure Wayne's already thinking about alternatives. He's not going to cancel shows."

Nori rolled her eyes. "I don't want to get a fill-in to play. Who knows who Wayne would throw at us. Probably some asshole guy."

I said, "We could ask Rhynn if she's interested."

"Do you think she would?" Toni asked.

"I don't know, but we can ask her. I mean, last night went great, considering. We have a few days before we leave for the cruise, so we could rehearse and get her up to speed."

"Let's find out where she is and talk to her," Nori said. "Then we'll talk to Wayne."

CHAPTER TWENTY-ONE

Earth Date: 1 November 2453
Moon Base Domed City

Rhynn

"Stacy quit the band. We need a drummer to finish the tour. Would you consider filling in?"

Ari's words rang in Rhynn's ears. She played them over and over in her head, not quite believing she wasn't dreaming. Standing dumbstruck in front of the media center in her apartment, she stared at the three women of Shattered Crystal Enigma while her hungover brain attempted to process Ari Walker's question.

Ari said, "Come down to the hotel and we'll talk about it."

"Are you serious?" Rhynn rubbed her face with both hands. "I'm sorry. I just—Really?"

Behind her, Leigh was practically jumping up and down on the couch.

Ari nodded. "Yes, really."

Toni Catone leaned into the camera. "Stacy is recovering, but she said, in no uncertain terms, she's done with the band."

"You were great last night," Nori put in. "We think you could do this. And it would seriously save our asses."

"Come down to the hotel and talk to us, at least," Ari said.

Leigh marched up behind Rhynn and put both hands on her shoulders. "She'll be there. Let me get some more caf into her hungover self, and I'll send her on her way."

An hour later, Rhynn plodded down the main thoroughfare that split Moon Base dome, winding her way through lazy Sunday pedestrian traffic toward the Aldrin Hotel. The five-story structure was the highest in the dome, though like most of the buildings on Moon Base, it was more functional than pretty.

Rhynn knew these streets like the back of her hand. She'd walked them so often she could do it in her sleep. She'd thought about leaving a hundred times but never did. Why uproot her life if she had no specific prospects somewhere else? She was a laborer with no transfer to Earth in her future employment plans. Of course, as her mother liked to point out, she could find a job on Earth if she wanted to. Or go to University, finish her degree and make a decent life for herself.

But she had no desire to pursue her mother's dreams. She was comfortable on Moon Base. This was a life she knew. People she knew. Her band was here. Her mom. Her friends.

She wondered what Cassandra Knight would say about this new opportunity. The band seemed serious about her filling in. The offer seemed almost too good to be true.

Rhynn passed through the entrance and into the hotel lobby. Green plants grew in waist-high marble pots placed among the chairs and couches in the open space to her left. Her boots scuffed over dull black marble tiles as she approached the front desk and caught the attention of the guest service attendant.

The young man gave her a somewhat wary look. "May I help you?"

She wondered how hungover she appeared and supposed that dressed in ragged cargo shorts, combat boots, and a band T-shirt, she didn't fit the image of the average businessperson. She pushed magenta bangs out of her eyes. "I'm here to meet some friends. They said to have the front desk call Suite Two. Tell them Rhynn is here."

The kid's expression perked up. "You're here to see the band? Just a second." He tapped open a com and spoke into his earpiece mic. "Yes, this is the front desk. I have Rhynn here to see you. Sure. I'll have her wait. Thank you." His expression grew more impressed. "Their security is sending someone down for you."

"Thanks." She wondered why they thought she needed security to bring her up to their suite. Did they think she was dangerous or something? Or was it just protocol on a big tour to have so much protection?

She knew the confetti hadn't been planned. And nobody said so, but it was pretty obvious to Rhynn that Stacy had flipped out. Whatever she was high on, she freaked like hell at the stuff falling. Did Stacy quit the band because of whatever had happened? The wary voice in her head told her she'd better ask a lot of questions. The other part of her, the musician and dreamer, was too excited about the prospect of touring with SCE to care.

She recognized the man who came for her as one of the guards who'd been at the club the night before. "Hello, Rhynn. Come on up."

She followed him to the elevators. He used a passkey for the fifth floor. When the doors slid open, they entered a hallway with thick dark red carpet. At the far end, a table with two chairs blocked access to one of the doors. A guard sat at the table. Another stood in front of the door itself.

As they approached, her escort said, "Go ahead. They're waiting for you."

Rhynn nodded. The man at the door knocked twice. A few seconds later the door opened, and Dia Caban looked out. She beamed when she saw Rhynn. "Hey, come on in!" She gave the guards a quick wave. "Thanks, guys!"

Rhynn walked into the band's suite, and Dia shut the door behind her. "We're glad you could meet us. Come in, make yourself comfortable. You want a beer? Fizzy? Caf? Water?"

Rhynn said, "Caf would be great."

"You like it loaded?"

"Yeah, thanks."

Ari stood up. "Hi, Rhynn, how are you?"

Rhynn ran a hand back through her hair. "Still feeling a little rough. My band kept me out late last night. I don't party much, usually. But it was a big deal, being able to open for you guys. That stuff doesn't happen here very often."

She perched on the edge of the sofa next to Ari, careful to keep a respectful distance. Dia returned with a mug of caf and handed it to her before folding herself onto the other end of the couch.

Toni asked, "Have you given our offer some thought? Do you have questions for us?"

Rhynn sipped her caf and tried to pull her thoughts together. "I've been thinking about it. but I'm not even sure what to ask."

"Let me try to lay it all out," Toni said. "We'd need you to stay with us at least through this leg of the tour, which includes the cruise ship gigs and the show at Luna City. You'd need to bring your drum kit. Stacy's equipment will go back home with her. We'll pay you for your time and for the gigs. We'll work out those details in a contract with our management, but it would be at least at musicians' union scale. As for what happens after this leg of the tour, we'll figure that out as we go, and see how this works out, you know?"

Rhynn leaned her elbows on her knees. Her brain kicked into gear. The timing was good. She didn't have a regular job, so she didn't have to deal with a leave of absence or anything. And the pay from the gigs would cover her part of the rent. Technically, there was nothing holding her back.

She looked up, glanced toward Ari. "Will you tell me what really happened on stage last night? I mean, with the stuff falling and Stacy freaking out?"

She noted the silent exchange taking place between the band members. Finally, Nori said, "It might be best if we start at the beginning." She launched into the story of Ari's stalker and Stacy's slide away from the band and into addiction. As Nori described the previous night's incident, Ari curled up into the corner of the sofa, putting a distance between herself and everyone else. Rhynn was horrified at the threats toward Ari, all the notes, and the bloody bouquet at the studio.

The stalking incidents explained the excessive security as well as the fear and anxiety Rhynn had seen in Ari's expression. If she took this gig, she could be walking into a potentially dangerous situation. Still, it was only for a month or so, and then she would return to her regular existence.

Touring with SCE was an opportunity of a lifetime. She'd be a fool to turn it down. She'd be spending time with her favorite band, playing for huge audiences, living a dream, maybe even getting to know Ari Walker. She immediately looked down at her boots. Damn. Not the time to be acting like a hormonal boy.

"What do you think, Rhynn?" Dia asked. "Will you do the tour?"

Rhynn wanted to turn so she could see Ari's expression, but she held herself still.

"Please consider it?" Ari's voice caressed her ears.

It felt like all the air had gone out of the room. "Yeah, I'm in. I'd like to play." She grinned as a weight lifted from her shoulders. She felt an intense urge to skip around and announce to the world she was living a dream come true. It was the right decision.

CHAPTER TWENTY-TWO

Earth Date: November 2453
Moon Base shuttle to cruise ship

Ari

I found myself staring out the large portal to my right as the space shuttle thundered away from Moon Base spaceport, flying toward the cruise ship *Star Rider*, which hung in stationary orbit above us. There was only the band and our road crew on the cramped shuttle, seated two on each side of a narrow aisle.

I had claimed a window seat with Rhynn beside me.

Taking advantage of our window, Dia stretched across my lap and Rhynn's, practically lying in Rhynn's arms to stare at the angular silver monstrosity of the *Star Rider*. She pressed her forehead against the shuttle window like a little kid. "It's fucking huge!"

Rhynn said, "Glad I'm not working the loading crew."

Dia snorted, "Practical kinda gal, aren't you?"

"Practical is my middle name."

"Someone around here should be practical," Nori said. She was behind us, leaning over Toni's and Friday's laps.

Toni laughed. "This is going to be such a crazy party barge. They did the same thing with the Epic Failure tour last year. The stories the fanzines published were insane. One of the bands didn't even make it through the whole two-week cruise."

"That will not be happening," Nori said flatly.

"Not to us, anyway," I said. We had no control over the opening bands or the other two headliners sharing the tour with us. Terestian and Zero Hour were sharing the headliner spots with us. We'd played with them in the past. The guys from Terestian were decent; they partied but they put on a good show and were reliable. Zero Hour was a little more aloof. They acted like they were better than the rest of us, and their lead singer, Angie Moore, was a nasty little bitch. She had a great voice, but she had an attitude. Nine other bands were scheduled to open the shows or play earlier in the day and evening.

Rhynn said, "Seriously, if you're playing almost every night, there's no way you could party the whole time and still be able to perform."

Rhynn's statement eased the worry niggling in the back of my mind. She didn't strike me as the party animal type. My instincts told me she was trustworthy, but I didn't know anything about her other than what we'd seen in the last four days. Shaine and Morgan vouched for her after running background checks. Shaine called it due diligence. They checked out everyone on our road crew, as well as Panther, who was accompanying us as part of the record company's tour security. It was disconcerting they felt the need to investigate people we considered friends, but it was reassuring to know nobody around us, including Rhynn, was a threat.

Goddess knew she's all I'd thought about since I met her on the loading dock behind Club Tranquility. She'd worked her ass off the last couple days, learning songs before the tour. The club allowed us to set up on their stage for rehearsals during the day, and we'd started early and put in nine-hour days to get the work done.

Rhynn proved to be a fast learner, a phenomenal musician, and seemed to be a genuinely nice person. She took Dia's teasing and Toni's musical direction with good humor. She wasn't afraid to ask when she wanted to repeat parts of songs to get them right. She didn't get pissed off and defensive when one of us made suggestions or wanted to go over sections that weren't quite working.

In the three days we had to run her through our set, she made the songs her own, putting her stamp on the rhythms. She approached the music a little differently than Stacy. Rhynn had a different ear. She cued in more closely to the melody and the subtle details in the arrangements. I don't know if she even realized how she shifted the feel as she translated Stacy's patterns from the recordings to what came out when she played them.

Our discussion with Wayne was short and sweet when we told him Rhynn was sitting in for Stacy. He'd seen the vid recording of her playing with us at Club Tranquility, so he knew she was a good choice. Even so, he was miffed we hadn't consulted him in our decision; he'd apparently been talking to a couple guys about filling in. Wayne always wanted to think he was in charge. We were dead set on working with Rhynn, though, so he gave in pretty quickly. It took him all of two hours to send a contract for her to sign.

I was relieved to have a drummer who was easy to work with. And I couldn't deny thinking Rhynn Knight was hot. I'd thought so the first time I'd seen her. She had a loose, casual way about her that said she was comfortable in her own skin. She didn't fawn all over us, though sometimes I could tell she was a little starstruck. She was talented, intelligent, and handsome in a plain but intriguing way. She appeared taller than she was, with her rangy, lean build. When she played, I got the impression of an octopus—all moving arms and legs. Watching her play was exceptionally distracting. And enticing. I caught myself aching in interesting places and wondering what it would feel like to be wrapped in those strong and flexible limbs.

Of course, the band didn't need me hitting on and distracted by our stand-in drummer. And on top of that, I worried that paying any untoward attention to Rhynn would surely garner a negative reaction from Celestian.

I'd hoped getting off Earth and on tour would be an escape from my stalker, but after the incident at Club Tranquility, I could no longer convince myself the cruise would be safe. I could only hope Celestian's behavior wouldn't escalate. Obviously, whoever this person was, they had access to concert venues, to our home, to hotels. I took some solace in the fact that so far, the threats were to my privacy and my sense of security, and there hadn't been any physical violence. Unfortunately, emotional threats didn't seem as important or urgent to the authorities as physical ones.

Shaine and Morgan and their security team seemed very capable. They were certainly attentive and serious about their jobs. Friday thought the world of her moms and continually told tales of their adventures on Mars and how she came to be their foster daughter. I hoped they could save me too. They hadn't kept Celestian from dropping bloody rose petals onto the stage, but the petals and release mechanisms were likely planted days before. What were the chances that Celestian had gotten onto the cruise ship early too? I shuddered inwardly.

"Attention. We are making our approach to the *Star Rider.* For your safety please take your assigned seats and put on your crash restraints."

Dia muttered, "Killjoy," as she pushed herself upright and into the aisle. She dropped a playful kiss on Rhynn's cheek. "Thanks, hon, for letting me lay all over you."

Rhynn's face turned bright red, the heat creeping up to her ears. "Uh, sure."

Dia laughed uproariously as she and Nori settled into their seats across the aisle and pulled the crash webbing across themselves.

CHAPTER TWENTY-THREE

Earth Date: November 2453
Cruise Ship *Star Rider*

Rhynn

Rhynn followed her new bandmates and Morgan Rahn off the shuttle and into the *Star Rider*'s docking bay, an expansive space rising three stories above their heads and stretching the length of two soccer fields.

Two similar shuttles were parked ahead of them, disgorging passengers to several waiting air-skiffs equipped with simple bench seating that carried ten to twelve passengers. At least a dozen loaded cargo skiffs scooted across the docking bay's marked-up surface, following color-coded and numbered tracks, pulling hover-trailers full of supplies from the shuttles to cordoned off storage areas where crates were stacked in rows rising nearly to the ceiling. Voices, warning beeps, and the grating and rumbling of working equipment echoed through the bay. Rhynn observed the action with a knowledgeable eye; this was a well-organized crew.

An air-skiff towing an empty low-sided trailer slowed to a stop near the back of their shuttle. Two of the band's roadies jumped out of the back of the skiff.

Toni raised a hand. "Hey, Butcher, Vinnie."

The shuttle's rear cargo ramp lowered with a hiss of heavy-duty hydraulics and the thick clunk of metal on metal.

"We're grabbing the last of the equipment from the shuttle," Butcher said. His bald head shone in the glaring docking bay lights. "Everything else is already at the concert hall."

Morgan put one hand to her ear as she spoke into her com. She turned away and snapped something at whomever was on the other end. Rhynn couldn't make out the words, but her tone didn't sound happy. Three other WR guards spread out around them. One stood near the end of the shuttle's boarding ramp, the others a few meters away. All three continually scanned the area.

Morgan said, "They're sending someone to bring you to your suite. I'll go with you."

One of the shuttle's crew piled the band's personal luggage on a handcart.

Ari sidled up to Rhynn, nudging her arm. "You ready for this?"

Rhynn couldn't wipe the grin off her face. "Ready as I'm going to be." A low-level electric current of excitement pulsed through her veins.

A few minutes later, two crew members in pristine white uniforms pulled up in a short air-skiff. The crew attached the luggage cart to the back of the skiff while the band and Morgan settled onto the outward-facing back-to-back bench seats. One crewman drove and the other introduced himself as Pat, and cheerfully gave them a running description while they motored out of the docking bay and eased through pedestrian traffic down the wide corridor bisecting the cruiser's main deck. Shops with enticing window displays lined either side of the central throughway, promising gifts of every type imaginable. Pat pointed out the direction they would go to get to the pools, restaurants, and the main buffet. At the end of the corridor, he detached the luggage cart and guided it manually as they stepped into a lift to the twelfth deck.

The elevator opened into a burgundy-carpeted hallway lined with doors. The crewman explained this section of the ship was for VIP guests and had the largest suites. The band, their road crew, and the security team had three suites on the far end. Morgan led them to the end of the hallway where the WR team had set up a security station. A narrow desk lined with monitors and a couple of data terminals blocked access to the last three rooms. Del Marin stood up from her position behind the desk.

"Hey, Boss," Del said, giving Morgan a casual salute. "The suites have all been cleared. Shaine is coordinating the concert hall sweep with Gohste."

"Thanks, Del."

"The band is in the room at the end. We'll get the palm locks set right away. Shaine wants the band to check in and out, and nobody should go anywhere without one of us."

Rhynn glanced at Ari. They hadn't talked much about the stalker situation since the first day when Rhynn had asked, but she could read between the lines. Ari was scared, or at the very least, unnerved, by the whole thing, though she did a good job of hiding her worries. But Rhynn had noticed the way Ari seemed to curl in on herself when the subject came up, and how her gaze darted around when they entered a new space. Even now, if Rhynn hadn't known better, she would have read Ari's expression as disinterested or unconcerned. She stepped a bit closer to Ari as she followed the others into the suite.

The space wasn't as cramped as Rhynn expected. The common living room had two couches and a pair of reclining memory-form chairs. There was a kitchenette with a breakfast bar, and four bedrooms and a bathroom opened off the main room.

Del had each of them log into the palm reader at the side of the door while the crewmen brought their luggage into the living room. Afterward it was a free-for-all to decide who got which of the four bedrooms. Rhynn hung back, letting the others work out sleeping arrangements and wondering if she should opt for one of the sofas so everyone else would have her own space. Toni called dibs on the master bedroom with an en-suite bathroom. Dia called the second bedroom, leaving Ari, Nori, and Rhynn to divvy up two rooms.

Ari turned to Rhynn. "Do you want to share?"

Rhynn swallowed, wondering if Ari meant sharing with her, or if she meant Rhynn should share with Nori. Either way, Rhynn didn't figure she was in a position to make the call so she simply nodded. "Sure, I'll share."

Nori sent Ari a curious look. "Maybe Rhynn would prefer a room of her own," she said.

"I don't mind sharing with someone," Rhynn blurted.

Ari asked, "Are you sure?"

"Yes." She would have sworn Ari looked relieved, but she couldn't quite figure out the dynamic.

Ari said, "Good, because I'm too freaked out right now to sleep in a room alone."

Nori shrugged. "Guess I'll take the third room then, and you two can have the double on the end."

Dia said, "I'm gonna take a nap. Wake me up if anyone orders food."

Toni gave her a friendly shove. "You're always hungry, D."

"Hungry for loooove." Dia laughed, grabbed her suitcase, and traipsed down the hall.

Rhynn carried her suitcase to the back bedroom. There were two double beds, a dresser with a compact comp terminal and vid screen on top, a narrow wardrobe and a tiny en-suite bathroom. A porthole maybe two hand-spans in diameter was set into the far wall. Rhynn set her suitcase on the bed nearest the door as Ari entered.

Rhynn said, "You can take the bed against the wall."

Ari looked at her, startled.

"Unless you'd prefer this one? I thought you might feel safer further from the door." Rhynn shifted from foot to foot, wondering if she'd said too much.

"Thank you," Ari said softly. She slipped past Rhynn, touching her arm as she did, and set her suitcase and guitar case on the other bed.

Rhynn started unpacking, putting her clothes in the three drawers on her half of the dresser. She tossed her comp pad on top of her bed and stowed her small bag of toiletries in the gold-tiled bathroom. There was barely enough room for her to turn around. A narrow set of shelves was built into the wall behind the door and she claimed a lower one, carefully securing her things behind the wide bar meant to keep them from falling.

Ari ducked into the bathroom when Rhynn stepped out. Not knowing what else to do, Rhynn stretched out on her bed, leaned against the pillows piled against the headboard and folded her hands behind her head. She didn't know why Ari had decided to room with her—not that she minded. Hell, no. She hadn't dared consider what the sleeping situation might be. Sure, she may have had the occasional fantasy, but as the hired help, she assumed she'd probably be on the couch or a spare cot. She'd certainly never imagined she'd be sharing a room with Ari.

Besides, Ari never gave her any reason to think she was interested in anything more than friendship. They hadn't spent any time alone, other than rehearsing, since the day they'd met on the loading dock, which hadn't been anything except two people making small talk.

Of course, meeting Ari Walker, talking to her and having a beer was huge. Rhynn imagined Ari probably met adoring fans all the time. How many others had bought her a drink, talked to her, told her how amazing it was to meet her? Goddess, she probably thought Rhynn was an idiot.

Ari ambled out of the bathroom and flopped down on the other bed.

"I didn't think the rooms would be this big," Ari said. "This is nice." She twisted her head toward the portal revealing a glimpse of space and stars. "Kinda reminds me of my room when I was a kid, with the little window, except I had barely enough room for a bed and a dresser. I think it might have been a closet."

Rhynn stared at her, drinking in the information, a glimpse into Ari's humanity. She fancied seeing a flash of a little girl in the woman's expression. Maybe she imagined the last part. "You grew up out-system?" She had read that, but it was different to hear it from Ari's own lips.

Ari continued to gaze out the portal. "Mom was an accounts admin in a couple of the mining facilities in the 'Belt. We moved back to Earth when I was a teenager." She rolled her head on the pillow to face Rhynn. "You're a spacer too, aren't you?"

"Yeah. Moon Base mostly, though my mom got posted to a few of the mining facilities too.

"Just you and your mom?"

"Yeah. Never knew my dad. He ducked out as soon as he knew Mom was pregnant. She never mentioned him until I was older. She said she didn't need a man telling her what to do. She was glad it was just her and me." Rhynn shrugged. Old history. She was over it.

"My folks split when I was still in diapers. I saw him a couple times after Mom moved us back Earthside. He turned up at a show once a couple years ago, tried to say I was a chip off the old block.

I walked away and Toni told him to fuck off and stay away from me or she'd beat the crap out of him."

"Toni rocks."

"Yeah. She's a good friend."

They settled back on their pillows. Rhynn closed her eyes, thinking she'd like to be a good friend too.

CHAPTER TWENTY-FOUR

Earth Date: November 2453
Cruise Ship *Star Rider*

Ari

"Hey, sleepyheads! Pizza's on. Come and get it if you want any!"

I jerked awake to Toni's voice. My stomach growled at the enticing smell of pizza wafting into the bedroom.

Rhynn rolled off her bed with a groan. "Fuck yeah, I'm starving."

I hadn't intended to nap, but I felt better for it as I followed on Rhynn's heels. Three pizza boxes lined the breakfast bar between the kitchenette and the living room. Dia and Nori held loaded plates and stood at the bar scarfing down their slices. You'd think none of us had eaten in years, the way we descended on the food, but it was automatic after so many years living as starving musicians. We'd had plenty of lean times with no guarantee we'd pay our rent or have credits left over for food. Old habits die hard.

As Rhynn and I joined the others, I had to stop myself from asking where Stacy was. We may not have parted on the best terms, but I still felt bad and I did miss her. She'd been part of the band from the beginning, and it was strange not to have her with us. Despite our differences, I considered her a friend and I felt like I'd let her down. Maybe there was something I should have done to have kept her from crashing so hard.

Dia had spoken with her a couple of times. Stacy refused to talk to anyone else. She was heading back to Earth as soon as she was able. Apparently, she'd freaked during the show because she'd bought a hit off a guy at the club, and it'd been laced with some chemical byproduct that screwed with her. I very sincerely hoped she'd get help and get clean, but it was out of my hands.

As we finished the pizza, an announcement blasted over the ship's internal PA system. "Welcome, guests. We'll be casting off in about thirty minutes. There is a departure celebration in the Starshine Lobby and Lounge on the main deck. We'll be serving champagne and snacks. Everyone is welcome. Also, please remember that at fifteen hundred you are required to meet with the crew in your cabin section to go over safety regulations and emergency procedures. Enjoy the Hammer Down Cruise!"

Toni said, "We should go to the party."

"You think security will let us?" Nori asked.

Dia made a face. "Oh, come on, we'll take them with us. Besides, Wayne would say we need to be available to our fans, right?"

I nearly choked on my pizza. "Damn, you have his lines down."

"How many times have we heard it, right?"

Half an hour later we trooped out of the room. Our intrepid security force in the hallway had grown. Morgan, Shaine, Mitch, Ben, and Athenon had joined Del.

Shaine said, "We heard the announcement and figured you'd want to join the cast-off party."

"Who knew you guys were mind readers too?" Nori quipped.

Morgan grinned. "They train us for that, you know."

Shaine circled a finger in the air, and security fell in around us. The elevator opened and the infamous Jo Lupine strode into the hallway. Spacer pale, with black crew-cut hair and a bad attitude, she dressed all in black, sporting thigh-high boots, skin-tight leather pants and a skimpy, front-laced leather vest. I groaned inwardly, and Nori muttered, "For the love of the goddess."

Our security contingent quickly and smoothly put themselves between us and Jo. Burly, steroidal Mitch, with a weirdly soft-spoken voice, said, "Sorry, ma'am, we need to see your room pass to be on this level."

Lupine glowered. "Seriously, little man, I wouldn't be here if I didn't have a room." She gave him a disgusted snort, then leered at me. "Hey, Ari, long time no see."

I managed a fake smile. "Yeah." *And it would have been better if it'd been longer.*

Shaine stepped forward. Her military bearing was unmistakable in the black uniform. "Your pass?"

Jo slid her an irritated glare and pulled a passkey from her back pocket. How she'd gotten it into the tight-fitting leather pants I have no idea.

Shaine handed the pass to Mitch, who scanned it quickly. "Thank you, Ms. Lupine. Sorry to bother you. Your room is right there."

"I know where my fucking room is." She brushed past him to her door, then paused and grinned back at me. She always managed to add a hint of feral to that toothy smile. "I think you owe me an interview, Ari. Maybe we can catch up later?"

"We'll see," I said.

She smirked and disappeared into her room.

Toni snarled, "How did the likes of that bitch manage a room up here?"

Shaine asked, "Who is she?"

I told her about Jo Lupine, obnoxious Central LA music reporter. Morgan spoke the name into her comp pad. Apparently, anyone in our hallway was going to get a little extra attention from security.

The departure party was as raucous as I expected. The majority of the crowd was slam-thrashers. Everyone had a drink in hand and everyone was happy. A DJ on a raised platform in the middle of the room cranked up slam-thrash favorites, and a handful of people stomped in rough patterns in a circle in front of the platform. Without a zero-g cube, it was as close as they could get to slamming.

The Starshine Lobby on the main deck took up a soccer-field length from the bow of the ship. Two-story glassteel panels graced the front of the room with a wide view of space. Tables and lounge areas were scattered throughout the room, and the lighting made it seem as though it were true daylight.

We stayed on the outskirts of the party, observing more than joining in, though we indulged in the ubiquitous cheap champagne being passed out by neatly dressed hosts, hostesses, and cruise staff. Our road crew joined us, and Toni's face absolutely lit up when

Friday arrived. My tall, dark, and intimidating friend was adorable, holding hands with Friday as they regarded each other like love-struck teenagers.

Everyone cheered when the *Star Rider* eased away from her dry-dock moorings. When I asked Morgan about that, she said it was likely the cruise ship had some maintenance done while in moon orbit, thus the gigantic scaffold-like structure enveloping most of the ship. The fully powered scaffolding allowed maintenance equipment and power sources to be secured and not float away, stabilized the cruiser, and kept her in orbit when her drive systems were shut down. Rhynn and Morgan focused on the windows, peering at two support ships moving alongside us.

At my curious expression, Morgan said, "They're maintenance boats. They'll stay alongside until we're clear of the moorings. Then they'll dock in the ship's main bay before we get to speed."

Shaine glanced over at her. "Did you ever work on one of these, hon?"

"Naw. Never got the chance. Had friends who did, though. It's a sweet gig if you can get on."

Shaine wrapped an arm around Morgan's shoulders. "Here's to safe travels, love," she said.

"Back at'cha."

We all raised our glasses to the DJ's toast before he cranked up the volume on his playlist. We could drink tonight since we weren't gigging, so we took the opportunity to hang out and wander around the shops a bit. I was constantly aware of being shadowed by WR security. The teams had switched out, and the group with us now were in plain clothes. I saw surreptitious glances as our fans pointed us out. Some waved but only a few came to talk to us. I bought a "Hammer Down Cruise" tour T-shirt. Rhynn bought a T-shirt and a miniature model of the ship. It was going to be an interesting cruise.

CHAPTER TWENTY-FIVE

Earth Date: November 2453
Cruise Ship *Star Rider*
Show #1

Rhynn

Rhynn wailed through the last verse of "Endless Ocean." Stage lighting flashed in time to the vocals; flash-bangs exploded on the sides of the stage and the back edges of the drum riser. The heat singed Rhynn's skin and hair. Her blood pounded with adrenaline. She blinked furiously as the smoke from the pyrotechnics drifted across the stage, making her eyes water, and she coughed when she got a lungful of the hanging particles, but still managed to continue banging out the rapid-fire rhythm. Her feet tapped out running sextuplets under the ride cymbal and snare drum hits.

The crowd cheered wildly and nearly drowned out the music as Ari's guitar screamed out the solo line around Toni's vocal. Rhynn glanced up to see Ari and Dia face-to-face at center stage, whipping through the guitar licks. Fuck, they rocked. She accented the riffs with cymbal crashes—her sticks snapping out to smash the pads between beats.

After almost two hours, her arms and legs protested the workout and Rhynn pushed her body to keep up the intensity.

Playing drums in a slam-thrash band was like running a marathon. Her entire body stayed in motion throughout the show. Thank the goddess she didn't have to sing too.

Two minutes later the song came to its swelling end chord, supported by a roar of applause. It was their second encore, and now they were done. Rhynn nearly stumbled off the drum riser, grateful for Nori's supportive hand on her arm as she got her footing. She waved her sticks at the crowd. A second later Ari was beside her too, her guitar lifted in one hand, saluting the crowd, her other arm around Rhynn's waist. Their stage techs took their instruments as they jogged through the wings, and the WR security team hustled them to the dressing room.

The whole experience felt surreal to Rhynn. How many concert vids had she seen where the band was rushed off the stage with the yells of the crowd echoing down the corridor? As she passed through the green room door, one of their road crew handed out water bottles, and Toni gave Rhynn a high five.

"Yeah! Rhynn, great job! What a show!"

Hugs went all around the band. Rhynn hadn't realized how affectionate they were toward each other. Like sisters, she thought. Until Ari embraced her. Then she felt anything but sisterly as her body molded itself against Ari's. She felt the heat between them, and then the dampness of her T-shirt against her overheated skin. *I don't want to let go. Goddess, even sweating and a mess, she is the most beautiful woman I've ever seen. And she feels so good.*

Ari's voice in her ear was like honey. "You did a great show, Rhynn. That was amazing."

"You weren't half bad yourself."

Ari squeezed her before stepping back. "Thank you for jumping in."

Dia hugged Rhynn from behind. "Rhynn, baby, you rock my world."

Rhynn laughed. "Flatterer. I'm having the time of my life!"

"You have fifteen minutes before the VIP guests come in," Del Marin shouted from the door. "Do what you gotta do."

Rhynn looked at the rest of the band. "What do we gotta do?"

Dia snorted. "If you got hair to comb, or whatever, now's the time. Personally, ain't nothing gonna make me look less like a hot sweaty mess, so fuck it."

Rhynn glanced down. Her T-shirt and shorts were soaked through. "Fuck. I look like hell." She ran a hand through her hair, pushing soaking wet strands away from her face.

Toni laughed. "Yeah, well, they like us all hot and bothered. Our fans are freaks, and they probably smell as bad as we do."

"Worse." Dia slammed back the remainder of her water bottle.

Ari said, "Don't worry about it. We never do."

Rhynn laughed. "Okay."

The caterers had set up a short buffet table of snacks and drinks, both alcoholic and not. Security escorted the enthusiastic VIP guests into the room.

Rhynn was quickly overwhelmed by fans who treated her as a member of the band. The attention was crazy and unexpected. She had no idea what to say and was thankful she didn't have to talk much. Admirers just wanted to tell her how great the band was and how they loved all the songs and had all the downloads, and how great it was to meet them. She even signed a few comp pads.

One very drunk and overly excited fan kept insisting she should sign his chest with a tattoo pen. Fortunately, one of the security guys came to her rescue, guiding him away. She really, really didn't want her name permanently scrawled on some guy's hairy chest.

CHAPTER TWENTY-SIX

Earth Date: November 2453
Cruise Ship *Star Rider*

Rhynn

The following day, Rhynn trudged toward the Betelgeuse Buffet with Ari, Toni, and Friday. Mitch and Adam, two of the WR security guards, wore "civvies," and trailed a couple meters behind them. It was early afternoon and they'd missed the lunch rush. Rhynn was too tired to deal with crowds of people, so missing them was a good thing as far as she was concerned.

They ambled down the main corridor, past gift shops and fast-food restaurants. She sniffed the cloying aroma of fried protein and hoped for the best. Her stomach had been growling since she'd gotten up an hour ago. Her legs felt leaden after the previous night's show, but she knew a little food and activity would help. She'd gigged two or three nights in a row often enough to know how to work through the aches and pains. It was tough, but she was tough, too, and at least she didn't have to make it to her day job between shows.

The cruise ship's sprawling main buffet easily held a few hundred people. Special order serving counters lined the back wall. Rhynn counted at least five rows of covered buffet islands piled with food and desserts.

They found a relatively secluded table toward the back of the restaurant. Mitch and Adam sat at a separate table nearby. Security wasn't concerned about physical altercations. The stalker hadn't made or attempted any physical threats, and for the time being, they didn't expect the fans to be dangerous. Drunk and stupid, yes, but having their people around, even in plain clothes, would be enough to keep the idiots at a distance. Rhynn was okay with that assessment. She wasn't sure if Ari felt that way, and she couldn't blame her for being worried. She decided she would do her best to stay between Ari and anyone who threatened her.

After Friday and Toni returned with filled plates, Rhynn and Ari made their way to the buffet. Rhynn took her time looking through the offerings, finally deciding on fresh fruit, a made-to-order sandwich and a bowl of vegetable soup. She laughed inwardly at her bland choices, but what she wanted was comfort food.

Ari was already eating by the time Rhynn reached their table. She smiled at Rhynn around a mouthful of food. "The stir-fry is average at best, but I'm so damned hungry."

"I don't think a slam-thrash cruise is a place you'd go for high-class meals," Rhynn said, tucking into her soup with a satisfied slurp.

Friday said, "I hope the rest of the shows go as smoothly as last night."

Toni elbowed her. "Don't jinx it, babe."

Rhynn lifted her glass. "Rule number one of gigging—if it can go wrong, it will go wrong."

"Absolutely," Ari agreed. "Like that huge storm in the Austin metroplex a couple years ago. Halfway through the first set, lightning hit the building's transformer and blew out half our equipment."

Toni pointed her fork at Ari. "Man, that sucked. I thought the whole fucking place exploded. Me and Dia both hit the deck. Sparks were flying, there was a boom, and a screech of feedback that just about made your ears bleed. Then everything went dead. Everyone was screaming and freaking out in the dark."

Ari said, "It took us weeks to get all our fried stuff replaced. Thank the goddess we were signed then, so the record company covered our lost equipment. Otherwise we'd have been so screwed."

Rhynn chewed thoughtfully. "I've lived out-system all my life. I've never experienced a thunderstorm."

Ari cocked her head. "You've never been to Earth?"

"A couple of times. Mom has some family there. We went when I was about six years old. I mostly remember it being hot and bright, but I don't remember any storms."

Rhynn relaxed as they chatted and ate. She sat back quietly when a few fans stopped to say hello. Ari and Toni responded cordially. None of the fans addressed Rhynn directly and she was relieved nobody called her out as the new drummer. It told her she was doing her job, filling in for Stacy without being noticed. They'd decided to downplay her role in the band, at least for the time being, and Rhynn was content with the decision. She didn't need the notoriety or the attention.

After eating, they wandered the ship's main deck and hit a few tourist shops. She didn't buy anything, but it felt good to walk and stretch her muscles. Friday needed to check in with Mykal at the concert hall, and Toni tagged along with her.

When Rhynn and Ari returned to the suite, they found Dia and Nori lounging in the living room drinking caf. Dia was curled up in the corner of one of the couches while Nori stretched out on the other, watching a soccer game on the vid screen on the wall.

Dia asked, "How was the food?"

Ari shrugged. "Edible."

"Nothing to write home about, but there's lots of it."

Nori wrinkled her nose. "I had leftover pizza from last night. Maybe I'll go down later. Or order something up."

Dia said, "By the way, housekeeping was in. I told the nice cleaning boy if he touched your guitar you'd chop his hands off."

Ari raised a brow. "I hope he was sufficiently fearful."

Nori snorted. "I thought he was going to pee his pants."

"Glad you still have the touch, Dee."

Rhynn followed as Ari marched to their room, stumbling into her when Ari froze abruptly at the doorway.

Ari said, "Please go get security."

Rhynn whirled and ran to the suite door, palming it open and yelling, "Del! Come quick."

Del's head snapped around, short dreads flying. "What happened?"

"I don't know. Ari said come."

Instantly, Del was on her feet and brushing past her. She stopped beside Ari, who pointed into the room. Her eyes were wide. "There's a note."

Del stepped inside. The rest of the band came to see what was going on. Rhynn rested a hand on Ari's shoulder and peered into the room. A red plas-sheet rested on Ari's pillow.

Del said, "Housekeeping was in here, yes?"

Nori said, "Yeah. Young kid. Real light hair. Small."

"Okay. I saw the log and just reamed Mitch a new one because he hadn't gone in with housekeeping, and Adam because he left Mitch alone at the desk. Ship security is supposed to be accompanying their crew into your rooms, but they weren't along. Shaine can bitch at them. On the upside, Mitch made a note that he scanned the kid and the cart—no weapons and no stowaway on board." Del fished in the cargo pocket of her pants and removed a disposable glove. "I'm taking the note. Stay out of here until I can grab a scanner and sweep the room, okay?" She bagged the plas-sheet.

Ari touched her arm. "What does it say?"

Del squinted at the paper. "*Ari, beloved, I was so excited to see the show last night. You were perfect as always. Be well. I'll be watching over you. Yours always, Celestian.*"

"I don't understand what she wants," Ari said. "Why is she doing this?"

Del herded them away from the door. "We'll figure it out. Come on."

Rhynn followed Ari into the living room and sat beside her on the couch. Ari perched stiffly on the edge of the cushion, staring at her hands clasped between her knees. Rhynn rubbed her arm, not sure what to say.

Shaine and Gohste arrived. Gohste continued to the bedroom with a hand-held scanner and Shaine crouched in front of Ari.

"Are you okay?"

"Freaked out."

Shaine patted her knee. "We'll figure out what's happening."

Ari raised her head. "People keep saying that. But she's still getting in."

"I know. We'll do our best."

Ari looked down again.

Shaine said, "You didn't touch anything in the room, right?"

"Right."

"Gohste will find any forensic evidence. Likely it'll only be the housekeeping staff who was in earlier. We'll check him out." Shaine stood.

Ari said, "Thank you."

Nori handed Ari a mug of tea. Rhynn sat beside her, feeling out of her depth, only knowing she had a great need to be close to Ari.

Shaine and Gohste went through their room a second time with forensic scanners. Rhynn felt helpless, like being at a doctor's office and waiting for test results. Nothing she could say would make Ari feel any better. In fact, speaking seemed like the absolute wrong thing to do. Somehow, she'd ended up holding Ari's hand, and Ari's leg brushed against hers. She honestly didn't know if she or Ari had intertwined their fingers, but based on the strength of Ari's grip, their connection was a good thing.

Agitation rolled off Ari in waves. Rhynn tried to answer that tension with calmness. She wanted to be Ari's protector, her rock to cling to. She wasn't afraid, although she supposed she should be. As far as Rhynn was concerned, there wasn't much chance some random crew member was a stalker, but if the kid had put the note in their room, he'd been put up to it by someone.

Shaine and Gohste finally came out of the bedroom. Neither of them looked particularly happy.

Shaine said, "We've gone over everything. The only prints in the room, and the only fresh forensic samples we're picking up are yours and what we believe are the housekeeping staff's. No trace of anyone else. Nobody is hiding in there. There aren't any heat signatures other than our own."

Nori said, "So, it's safe?"

"Yes."

Rhynn asked, "What happens next?"

"Next we track down that kid and find out who gave him the note. We do additional crew background checks. And we make sure any staff who come into your rooms are accompanied by security, no matter how innocent they look, even if it leaves the desk temporarily unmanned."

Ari looked up at Shaine. "Thank you for taking this seriously."

Shaine gave Ari a tight smile. "It's a serious situation. We want to do the best job we can for you."

She and Gohste left.

Rhynn thought Ari looked incredibly vulnerable and she had a nearly overwhelming desire to hold her and make it all better. Rhynn stood, holding Ari's hand. "I don't know about you, but I'm feeling beat up. I need a nap. Do you want to come? Or do you want to stay?"

Ari looked from Rhynn to her bandmates. "I can't spend the rest of the tour avoiding our room. And I'm exhausted."

"Come on then."

Nori said, "We'll be out here."

"And we'll let Toni know what's going on."

Ari gave Nori and Dia a grateful look. Rhynn led the way back to the bedroom, and then stretched out on her bed and pulled the comforter up. Ari perched nervously on the edge of her own bed. Exhaustion painted her face. Rhynn debated her words for all of a second before she offered, "Come and lay down over here?"

Ari gazed at her. Rhynn held her breath, wondering if she'd said the wrong thing. Trying to read Ari's expression, she thought she saw relief, but also apprehension.

Rhynn shifted and pulled the comforter back. "Come on, we both need a nap before the reporter shows up."

Ari relented. Rhynn flipped the comforter over them, careful to keep her hands to herself and leave space between them. She didn't want to crowd Ari or make her feel any more uncomfortable than she already was. Rhynn's heart pounded. She felt the heat from Ari's body. *Holy fucking lunar hells! You are lying in a bed with Ari fucking Walker.*

Rhynn shoved down her raging hormones and panic and tried to convince herself she was just being a friend. Friends helped friends. Rhynn hoped if she were between Ari and the door, Ari might feel a little safer. What she wanted to do was pull Ari into her arms and hold her. She wanted to make Ari feel safe and protected.

Instead, she folded her hands over her stomach and closed her eyes. She felt the bed shift as Ari relaxed. She wanted so badly to watch Ari sleep, but she kept her eyes shut and breathed slowly and evenly.

Rhynn must have dozed off for a while because when she woke, she felt warm breath on her arm. She cracked her eyes open, carefully rolling her head to the side. Ari had curled up facing Rhynn, her head only inches from Rhynn's shoulder. Tucked into a tight fetal ball, Ari's knees pressed lightly against Rhynn's side.

Rhynn forced herself to remain still and relaxed. The chron on the nightstand told her they still had more than an hour before their first scheduled interview with J'Nell Inagayle. She was warm and cozy under the comforter and didn't want to wake Ari until she had to. Even in sleep, Ari's brow furrowed. Rhynn wanted to smooth the lines away, but Ari didn't need yet another fangirl smothering her, and as the contract drummer, it wasn't appropriate. Rhynn closed her eyes and drew in a deep breath, tasting the slightly flowery scent of Ari's shampoo, reveling in the warmth of her skin so close. Rhynn exhaled slowly, letting her body relax back to sleep.

CHAPTER TWENTY-SEVEN

Earth Date: November 2453
Cruise Ship *Star Rider*

Rhynn

"Looks like it's about time for the interview," Ari said.

She and Rhynn rested on Rhynn's bed. Rhynn wasn't in a hurry to get moving, nor was she particularly looking forward to participating in an interview. She groaned and rubbed her hands over her face.

Ari slowly straightened and eased into a sitting position. She gave Rhynn an embarrassed look. "I didn't mean to crowd you earlier."

Rhynn stretched her arms out and smiled. "You didn't. I'm just glad you got some sleep."

"I did. Thank you."

"My pleasure." Rhynn felt her face go hot. "I mean, well, you know. No worries, yeah?"

Ari laughed softly. "I know. It's all good. Dibs on the bathroom." She stood and slipped into the cramped en-suite.

Rhynn sighed as the door closed. Damn. Standing, she rubbed her face again and pulled her clothes straight. She glanced in the mirror and ran her fingers through her unruly hair. Ugh. She looked like she'd just woken up, which was not good if this interview was going to be on vid. She needed a comb and some water. And a hair tie.

She didn't plan on participating in the discussion unless someone asked her a direct question. After all, she was only the fill-in drummer, not really a member of the band. Her knowledge of their history and the music was what she'd read or learned in conversations with them. None of it was her own experience, so she didn't feel right talking about it.

Ari stepped from the bathroom, looking much more awake. "Nothing like cold water on your face to get your blood flowing."

"Hope it works for me."

"You think this will work for the interview?" Ari gestured at herself.

You'd look incredible wearing a belted garbage sack. "I think you look great." Rhynn ducked into the bathroom. She splashed cold water on her burning face, then wet down her hair in attempt to get the goofy sleep kinks out. After running a comb through it, she left a flash of magenta bangs and pulled the rest into a single topknot and called it good.

When she came out, Ari was brushing her hair. "You ready?"

"Ready as I'm going to be." Rhynn followed Ari from the bedroom, not sure she was at all prepared.

As they entered the living room, all conversation stopped. J'Nell Inagayl rose from her seat on one of the recliners, greeting them with a wide show of teeth. "Well, there you are! Now we have a quorum."

Ari said, "Hi, J'Nell. Sorry. We fell asleep. I think all the craziness the last few days caught up to us."

Rhynn managed a weak smile, trying to gauge the mood in the room.

Ari took a seat between Toni and Dia on the couch. Nori sprawled in the second recliner. Feeling the need to stay close to Ari, Rhynn sat cross-legged on the floor between her and Dia.

Dia playfully pulled on Rhynn's colorful topknot. "Rhynn's been working her ass off learning all our tunes. We had a couple days before we boarded the cruise ship and she and Ari even worked together outside of rehearsals, smoothing out some of the transitions in the songs."

Rhynn was acutely aware of J'Nell's piercing gaze as the reporter sized her up and she wished Dia hadn't brought any attention to her.

"We haven't formally met," J'Nell said, extending her hand. "J'Nell Inagayl."

The reporter's grip was firm. "Rhynn Knight."

"You are an absolutely gifted drummer. Truly, you'd never know you weren't part of the band. The show last night was superb."

Rhynn smiled warily, not completely buying J'Nell's hype, but figuring it was best to be polite.

J'Nell set up a portable vid-cam on a stand beside her. "It's all right if I tape this?"

Toni said, "Yeah, for sure."

J'Nell used a palm-size remote to activate the camera and focus it in on the band. "Hello, fans! I'm here on the Hammer Down Cruise, visiting with the ladies from Shattered Crystal Enigma. Say hello, ladies."

She paused while the band members smiled and waved at the camera and called out their greetings. "For you newbs who don't know the lovely ladies of SCE, we have Ari Walker on lead guitar, Dia Caban on rhythm guitar, the venerable Toni Catone on lead vocals, and Nori Beaty on bass. Sitting in for drummer Stacy Rowe, who couldn't make the tour, is Rhynn Knight."

Nori said, "Rhynn stepped in on Moon Base when Stacy wasn't able to finish the show. She impressed the hell out of us, so we asked her to fill in for this part of the tour."

"Rhynn's our fairy god-drummer," Toni joked, and Dia and Nori groaned playfully.

J'Nell said, "Last night's opening show was a huge success, and the fans were super hyped. You played a couple new songs. Will we hear more from the new release throughout the tour?"

"Absolutely."

Nori, Dia, and Toni ran with the interview. Ari commented from time to time, but to Rhynn she seemed subdued. For her part, Rhynn answered a couple questions directed specifically toward her, relieved she managed to do so without tripping over her tongue or sounding like a complete idiot.

J'Nell handled the interview energetically. Nobody said Stacy had quit the band, and J'Nell didn't ask directly. Rhynn figured it would come out soon enough. There'd been no decision she was aware of to hide Stacy's exit. Maybe Wayne or Nelda had told them to keep it quiet. Maybe they just didn't want to talk about it until they'd figured out who would fill the position permanently.

After about forty minutes, J'Nell switched off the vid camera. "That was great, ladies, thank you."

Nori said, "You know you're our favorite reporter, J."

J'Nell laughed. "Well, I'm sure you'll be tired of me by the end of this tour. Do you think we can meet up again in a day or so?"

"Sure. You know where to find us."

"I'd better get going. I need to clean up the video before I post it. Thanks again for the time."

As she packed her camera into a small handbag, she glanced at Ari. "You were quiet today, hon. You doing okay?"

"I'm fine. A little tired."

J'Nell said, "Well, be sure to take care of yourself, okay?"

"I will."

J'Nell said her goodbyes and headed toward the door with Dia and Toni on either side. Rhynn slipped into the kitchenette to grab a container of fizzy ale while J'Nell swept out the door.

Toni walked into the kitchen. She pointed to Rhynn's drink. "Any left?"

"Yeah." Rhynn opened the cooler and handed Toni a bottle.

"Did Ari get some sleep?"

"She did. But I think she's still pretty weirded out about the whole situation."

"I hope they can figure out who it is and stop it, because it's wearing on our girl."

"I hope so too."

CHAPTER TWENTY-EIGHT

Earth Date: November 2453
Cruise Ship *Star Rider*
WR Security suite

Shaine and Morgan

"Have a seat, Mr. McCloud."

"Look, man, I ain't done nothin' wrong."

Del pushed the man into the hard-backed chair next to the table in the security suite's kitchenette. Staring at him with a hard, no-nonsense expression, she looked every inch the badass.

Leo McCloud had stringy blond hair hanging damply onto the towel around his shoulders. His loose swim shorts dripped onto the tiled floor. His gaze shifted uneasily between Del, Shaine, and Morgan.

Del said, "I didn't say you did anything wrong. We just want to ask you a few questions."

Shaine took the chair across the table. She pushed a holo photo at him. "Know this kid?"

McCloud squinted at the holo and looked away.

Del loomed over him. "Do you know him?"

McCloud avoided her glare and said nothing.

Shaine said, "You gave him fifty credits to put a letter on Ari Walker's bed."

McCloud looked at her and she held his gaze.

"Your prints are on the plas-sheet, so we know you had it in your hands." She glanced over at Gohste, who sat behind a computer terminal in the living room. He nodded briefly. "Did you write the note?"

"No! I didn't write it, okay?"

"Then who did?"

"I dunno."

Del leaned closer. "Come on, McCloud. Fess up. There's no crime in writing a love note. We need to know who did so we can ask them to stop. If you didn't write it, where did it come from?"

"If I tell, you'll leave me alone?"

Shaine's expression remained calm, empty, non-threatening. "As long as you tell me the truth."

"This babe came up to me last night, in the bar, after the show. We was talkin', if you know what I mean. And I was gettin' somewhere, and then she asks if I would deliver a letter for her, to one of the chicks in the band. And I was, like, not sure about that. Then she pulls a credit chit from between her tits—and she was built, man—and I was like, okay, sure."

Del growled from above him. He swallowed visibly.

Shaine said, "But you didn't deliver it."

He shook his head. "I went up, but there was all you guys in the hallway, and I thought, naw, I don't wanna do that, so I just took the elevator back down without getting out. But she said she'd see me later, if I delivered it, so I wanted to do it for her, and see her again, you know? She was real sweet-lookin'. So, there was this kid doing cleaning, right? Housekeeping? And I said, hey, I'll give ya fifty chits if you'll put this letter in the guitar chick's bedroom, and he was like, sure, I can do that."

Shaine asked, "The woman who gave you the note, what did she look like?"

"Like I said, she was built, like out to here." He gestured with his hands out from his chest.

Del snapped, "What color was her hair?"

"Uh. Brown, I think. Yeah. Kinda brown, but you could tell it was a wig. She had those weird red cat-eye lenses in her eyes too."

Shaine asked, "Light or dark skinned?"

"Light, like tan."

"Do you remember what she was wearing?"

He screwed up his face. "Uh. Her skirt was real short. And her shirt left a lot showing, you know?"

"What color skirt or shirt?"

"Uh, red, maybe? With black. I wasn't lookin' at the color, y'know?"

"Okay. If you think of anything else, this is my calling code." Shaine handed him a card. "Thank you for your time, Mr. McCloud."

He took it tentatively. "Can I leave now?"

"Sure. Thank you for answering our questions."

"Uh, yeah. Sure." He stood, and Del moved back a couple paces, allowing him a path to the door. He nearly tripped over himself getting out of the suite.

Del slouched against the counter next to Morgan. "What a loser."

Gohste said, "Bio scans say he's telling the truth."

Shaine said, "Get the elevator video from ship security and look for this guy, verify he was up here."

"So, who's the chick?" Morgan asked. "And why aren't her prints on the letter?"

Shaine leaned back, frowning. "Wearing gloves, which he'd have noticed, or Nu-skin fingertips to hide her prints. Or clear finger covers."

"Fucking expensive for good ones," Morgan said.

"So's a chameleon suit."

"So, we try to ID all the well-endowed women on this cruise who have money and wear wigs and cat-eye contacts?"

"Looks like."

"Fuck."

CHAPTER TWENTY-NINE

Earth Date: November 2453
Cruise Ship *Star Rider*
After-party meet and greet, show #2

Ari

The second show went off almost as well as the first, except for me worrying about Celestian sending another calling card. Anxiety kept me on edge and not fully engaged in the music. No one besides me and my bandmates noticed. I didn't make any blatant screw-ups, but I wasn't satisfied with my performance.

My unease continued while we attended the after-party in the Starshine room. Our security contingent was present in full force and in uniform. I saw Morgan and one of the guys talking with some of the slammers, and from the gestures, I gathered they were talking about slamming in the zero-g cube. I guessed it was good public relations if security made friends with the fans. Either way, the security presence kept me from completely freaking out.

I didn't feel physically threatened, but I continually scanned the room, studying faces, wondering if any of them were Celestian. I considered men and women alike, especially if anyone seemed to pay too much attention to me, certain I was being watched and not in a good way.

Rhynn stayed close. I didn't know if she did it unconsciously or if she had taken her promise to protect me to heart, but I didn't mind. She was sweet. The two of us, more than the others, had spent time getting her caught up on the music, so it made sense we were more comfortable together.

The more time I spent with her the more I enjoyed her energy. Rhynn was easy to be around. And yesterday—I couldn't believe I'd slept, dreamless, at her side while we'd napped in the afternoon. She hadn't come onto me. Didn't take advantage. She could have. But she didn't. That meant more to me than anything. And if she'd held me, I don't think I'd have minded.

I shook off the thoughts and focused on the fans milling around. Two women came up to talk and I accepted their compliments. I didn't get a creep-out factor, so we chatted a little about how huge the cruise ship was and how none of us had ever been on a cruise before.

Rhynn and I eventually joined Toni, Friday, Dia, and Nori at a couple of high tables pushed together, adding our plates of snack food to theirs. Our fans continued to stop by to visit.

At some point, J'Nell swept into the party, dressed to kill in a form-fitting gold jumpsuit and high boots, her blond hair spritzed around her head. "Ladies, great show as usual."

Dia lifted her glass. "Hey, J'Nell. I saw the spread you posted earlier. Got some great shots of the bands."

"I loved the two new songs you added. Very intense."

Nori said, "Toni wrote the lyrics." She reached over and stole a hot sauce-drowned protein bite off my plate with her fork.

"Hey!"

"It was calling my name."

"Then you can go up for the next plate," I said, playfully threatening her with my own fork. Then, without even thinking about it, I stole a similar protein bite off Rhynn's plate. She elbowed me playfully, and I gave her a shoulder bump.

J'Nell laughed and snapped a few photos of us fooling around. "It's so great you get along so well."

Toni said, "One big happy family, right? Hey, have you met Friday? She's doing all our stage and lighting design this tour, and she put together the background vids too. Friday, this is J'Nell Inagayl, famous and amazing entertainment reporter."

Friday smiled, and Toni kissed the side of her head.

J'Nell asked slyly, "I take it you're a couple?"

Toni and Friday giggled like schoolgirls. Toni said, "Yeah, I think that's a pretty fair description."

J'Nell snapped a photo. "Congratulations."

Dia smirked. "No wonder Toni wanted a room to herself."

"Jealous much?" Toni tossed a balled-up napkin across the table at her.

Rhynn snickered and grabbed a fried veggie off my plate. "Just keep the volume down. Some of us need our beauty sleep."

I laughed out loud. I'd never heard Rhynn join in the band's teasing before. I hardly even noticed she'd stolen food from my plate, as if it were the most normal thing in the world. My heart felt strangely full when Rhynn met my gaze. Her quick glance and a quirky half-smile warmed me to the core. It wasn't until later that I wondered what our interactions must have looked like to J'Nell.

CHAPTER THIRTY

Earth Date: November 2453
Cruise Ship *Star Rider*

Ryhnn

Rhynn yawned. Mid-afternoon, and she was still wiped out. Being on tour was a lot more work than most people thought. As she walked through the cruise ship with the rest of the band, plus Morgan and two additional bodyguards, she did her best to stretch her stiff limbs. They'd played two shows in two nights. Her hands felt stiff and a little swollen when she clenched her fists, and she'd woken up early in the morning with a pounding tension headache from the tightness in her shoulders and neck. She tilted her head back and forth as she walked and told herself to quit whining and deal with it.

Ship security officers allowed them to enter the darkened concert hall as the second of the two opening bands finished their sound check. The Meteor Music Hall was three times the size of Club Tranquility on Moon Base, with a huge zero-g cube at the center of the hall. Both the cube and the floor of the hall had been packed wall-to-wall with thrashers for every show.

Terestian's road crew rolled their equipment racks and drum riser off to the side. Rhynn slouched into a chair at a table toward the front of the club, surrounded by her bandmates. They settled in to wait until their own crew was ready for them. One of the club's staff brought a tray of beverages to their table—a mix of fizzy ale, which had a low alcohol content, or fizzy soda, which had none. Rhynn opted for soda with the hope the caffeine would give her a lift.

She leaned an elbow on the table and sipped her drink. Two shows down and two more to go before they shuttled off the cruiser for two shows at Mann-Maru mining facilities in the Asteroid Belt. The cruise ship would stop outside the 'Belt, and the band and road crew would take smaller transport shuttles to the gigs, with a minimal stage show and without any of the other bands. Rhynn looked forward to the mining facility shows. In some ways it would be like returning to her childhood, though the facilities weren't ones where she and her mom had lived.

As she watched the stage crew hard at work, she realized that she'd easily fallen into the rhythm of sleep, eat, chill, play, eat, sleep and start all over again. At the same time, the routines still seemed larger than life. The stage was bigger, the accommodations fancier, the audience larger and more enthusiastic, but it felt strange without her familiar group of friends from Moon Base.

It was definitely odd not seeing familiar faces in the crowd, and she wished she could have brought her friends along with her. She even wished that her mom could see her play, just once, with SCE. She'd exchanged messages with Leigh and Vicki and her mom, trying to explain all the things she'd seen and experienced. Leigh called her a fangirl, and her mom told her to enjoy herself and do her best.

Their stage manager Mykal consulted a comp pad as he directed the techs. His deep, gravelly voice boomed across the empty hall. The drum tech and two others pushed her drum riser forward. Mykal walked the front of the stage, talking into a mic, his ear cocked toward the monitors. "Check. Toni's mic. Check. Hey, Toni, come get your mic."

Toni pushed up from the table and jogged toward the stage. "You know, Myk, you could tie a bow around it and leave it on stage for me."

"Don't push your luck, Catone."

She laughed as she vaulted onto the stage and took the wireless from his hand. "Get your asses up here, you guys," she called back to the table.

Groaning, Rhynn and the others followed. Rhynn joined her drum tech, Jax, as he plugged power leads into the floor outlets and checked around the outside of the chrome rack holding all her drum pads. "Hey, Rhynn. You ready to go?"

"Sure. At least I wasn't drinking myself into oblivion last night," she added, nodding toward a couple of Terestian's road crew, who looked like twice-used rocket fuel.

"Yeah, they're all bitching. Myk told 'em to shut the fuck up and do their jobs or he'd toss them head first off the stage."

Rhynn laughed, imagining their sweet but grumpy stage manager laying down the law. She circled behind her drums and was about to sit down when she noticed the small black envelope on her snare drum pad. She picked it up and waved it at Jax. "You sending me notes now?"

"No. Where'd that come from?"

"It was on my snare drum."

"Maybe you should put it down and let the security guys look at it."

Her hand jerked and she dropped the envelope back onto the pad as though it were on fire. Her voice squeaked as she called out, "Hey, Morgan, can you come up here?"

Ari spun around where she stood facing her amps. "Rhynn?"

"Someone left me an envelope."

Ari's face paled.

Rhynn added hopefully, "Maybe it's from a fan."

Ari slung her guitar off her shoulder, leaning it against a speaker cabinet.

Morgan jogged from the side of the stage and bounded onto the drum riser. Rhynn pointed to the envelope and moved out of the way. Ari slipped her hand into Rhynn's as Rhynn joined her, and Rhynn looked at her, surprised. Ari watched Morgan, her jaw clenched and fear in her eyes. Rhynn squeezed her hand and shifted closer. She wanted to say something brave and comforting, but nothing came to mind, so she held her tongue and silently berated herself for taking too much pleasure in holding Ari's hand.

Morgan drew a scanner out of her pocket and ran it over the envelope and the drum pad. After a few seconds the unit beeped and she pocketed it. She pulled on a pair of gloves and gingerly picked up the envelope. Flipping it over, she scanned the back side and then tapped the com unit in her ear. "Shaine. Someone left an envelope on the drum kit. I've scanned it and the pad it was on. Scanner says it's clean, except for Rhynn's prints. You want me to open it?" After a pause, she turned toward Rhynn and Ari. "I can open it, if you want."

Rhynn said, "Do it."

She felt a tremor shudder through Ari's body.

Morgan broke the seal on the envelope and removed a folded piece of white paper from the black envelope. Before she read it, she ran the scanner over both sides until it beeped.

"It says, *Drummer, you are only temporary. Don't get comfortable. Arienne is taken.*"

Rhynn tried for a light mood, "Guess they don't like my playing, huh?"

Ari muttered, "I don't think that's the issue." Rhynn heard her voice break. The color had leeched from her face, and she seemed to be on the brink of crying.

Rhynn said, "It'll be okay."

"Will it?"

"Yes," Rhynn said. She wouldn't let this freak hurt Ari. She would protect her, even if it meant putting herself in the crazy stalker's path. Ari's hand gripped the waistband at the back of Rhynn's shorts, as though holding on for support.

"We'll get whoever is doing this," Morgan said. "I'll take this back to the suite, and we'll start going over the surveillance vids. We've got scanners and cameras running everywhere around the stage. Something's got to show up."

Morgan sounded so positive. Rhynn tried to project the same certainty. Who knew? Maybe the freak was a big fan of Stacy Rowe and pissed she wasn't on the tour. Rhynn caught Ari's other hand and squeezed it. "We're not gonna let anything happen to you."

She felt the tremor in Ari's hands and thought about what they looked like right now, with Ari holding onto the back of her shorts and her holding Ari's hand. Maybe whoever it was thought she was sleeping with Ari. The thought sent a flash of heat through her. She took a deep breath. Ari was her friend, and she would stay strong for her.

CHAPTER THIRTY-ONE

Earth Date: November 2453
Cruise Ship *Star Rider*

Shaine and Morgan

"There." Gohste stopped the scanner log video and ran it back a few frames. "See it? For a couple seconds, there's a heat signature at the back of the drum riser."

Leaning over his shoulder, peering at the monitor, Shaine muttered, "Fucking chameleon suit again."

"Let me see if I can isolate the data and get some kind of form out of it." He bent over the keyboard, pecking madly at the keys and then swiping at the screen to enlarge the image.

After a while he shook his head. "This is the best I can do. The stage was really warm right after the show, and it's canceling out the body's heat signature. You can see a faint outline. I think that's your person." He grabbed a stylus and drew a line. "See? Here, and a little bit here. Not much to go on." He did a screen grab from the vid and tapped forward a frame at a time. "See it moving? It's a pretty small person. If I'm reading this right, no more than a meter and a half tall. More likely a woman than a man, I'd say. Unless it's a real small guy."

Morgan said, "That's what the reports said, too, about the size of the person. The heat signature they got suggested a woman."

Shaine frowned. "Save anything that looks useful and we'll add it to the very small pile of information we have. Thanks, Gohste."

"I'll see if I can track it across the stage, maybe into a cool spot or something."

Morgan said, "So, we're still pretty much at square one. Probably a female, but who? There are probably a couple hundred women with enhanced chests on the security shots from the ship's manifest. So far, none of them fit a stalker psych profile."

Gohste said, "Someone in disguise?"

"That opens the list to almost anyone under one and a half meters," Shaine said.

"Do we start interviewing anyone who fits the profile?"

Shaine shook her head slowly, thoughtfully. "System Investigation Bureau should be dealing with this, not us. I signed on for security, not investigation. Unfortunately, we're out here, and they're not. We need to step back and start looking at this like investigators, not a security detail."

Gohste said, "So, we need to look at the whole situation and try to figure out who would have been doing this the whole time, not only on this ship, or on this tour."

"Right. We need motive, and someone with the means to get to Ari."

"And someone on this ship."

"Not necessarily. Could be someone directing things from a distance."

Gohste scratched his head. "That just doesn't seem likely."

Shaine scowled. "At this point, we can't rule out anything."

CHAPTER THIRTY-TWO

Earth Date: November 2453
Cruise Ship *Star Rider*

Rhynn

Rhynn settled on the throne behind her drum kit, scooping up a pair of sticks and looking out toward the sound booth. Kevven, SCE's primary sound engineer, leaned over the control boards and his voice echoed over the PA. "Rhynn, give me some bass drum. Right and then left."

She dutifully set a steady beat first with her right foot and then the left. Kevven had her go foot to foot after that, evening out the levels. They continued around the drum pads, and she followed his direction, but found herself repeatedly glancing to her right, watching Ari.

Ari's posture seemed slightly hunched, her hair hanging down over her face, as though she was hiding behind it. She faced her amps and fiddled with the settings as she played warm-up scales. Rhynn could hear the low tones of her guitar under the thick, edgy smack of bass drums over the main PA. Normally, she reveled in the powerful sound of her drums over the concert PA, but she couldn't shake her worry about Ari.

After the envelope showed up, Ari had withdrawn into what Rhynn interpreted as self-protective silence. Ari's unease wasn't unexpected and Rhynn didn't blame her.

Rhynn tried to push the note out of her mind and focus on the job at hand. She wasn't scared of Ari's stalker, at least not for herself. But this Celestian was getting way too close. Even if there wasn't any overt physical threat, the constant mental pressure on Ari had to be unnerving. Ari said she hoped being away from Earth would have given her a break. How disturbing was it to realize the threat continued unabated?

Rhynn finished her sound check and sat back while Kevven ran the others through their paces. J'Nell showed up at the concert hall and marched onstage, interrupting Kevven so she could explain how she planned to interview the band over the course of the evening so she could show their fans a behind the scenes perspective.

Mykal stomped out from behind the monitor boards on stage left. "Then how about you show the fans how we don't have time for this crap," he growled. "We need to finish the sound check."

J'Nell rolled her eyes at him.

"Just stay the fuck out of the way, so we can get our work done," he snapped, shaking his head and returning to the soundboard. He made a circling gesture to Kevven to continue.

The soundman's voice had an amused tone. "Dia, let's get that clean level."

Dia started playing chords with a clear, undistorted tone.

J'Nell prowled the stage with her palm-sized vid-cam, documenting the band and stage crew.

Rhynn was annoyed by the interruption and J'Nell's intrusion on what she now considered her territory. She recognized the shift in her perception from "their" stage to "her" stage, as well as *her* band, even if the job was only temporary. J'Nell could have shown up earlier or waited until they'd finished the sound check to do her presentation.

She smiled when she saw the WR security contingent stop J'Nell at the side of the stage, Del and Mitch talking to her with serious, business-like expressions before they stepped back and J'Nell continued filming.

With Kevven's go-ahead, Rhynn clicked off the first song on their usual sound check playlist. Dia started with a sparse rhythm line before everyone else jumped in and they kicked into the first verse.

J'Nell glided around the drum riser, pointing her camera at Rhynn who pointedly kept her focus on her hands and feet, not looking up. Still, she wasn't above a little arrogance, so she dropped a few extra fancy fills into the song. *Take that, boys. Ain't nothing you got that I can't do too.*

She supposed her attitude toward competing with the guys was cliché, but honestly, slam-thrash was mostly a guy thing, and they rarely took female musicians seriously until they got their musical asses kicked.

J'Nell backed toward the front of the stage. Nori and Dia posed and swaggered for the camera with exaggerated flair while Toni laughed at their antics. J'Nell filmed it all with a wide smile of encouragement. Before they were finished with the sound check, Rhynn asked to run over the verse-bridge-chorus transition of one of the new songs. Ari and Nori grouped around the drum riser to better communicate. She played easily through the verse, and when they hit the transition into the odd-time bridge, Rhynn's focus went to Ari.

Ari directed, motioning with the head of her guitar. Rhynn followed, shifting her focus to Nori as Ari played the bridge solo. Rhynn added some supporting syncopation to Ari's riff that Stacy hadn't done in the recordings. Ari caught her eye, grinned appreciatively and guided them back out of the bridge and into the chorus.

Rhynn acknowledged her bandmates with a flash of sticks. "Thanks, guys."

Ari winked. Rhynn watched, fascinated, as Ari moved with a sway of her hips to her usual place.

Kevven asked, "Do you ladies need to run anything else, or are you good to go?"

Toni looked around the group. "Anyone?"

Rhynn shook her head, forcing her focus away from Ari's perfect ass. "I'm good."

Ari swung her guitar off and handed it to Gavin.

J'Nell clapped her hands. "That was wonderful! The fans will love the video."

"It's been fun." Dia spun her guitar in her hands before handing it off to her tech.

Rhynn stood behind her drum kit, stretching her back and leaning forward with her arms resting on two cymbal pads. "We done, then?"

Toni said, "Yeah. Who wants to go get some grub?"

A sharp, explosive bang echoed across the stage.

J'Nell screamed, "Look out!" She grabbed Ari's arm and yanked her sideways. Ari stumbled and sprawled face-first as a meter-long stage light crashed to the floor with a shattering explosion of noise, landing where Ari had been standing a second before.

Rhynn vaulted over her drum kit and leaped off the riser, dropping beside Ari amongst the shards of shattered glass and debris. Not feeling the splinters digging into her knees, she brushed the glass out of Ari's hair, from her back. "Are you okay? Ari?"

Ari had fallen face down, both hands trapped under her body. She groaned and pushed herself to her hands and knees. Blood gushed from her nose. "Oh, shit."

Without thinking about it, Rhynn stripped off her shirt and balled it up, pressing it to Ari's bleeding nose as she helped Ari shift awkwardly into a sitting position.

Ari grasped the cloth, muttering, "Fuck. I think by nothe ith broken."

Security surrounded them.

Rhynn only had eyes for Ari, frantically searching her for other injuries. When she ran her fingers through Ari's hair, her fingers came away bloody, and she felt a sharp jagged edge of glass come free from her scalp. She didn't have anything to stop the bleeding, so she just held a hand against Ari's head.

Someone asked J'Nell if she was okay and Rhynn glanced over as one of the security guards helped her sit up. J'Nell looked shell-shocked and pale, but she seemed unharmed.

Rhynn said loudly, "Ari needs to get to the infirmary. Her head's bleeding too."

Morgan squatted at Ari's side. "I called for medical."

Rhynn frowned at the blood starting to drip between her fingers on the back of Ari's head and still soaking the balled-up shirt under Ari's nose and felt her own panic rising. Ari leaned against her with her eyes shut.

Rhynn noticed J'Nell watching her and gave the reporter a grateful smile. "You saved Ari's life."

J'Nell smiled wanly. "That's me, the reporter superhero."

Eyes still shut, Ari mumbled, "I owe you wud, J. Thag you."

CHAPTER THIRTY-THREE

Earth Date: November 2453
Cruise Ship *Star Rider*

Ari

My nose had almost stopped bleeding by the time medical showed up, and Morgan had found a towel to hold against the cut in the back of my head. J'Nell insisted she was fine and needed no assistance, but Rhynn and I rode a hover-cart back to the ship's med bay. Del and Morgan rode behind us in a security cart.

The doctor did a scan and quickly determined my swollen nose wasn't broken, merely battered. The med tech gave me a handful of wipes with which to clean my face. I had a few minor cuts from the flying glass and the one on the back of my head which needed a couple stitches. Rhynn got a few stiches in her right knee from the glass on the floor.

All in all, though, we were damned lucky.

In the curtained space at the side of the trauma room, Rhynn sat next to me in a memory-form recliner, while I lay propped up on a narrow bed with an IV in one arm. I had lost what seemed to me to be a lot of blood between my head and my nose, and was feeling light-headed, so the doctor wanted to get some fluids in me before he let me go. Still shaking inside from the close call, I wasn't ready to face the world. If the doc wanted to give me fluids, that was fine by me.

Rhynn tucked the light blanket around my shoulders. "You look cold."

I rolled my eyes at her concerned attentiveness. With the gashes on her knee and lower legs, she looked like a kid who'd fallen off her bicycle. "I think you're more beat up than me."

"You're just saying that because you can't see how swollen your nose is. Bet you'll have black eyes in the morning."

I sighed. *Wonderful.* Oh, well. I'd get Dia to help with a little makeup. At least they hadn't needed to cut away much hair, but the synth-skin glue sealing the wound made a weird, rubbery bump I'd need to be careful of combing over for a couple days.

Rhynn shifted in her chair. She blurted, "It scared the hell out of me. I thought you were dead."

I studied her face, full of earnestness and intensity. I snaked my free hand out from under the blanket and squeezed hers. "It still scares the crap out of me. Thank you for staying with me. And giving me the shirt off your back." I smiled at that last part. I had no problem with Rhynn wearing only a sleek black sports bra with her shorts, though now she wore a disposable scrub shirt against the chill in the med bay.

Her face reddened. "Yeah, I could probably have thought that through a little better."

"It was very gallant."

This time she laughed. "Yeah, and stupid embarrassing. Anyway, I'm glad you're okay."

"Thank you." I looked into her serious brown eyes and saw something that grabbed at my heart and made my chest ache. A bright current ran between us and took my breath away.

Then the curtain whooshed open and J'Nell stood in front of us.

I felt Rhynn's hand slip out from under mine and disappointment washed over me.

"I wanted to make sure you were both okay. The doctor said you were back here." Worried furrows marred J'Nell's brow and she looked us over with concern.

Rhynn said, "We're good. All patched up. They're giving Ari some fluids because she was feeling light-headed."

I said, "I need to thank you properly. So, thank you, so very much, for saving my life. If you hadn't thought so quickly and pulled me away, I'd probably be dead."

J'Nell waved it off, though her expression was pleased. "No thanks needed. I'm glad I was able to help."

"You're okay, right, J'Nell?" Rhynn asked.

"I'm fine. A little sore, but fine. Did they say why the light fell?"

I said, "Nobody's told us anything. Probably a just freak accident." I had no intention of making my stalking story public, but Rhynn and I both thought the incident had something to do with Celestian.

"I was thinking maybe I could do a quick interview since we're all here? Rumors are already flying around the ship."

Seriously? An interview? I was lying in a trauma bay, my nose hurt like a bitch, and I had an IV in my arm. I wasn't up for an interview. I glanced over at Rhynn and caught her watching me.

She said to J'Nell, "I think, for now, we'd rather have you just let everyone know we're okay. The stage crew is having a look at the lights. Something must have come loose from the rigging during the show last night."

J'Nell turned her gaze toward me, as though I might have a different answer. I wasn't all that sorry to disappoint her. "I'm really wiped and my head hurts. I just want to rest before the show."

J'Nell blinked and nodded. "Oh. Well, yes, you should rest. I'll let everyone know you're fine and you'll be playing tonight."

"Thanks, J'Nell. I appreciate it."

"I really am glad you're all right. I'll leave you to rest then, and I'll talk to you later."

Rhynn said, "Thanks, J'Nell. Truly."

She slipped away, leaving the curtain fluttering behind her.

I was relieved to be alone again with Rhynn. She laid a warm hand on my arm, her thumb gently rubbing my skin, shooting tingles through my body. She said, "Close your eyes and try to sleep for a while. I'll be here."

"Thanks, Rhynn."

"Anytime."

I closed my eyes and exhaled slowly, concentrating on the warmth of her hand on my arm and her gentle touch. *My protector*, was the last thing I thought before I fell asleep.

CHAPTER THIRTY-FOUR

Earth Date: November 2453
Cruise Ship *Star Rider*

Shaine and Morgan

The light rigging was suspended a story and a half above the stage, a spider's maze of grated metal walkways, narrow beams, and cabling. Shaine watched anxiously as Morgan hung over the edge of the grating, using a hand-held comp pad to take scans and vid of the broken hinge that had secured the fallen light.

Shaine watched the transmitted data on her comp pad and kept a tight grip on the back of her partner's pants. Thank the universe she'd thought to clip a safety line to Morgan's belt. It made her crazy when Morgan pretended to be a monkey when she wasn't in low or zero-grav.

"Are you getting this?" Morgan's voice came up to her, muffled by her position.

"Yes. I wish we had Grey Tannis here. I need to send this to her. Looks like plastique explosive damage."

"Whatever it was, it pretty well shredded the light's connection to the C-clamp and the wiring and safety cable holding it."

Shaine studied the video on her screen. "Get closer to the wiring. Do you see the embedded metal pieces? Yeah. There. I think that's a piece of a remote detonator—military hardware."

"Is that good or bad?"

"Likely it's bad."

"How the fuck is this person getting stuff into place under our noses, Shaine?"

"Too much space for us to cover twenty-four-seven. And this could have been here for a long time, waiting to be used. That light was part of the standard house lighting, not the equipment SCE brought in."

"But if military explosives are coming on board, how is the Customs screening not catching it? They fucking bitched at me for having a multi-tool in my kit."

Shaine shrugged, though she knew Morgan couldn't see it. "If you have money, there's always a way. Scan-proof a section of a suitcase, buy someone off, bury it in a food delivery or something."

"Whoever this is has connections."

"I think so."

"I don't get it, though. I mean, someone with military connections, with the money to get this kind of equipment, that's not usually the kind of person obsessing on a guitar player in a slam-thrash band. What dumb-ass thrasher would have both money and skills?"

Shaine laughed. "Honey, you're a dumb-ass thrasher, and look what you've accomplished."

"Shut up."

"I think you've gotten vid from every possible angle. Come on back up." She tugged on Morgan's pants, and Morgan pulled herself back onto the narrow walkway suspended above the stage. When she was sitting safely, Shaine said, "I've got Gohste, Rich, and Bagger looking at the surveillance video and scanner readouts. I doubt they'll come up with much. Del is going through the ship's personnel records to see if anyone might even vaguely fit who we're looking for. Rae and Jorge are at the med center keeping an eye on Ari and Rhynn."

"Where do you want me to be?"

Shaine leered and wondered for a second if they could manage to get away with it up in the rigging.

Morgan snorted. “Man, you’re a horny bastard.”

Shaine laughed. “Yeah, I am. Come on. Let’s take on the passenger list and see who looks suspicious.”

CHAPTER THIRTY-FIVE

Earth Date: November 2453
Cruise Ship *Star Rider*

Rhynn

For the first time since she joined the tour, Rhynn could honestly say she was glad the night was over. Exhaustion had leeched away any remaining adrenaline from the show, leaving her with barely enough energy to jam some high-carb food into her mouth. Leaning heavily against the counter in the suite's kitchenette, she chewed slowly on a handful of protein crackers and sipped a sugar-laden fizzy drink.

She should have grabbed food during the obligatory VIP meet and greet after the concert, but she and Ari hadn't stayed long enough. After about twenty minutes of mingling, Ari's face had taken on a pale, pasty tinge, her eyes glassy with fatigue. Rhynn had grabbed Morgan and asked for an escort back to the room.

Rhynn's main concern was with Ari, but her own sock was soaked with blood. The stitches on her right knee had broken open, and she'd played the second half of the set with blood dripping down her leg. Now it throbbed like a bitch.

When they reached the suite, Rhynn sent Ari into the shower before hobbling back into the kitchenette to find something to eat. She shifted to take the pressure off her knee. The gaffer's tape she'd hastily wrapped over the wound was holding, but as soon as she removed the tape, the cut would start bleeding again.

She pushed off the breakfast bar and limped across the kitchenette. Palming the lock, she poked her head into the hallway to get the attention of the uniformed woman sitting at the table in front of their door. "Hey, Rae, do you guys have a med kit?"

"Sure. You want me to get a doc or a med tech for you?"

"Naw. Just the kit. I'll tape myself back together."

Rae typed a message into her comp pad. Moments later, Mitch stepped out of the security suite with a med kit in a red case. He tossed it to Rae, who walked it over to Rhynn. Her gaze dropped to take in the blood leaking down Rhynn's leg. Rae raised a brow. "That should probably be re-stitched."

"Tomorrow. I'll deal with it tomorrow."

Shrugging and shaking her head, Rae returned to her post, and Rhynn locked the door carefully behind her. She finished her crackers and drink and limped to the bedroom with the med kit.

Ari sat on the edge of her bed, wearing lounge pants and a T-shirt, combing out her hair. She looked up when Rhynn came into the room. "Shower's open. I think I feel a little better now."

"Thanks. Hey, at least you didn't end up with black eyes."

"No. Just a bruised, red, swollen nose. Your knee is bleeding again."

"I got a med kit from security. I'll tape the crap out of it when I get out of the shower."

"I can help, if you want."

Thoughts of Ari's hands on her skin made her shiver. "Yeah, sure." She set the med kit on her bed, pulled boxer shorts and a sleep shirt from the dresser and retreated to the bathroom. "Be back in a flash."

She was glad to strip off her sweaty clothes. She cranked up the steam as much as she could, stepped into the shower, and hung her head under the single overhead mister. The sonic waves loosened the sweat and dirt from her body as the hot steam relaxed her aching muscles, but the cuts on her legs stung like hell as the steamy mist dripped down her skin. Clamping her jaw, she prepared herself, then ripped the tape off her knee. She bit back a squeak at the sting and frowned when it started gushing blood again.

Biting her tongue on a string of obscenities, she let it bleed and cleaned the wound with soap. Groaning, she held her leg in front of the misters to rinse it. She finished her shower, squeezed the water from the washcloth and draped it over her knee while she dried herself.

Getting dressed without bleeding on everything was a bit of a challenge. She sat on the commode with a twice-rinsed bloody washcloth on her knee. She realized she did need Ari's help, and wondered if Ari was still awake. She stood, feeling more than a little unsteady and shuffled awkwardly toward the door, holding the cloth against her knee. Cracking it open, she peered out.

Ari sat on the edge of her bed, hands in her lap, frowning and pensive.

Rhynn cleared her throat. "Um, if you're still willing to lend a hand, I'm kinda bleeding all over everything."

Ari jumped to her feet. She was in the bathroom before Rhynn settled again on the closed commode. Kneeling on the floor in front of Rhynn, she opened the med kit on the floor and reached for a clean, dry washcloth. After a bit of searching, and she found self-dissolving tape strips and nu-skin patches. Rhynn held the washcloth against her knee and waited for instructions.

Ten minutes later, Ari had Rhynn fixed up, the cut on her knee reasonably sealed and the blood cleaned away. Rhynn watched, amazed at the gentleness of her touch and the sureness of her actions. Ari had either done this before or was a quick learner. Either way, when she'd finished, Rhynn missed the warmth of Ari's strong fingers on her skin.

"Thank you," Rhynn said.

"My pleasure." Ari yawned, and Rhynn felt bad for keeping her up. Ari packed the med kit, stood and held out a hand, which Rhynn took, though she used the edge of the sink to help pull herself to her feet. A wave of dizziness washed over her, and she immediately felt Ari's hands on her waist, steadying her.

Rhynn blinked and took a couple deep breaths. "I'm okay."

Ari studied her for a couple beats before taking the med kit and leading Rhynn into the bedroom. Ari set the med kit on top of the dresser and returned to sitting on the edge of her bed. Rhynn pulled down the covers on her bed and faced Ari. She stretched out her neatly bandaged knee while Ari stared at the floor with her hands folded between her knees. Her still-wet hair hung over her shoulders, dampening her T-shirt.

She glanced at Rhynn and said, "I'm sorry you've been dragged into all this craziness. And I'm sorry you got hurt on my account."

"Hey, nothing for you to be sorry about. And I'm fine. Hell, if I could have kept you from smacking your nose, I would have. You're good people, Ari. You don't deserve this stalker making things so difficult. I like you. All of you guys." Rhynn took Ari's folded hands into her own. "Seriously, I don't kneel in broken glass for just anyone."

Rhynn wasn't sure where her words were coming from, except that she was tired and her filters were down. But it was true. For Ari, she would have done anything. Not because Ari was an incredible guitarist and rock star, but because she was Ari, a friend, and because Rhynn felt a connection between them. She was drawn to Ari in a way she had no words to describe.

"You're a very special person, Rhynn," Ari said softly.

"No more than you."

Ari shook her head. "I'm scared," she whispered. "I don't understand why this is happening. I don't understand how someone can, at the same time, be obsessed with me and want to hurt me. I'm scared you, or one of the others, are going to get hurt by mistake, more than you already have been."

"It's okay to be scared." Ari's hands felt so cold. Rhynn leaned forward, lifting Ari's hands and placing a chaste kiss on her knuckles. She wasn't sure what else to do. Or say. She knew she wanted to be there for Ari, to hold her up, keep her from drowning.

"I'm so tired," Ari whispered.

"Then let me tuck you in and we'll get some sleep."

Ari lifted pleading eyes toward her. "Stay with me? Hold me?"

"Anything."

They stood and Rhynn pulled back the covers on Ari's bed. Ari slithered between the sheets. Rhynn eased in beside her, pulling the covers up and cuddling Ari into a tight embrace.

Goddess, it felt good. She smoothed a hand over Ari's damp hair, holding her head against her chest. Rhynn's heart felt full to bursting, emotions bubbling up inside, almost overwhelming her, and she felt tears prick at her eyes. "Lights, out," she said quietly into the room, and they were plunged into darkness.

Ari's hand tightened in the fabric of Rhynn's T-shirt, and Rhynn hugged her. "Sleep well."

She felt the warmth of Ari's sigh through the thin material of her sleep shirt and heard a whispered murmur that could have been anything from "you too" to "thank you," and almost could have been "love you."

CHAPTER THIRTY-SIX

Earth Date: November 2453
Cruise Ship *Star Rider*

Ari

Hands grasped my clothes, pulling the neck of my shirt tight, and I struggled in the darkness. I screamed. No! Leave me alone! I wanted to say the words aloud, but they were stuck in my aching throat. Fear hissed through my blood. I thrashed against the suffocating hold, trapped against my will, unable to move.

I jolted awake, my heart slamming wildly against my chest.

Then I recognized the bedroom of the cruise ship and realized the arm trapping me, the leg sprawled over mine and the warmth against my back was Rhynn spooning me.

I sucked in a shaking breath and felt my body tremble violently in reaction to the nightmare.

Fuck.

Scenes from the previous day played in my head: J'Nell pulling me out of the way of the light, Rhynn's panicked expression as she knelt beside me, her T-shirt against my bleeding nose, cradling me against her as she tried to stop the bleeding, holding my hand in the infirmary.

I thought about Rhynn playing through the show last night with blood dripping down her leg, seemingly unaware of it as she wailed through the set. Her whole body was in motion behind the drums, fluid, forceful and graceful. Her intensity fascinated me.

She was so different from Stacy. Stacy was a technician, flawless, measured, steady. But Rhynn felt the music, flowed with it, was part of it. She understood music the way I did, from inside her heart, driven from the emotion rather than the mechanics of it. I got the sense she reacted to the universe the same way, as a part of it, rather than fighting against it.

I listened to the slow rhythm of her breathing, aware of my body reacting to her nearness. A day ago, two days ago, I could have gone on shutting down my emotions, pushing away the growing attraction. The goddess knew I had learned that technique over the years—nobody came between me and my music. This afternoon, though, Rhynn's fierce protection made me want to roll her over and kiss her senseless, to feel her skin against mine. I shuddered and felt the flush of heat wash over me.

Damn. I needed to get up. I needed to stop this. Not the time or the place. *And when would that time or place be?* The devil on my shoulder prodded me. *I'm a damn thrash musician. Why shouldn't I be sleeping with Rhynn?* After all, it was expected—twisted sex, intoxicants, wild parties. The temptation was there. I knew others who played that game. Stacy did. Of course, where had it gotten her?

I eased out of Rhynn's embrace. She murmured, and I tucked an extra pillow beside her, stopping to watch her sleep, curled around the pillow, looking incredibly vulnerable. Goddess, she was beautiful.

I forced myself to breathe evenly and padded into the bathroom. I splashed water on my face and squinted at my reflection in the mirror. My nose was still red and a size too big, but it would heal. My hair was a kinky mess after sleeping on it wet. I ran over it with a brush, careful of the tender cut on the back of my head, and made a face at myself in the mirror, and then changed into pants and a cut-off T-shirt. I sneaked out of the bedroom with one last look at a soundly sleeping Rhynn.

Dia sprawled on the couch playing on her comp pad. A cup of caf and a bowl of chips rested on the low table in front of the sofa and a soccer game played quietly on the vid screen on the wall. "You get some sleep?" she asked as I wandered into the kitchen.

"Yeah. You?" My voice sounded scratchy.

"Just got up a little bit ago. I think Nori went down to the main deck for a walk or something. Toni and Friday are still in their room."

I smirked. Their room. It hadn't taken long for Friday to move her stuff in with Toni. They were adorable together, and I didn't think I'd ever seen Toni so, well, giddy.

I got a cup of caf from the dispenser and joined Dia, stretching out on the sofa so I could watch the game. I sipped my caf, enjoying the warmth as it slid down my throat.

Dia gave me an assessing look. "The nose isn't too bad."

"The med tech said it would be back to normal in a couple days. Rhynn needs to get her knee stitched up again, though."

I supposed I asked for it, bringing Rhynn up, and Dia, typically, jumped right in.

"That sure was something the way she came over those drums to your rescue yesterday."

I gave her a raised brow and sipped my caf.

She laughed. "I think she likes you."

Yeah, and if you'd seen us sleeping together last night you would be thinking more than that. "We get along well."

Dia's unladylike snort made me laugh.

We watched sports and she flipped channels while I finished my caf. Rhynn hobbled out of the bedroom, tousled with sleep, still wearing her T-shirt and boxer shorts. "Morning," she mumbled groggily.

Dia gave her the same once-over she'd given me. "Hey, girl, how you feeling?"

"Ask me after caf." Rhynn shuffled into the kitchenette. I watched her take a mug from the counter and set it under the dispenser. She drank half of the mug standing there, refilled it and joined us in the living room. I swung my legs from the sofa to the table, and she sat stiffly beside me, carefully stretching her knee in front of her. Blood stained the bandage.

"How's your head?" she asked. "Looks like the swelling is down some."

"I'm fine. You need to get your knee stitched up properly."

She shrugged. "It'll scab over eventually even if I don't."

Dia rolled her eyes. "Badass."

"Drummer thing," Rhynn said.

I patted Rhynn's leg.

Rhynn swallowed more caf and leaned into the overstuffed cushions with a sigh. "I'm starving. Who wants to go down for food at the buffet?"

"Infirmary first," I said.

She made a face. "Hopefully they'll be fast. You think they'd let us borrow one of those little carts?"

Dia said, "Yeah, I can see you two, whipping around the deck, bodies flying down the hallways."

In the end, after we got cleaned up and showered, we decided to eat first, since we'd pass the buffet on the way to the med center. Once we piled on the food and found a table, a handful of fans dropped by to say hello. I thought it was cute that Rhynn didn't think they were including her when they came to talk to "the band." She continued to be so surprised when they asked for her autograph as well. But in the last week, at least in my mind, she had become one of us.

We plowed through our first plates and went for seconds. We both headed for the build-your-own pocket sandwiches, teasing each other about the choices we made, and we each grabbed an extra plate for desserts.

Rhynn led the way back through to our table but stopped short as she approached. "Oh, fuck," she muttered.

"What?"

Two roses lay on the table where our emptied plates had been—a red one in front of my chair, a black one in front of Rhynn's. I almost dropped my plates. We only had one security guard with us, a youngster named Athenon, and he rushed up as he realized something was wrong. He'd been shadowing us and not watching the table.

I stared at the roses, swallowing as my breakfast threatened to make a reappearance. Couldn't I have a day without this? What was next? As much as I didn't want to fall apart in the middle of the buffet, I was relieved when Rhynn enveloped me from behind, her chin on my shoulder, murmuring, "It's gonna be okay."

Shaine called a meeting later that afternoon to fill us in on what they'd learned. We gathered in our suite and Wayne and Nelda participated via vid call, though what they could do from Earth was minimal. On the other hand, at least they weren't with us for the cruise, because Wayne's posturing would likely have driven us to attempted murder.

Shaine described how the light had fallen when an explosive was detonated, but neither the remains of the light nor its fixture had left any clues as to who had set or detonated it. The vid cameras that should have shown us who left the roses at our table in the buffet had been electronically jammed and showed only static. Shaine's people and ship security were trying to track down anyone who'd been in the buffet at the time and might have seen something.

Toni asked, "So, whoever this Celestian is, they know how to make bombs and jam the ship's vid systems?"

"A couple possibilities. One, that this person is a tech wiz and a demolitions expert, likely military. Two, this person has a lot of money and contacts. There are gadgets that are easily hidden in someone's clothing or belongings that will jam electronics within a certain range—maybe ten or fifteen meters, tops. But they're pricy. And the plastique that blew the light down didn't take a lot of know-how other than to wrap the plastique around the coupling, stick the detonator into it, and click a remote. Again, all those things are accessible if you have the right contacts and the money to pay for it."

Dia said, "I don't think that's particularly comforting."

I had to agree with her.

Wayne didn't want to stop the tour. Nelda wanted to keep things under wraps as much as possible, but a couple of slam-thrash fanzines and gossip blogs on the net were already talking about the falling light, posting holos of me with my nose swelled up and touting J'Nell for saving my life. I publicly thanked her at the concert last night.

Shaine said they were still going through the crew and passenger lists for likely suspects, but the going was slow. This far into space, the net connection was sketchy, so running background checks took three times longer than normal.

As the meeting ended, Del and Morgan rushed into the room wearing sober expressions. Morgan had two cards in her hand. "These came from the Purser's office. One is addressed to Ari and one to Rhynn. Exterior scan just shows staff prints."

"Go ahead and open them."

Morgan eased her finger under the seal and began to read. *"Dearest Arienne, as always, your performance last night moved me. I am so very glad your life was saved. The world would be a much darker place without you in it. I hope you enjoyed your flower at lunch. Be well, my love. Always and forever yours, Celestian."*

I shuddered, understanding how close she was, this faceless freak who got off on taunting me, poking at me. No place was out of her reach. Had she set up the light to fall? Why? If she loved me so much, why would she put me in danger? It made no sense.

Morgan opened the second letter. *"Interloper. You are not wanted. You are not needed. You suck the light from me."*

Rhynn cocked her head. "Is that intended to be a threat?"

"Well, I don't think she likes you very much," Nori said.

Morgan frowned at the plas-sheet in her hand. "Sounds pretty threatening to me."

Shaine said, "We need to treat it as a threat."

"I'm not going to let someone tell me what I can and can't do," Rhynn said. "She may not like that I'm the drummer, but I sure as hell am not quitting."

Dia asked, "What does the sucking the light thing mean?"

"Melodramatic bullshit," Toni said.

Rhynn muttered, "If I get a hold of this freak, I'll put out her damned lights."

CHAPTER THIRTY-SEVEN

Earth Date: November 2453
Cruise Ship *Star Rider*

Rhynn

Rhynn sat silently in the dark. Her set list, illuminated by a micro-LED on the floor between her foot pedals and triggers, was marked with notes about song transitions, beginnings and endings. She'd snuck on stage before the others so she had time to get settled. Sticks in hand, she waited, glancing at the backlit controls on her sound mod controller and amps, verifying for the umpteenth time that everything was ready.

The audience chanted, restless for the show to start. Vapor machines flooded the stage with billowing white fog.

The techs, with shadowed lights, led the rest of the band on stage. Jax crouched in the corner of her drum riser with a hand over his earpiece, listening to Mykal's stage directions. She watched Jax for her cue to start. He held up a hand. Almost ready. She waited, playing out the beginning of the song in her head, bouncing her left foot to the tempo she needed to set.

Jax held up three fingers. Two. One.

She took a breath and slapped out the count on the hi-hat-cymbal pad. On five, the stage exploded with sound, lights, and pyrotechnics flashing. She, Ari, Dia, and Nori slammed out syncopated hits in unison, then a fast, rolling drum riff brought them into the song.

Toni's voice broke over the monitor PA, guitars and bass driving underneath her distinctive growl. Rhynn laid into her drums, hands and feet pounding out what had become familiar patterns. The music and the energy of the audience's approving roar flowed through her.

Glancing to her right, she saw Ari framed in the space between two cymbal pads. Their gazes locked. Ari winked and lifted the neck of her guitar.

Nori and Dia crossed back and forth on Rhynn's left. Dia stopped at the backup vocal mic and added her throaty tones to Toni's lead vocal.

Rhynn focused on the song, thinking ahead and making the transitions smoothly, cranking out a break with hands and feet, then driving the main rhythm to a flurry of unison hits with Nori and Dia. Then into the guitar solo. She rhythmically supported Ari's melody line, accented her high points and shifted the tempo to hold the last line a tiny bit longer.

Ari grinned at Rhynn, a quick expression of musical appreciation. Rhynn's insides glowed with warmth.

After the third song, they paused long enough for Toni to talk to the crowd. Rhynn swallowed a few mouthfuls of water and glanced down at her set list, thinking through the next song while Toni finished talking. Ari kicked off the next tune with a tasty little guitar lick and they were off and running.

The ninety-minute set expanded to one hundred and twenty after two encores. As the final notes of the final song echoed and drowned under the roar of the fans, Ari held her guitar in the air with one hand and waved to the crowd. Rhynn jumped off the drum riser to join her. A strong arm closed around her waist when her knees almost buckled as her feet hit the floor. Rhynn took a second to hold on to Ari's shoulder as she got her footing and tossed her used drumsticks into the crowd as they ran off the stage. Toni followed and they slowed to a walk down the narrow hallway to the dressing room behind the stage.

Mitch and Ben opened the door and a roadie handed each musician a towel as she entered. Rhynn wiped the dripping sweat from her face and looked around for a bottle of water. A ship's crew staffer passed her one from a bucket of ice and pointed her toward a table full of sandwiches, snacks, and sweets.

Rhynn wasn't ready for food, but she gladly took the water.

As the adrenaline wore off, exhaustion settled in. Her muscles felt like jelly and her hands ached. She looked around for the guy with the ice bucket and walked to him on slightly rubbery knees. "Hey, can I have that ice?"

He gave her a curious look, took the two remaining waters out, and handed it to her.

She noticed he was also holding a damp towel. "And, maybe the towel too?"

He smiled and folded the towel over her arm.

Rhynn gave him a grateful smile, held the bucket against her middle and took turns plunging first one hand and then the other into the ice. Over-playing was a bitch. Over-playing five nights in a row pushed her past her limits. The ice would take some of the swelling down. The Moon Base docs told her years ago to expect pain the rest of her life. A small price to pay for doing something she loved.

She carried the bucket and two bottles of water and collapsed onto the couch with her legs sprawled in front of her. Unfolding the towel, she wrapped it around a couple handfuls of ice and laid that on her aching knee.

Nori dropped onto the sofa beside her. "Fuck, what a sweet night. You are so rockin' this gig, Rhynn."

Rhynn gave her a tired grin. "Thanks, Nor. I'm having a blast."

Nori gestured at the bucket. "You doing okay?"

"Yeah. I'm good. Glad we have tomorrow night off, though."

"Me too. I think I'm going to treat myself to an expensive meal at the Golden Sun, drink a bottle of wine and pretend I'm a VIP."

Rhynn laughed. "I was thinking an evening in the hot tub myself."

"You should set yourself up with one of those spa things—get a massage and all that."

Rhynn snorted at the thought of herself wrapped in a towel with someone slathering crap all over her hands and feet. She switched hands in the ice.

Mykal poked his bald head into the room. "Hey, VIPs in five."

Nori stuck out her tongue and dragged herself to her feet. “I’m gonna clean up my face before they start snapping pictures of me looking like shit.”

Rhynn thought about doing the same but didn’t have the energy to move from her slouched position on the couch. She downed a second bottle of water and a solicitous crew member came past offering more water and asking if she wanted anything to eat.

She felt awkward asking for a couple of the protein bars from the table. If she’d had more energy, she’d have gotten up and gotten them herself, but since he offered, she thanked him again and let him fetch her a treat.

Ari sat down beside her, shoulder-to-shoulder, her leg resting against Rhynn’s. *Fuck, I’m a sweaty, smelly mess. Don’t get too close.* Ari patted Rhynn’s thigh. “Great show, Rhynn. You amaze me.”

Rhynn automatically deflected the compliment as she switched hands in the bucket again. “It’s what you’re paying me for. You, of course, are a guitar goddess, and made the boys and girls drool all night.”

Ari screwed up her face. Rhynn noticed her nose was barely swollen now. “All the drooling is on the other side of the stage where Dia is teasing the front row.” Ari scrubbed a hand over her face and leaned her head against Rhynn’s shoulder. “I am fucking wiped. At least we didn’t have any surprises tonight.”

“Yeah. Definitely a good thing.”

The door opened and security ushered VIP fans into the room. Toni, Nori, and Dia were positioned right up front to greet the crowd, including J’Nell and her ever-present vid camera. Most of the VIPs had become familiar faces, mostly fans who paid extra to hang with the band, along with others who’d won backstage passes or meet-and-greet prizes in casino games or on-deck events.

Rhynn set her bucket on the floor, removed the wet towel from her knee, and dried her hands on her damp, sweaty shirt.

Ari stood. “Come on, time to meet and greet.”

Rhynn managed a tired smile as Ari pulled her to her feet, holding Rhynn’s sore hands a couple beats longer than necessary.

CHAPTER THIRTY-EIGHT

Earth Date: November 2453
Cruise Ship *Star Rider*

Shaine and Morgan

Shaine typed a final note into the report on her comp pad and reached for the mug of caf on the kitchen table. In the main room, Rae and Jorge had their heads bent over mini terminals. Gohste had three monitors lined up on the breakfast bar, a cup of caf in one hand, and the other alternately flitting over the keyboard and swiping the screens. Scanning her report a final time, Shaine yawned as Morgan trudged into the security suite. Her shoulders sagged as the door shut and locked behind her.

"Everyone's locked in and accounted for. No envelopes, no flowers, no surprises." She slouched into the chair across from Shaine. "You know, I must be getting old because these hours are wearing on me."

Shaine laughed. "Ah, my little thrasher babe, you're not getting older. You're getting smarter."

"Tell that to my aching head."

Shaine pushed her steaming cup across the table. "This might help."

"Thanks, love. Anyone come up with anything?"

Shaine said, "I think so. We got two hits. Gohste is digging deeper, but the net's been spotty. Ship techs say it's the space we're in now and it'll get better. Something about solar wind or sunspots. In any case, they found two passengers with stalking or predatory behaviors in their incarceration records."

"That sounds reasonably hopeful."

Shaine shrugged. "Maybe. I'm getting tired of being two steps behind this bastard."

Morgan took another sip and pushed the mug back across the table. "I think I'm going to call it a night. You should too. Let them work their magic and we can review the results when we've got a few more awake brain cells between us."

Shaine rested her chin on her knuckles. "You go ahead. I'll be there in a few minutes."

CHAPTER THIRTY-NINE

Earth Date: November 2453
Cruise Ship *Star Rider*

Ari

My first cup of caf was going to be a reward for actually dragging my ass out of bed. Of course, I didn't have much reason to lie around once I woke up, even though it was earlier than I'd have liked. Rhynn and I had slept in our own beds last night. Rhynn showered first and was sound asleep by the time I got out of the shower.

The wave of disappointment had been undeniable, even as I told myself it was better not to get involved. I didn't want to sleep alone. The previous night had been comforting, even if we'd done nothing but sleep. The cold sheets on my bed were not inviting, but exhaustion took over and I was asleep practically before my head hit the pillow.

This morning, the living room and kitchenette were dark and empty. Bleary-eyed, I flipped on a couple lights, slid a mug under the beverage dispenser and punched in a request for double caf, heavy sweetener, heavy creamer. The steaming liquid smelled heavenly as it dribbled into my mug. I carried it to the couch and sat down, curling my legs beneath me and cradling the warm mug in my hands.

Tonight was a free night with the whole day and evening to ourselves. I hadn't thought about what I was going to do with my time. My inclination was to hole up in the suite with a couple vids or a book. Maybe take a nap or two. Celestian was out there somewhere, and I didn't feel like going out for dinner and finding roses at my table or notes on my chair. Or having equipment fall on me.

Walking onto the stage last night had been unbelievably nerve-racking. My heart pounded, my hands sweated, and I couldn't stop looking into the rigging. The anxiety of not knowing, of walking out into the darkness, even with my guitar tech at my side, was terrifying. The roar of the crowd rang in my ears. If a light fell, nobody would know until it hit me. I forced myself to focus on the smooth wood of the guitar's neck against my palm and the tension of guitar strings under my fingers. The crisp slashing of cymbals bit across the stage as Rhynn counted off. The music became my world as our first chord exploded into existence and the lights flashed in a blinding display.

Despite my anxiety, we had a good show. No incidents. The crowd was crazy, the monitors didn't cut out, and I didn't break strings at inopportune moments. The after-party meet and greet stayed relaxed, with only a couple fans over-the-top in our faces.

This morning I was immensely relieved to have nothing to do, nowhere to be, and no excited fans or inquisitive reporters to talk to. I sipped my caf and enjoyed the silence through the low ringing in my ears.

A door opened and Friday slipped out of the bedroom she shared with Toni. She wriggled her fingers at me and let the door shut quietly behind her. She looked so young with her blond curls tousled wildly around her head, wearing one of Toni's T-shirts, which was about three sizes too big.

"Morning," she said softly as she headed to the kitchenette. "Man, I need some caf."

I lifted my mug mutely. She got her own and stretched out on the recliner facing me. She took a couple minutes to sip her caf, closing her eyes and savoring the drink.

She asked, "Did you sleep okay?"

"Like a rock, but once I wake up, I can't go back to sleep. So, here I am."

"I think Toni could sleep through a hurricane."

I laughed softly. "Well, minor earthquakes and windstorms for sure."

"For real?"

"For real."

"How are you doing, Ari? I mean, with all the craziness going on."

"I'm okay." What else could I say? "It's hard, not knowing what's going to happen next. But I'll be damned if I'm going to let some freak get the best of me."

"You're very brave."

"Stubborn, maybe."

Rhynn wandered into the living room, rubbing her eyes and moving with a stiff, limping gait. She blinked and managed a tired smile. "Hey," she croaked. She crossed the room and folded onto the sofa next to me, grabbing the fuzzy throw in the corner and pulling it over herself.

"Hey," I said. "You doing okay?"

"Sore." Grimacing, she flexed her hands slowly. "It'll loosen up, always does."

I frowned, feeling the ache in my own hands. "You want a cold pack for your hands? Or I can get you some caf?"

"I'm okay for now. Need to sit a bit and wake up. Hey, Fri."

"Morning."

I took the last swallow of my caf. "I'm getting another cup. Anyone need some?"

Friday stood too. "I'll get mine. Why don't you get some for Rhynn?"

Rhynn glanced sideways at me. "Conspiracy," she mumbled. "Thanks, Ari, I'd love a cup."

"Be right back."

Friday elbowed me playfully as we stood in the kitchenette waiting for the dispenser to fill our mugs. She said in an undertone, "You guys are so cute together."

I blinked. "What?"

"Oh, come on. Toni thinks so too." She moved her filled cup and took mine out of my hand, putting it under the dispenser and filling it.

I opened my mouth and shut it. Was it so obvious? Because I was only figuring it out for myself. "We're friends," I murmured, purposefully stirring sweetener and creamer into my caf.

Friday filled a third cup and raised a brow. I said, "Heavy creamer and sweetener." And felt my face go red when she giggled because I knew how Rhynn liked her caf. I sighed and took the mug after she'd doctored it. We returned to the living room and I handed Rhynn her mug and took my place in the corner of the couch.

"Thanks." Rhynn shifted until we were touching, stretched her legs onto the low table in front of the sofa and spread the throw blanket over both of us.

Friday asked, "What are you guys going to do today?"

Rhynn yawned. "As little as possible."

"Toni and I were thinking about hanging out at the pool and hot tub."

Uh, no. Being out in the open in the middle of so many people, wearing a swimsuit, was not on my to-do list. Celestian had watched me in our own pool, spied on me in the privacy of my own home, lying naked in the sun and swimming. I shuddered.

Rhynn laid a hand on my leg. "As much as the hot tub would feel great, I could do without the crowd."

I wondered if Rhynn's words were for my benefit.

Friday said, "If you guys are worried about anything happening, I'm sure a bunch of Shaine and Morgan's gang will go along for crowd control."

Rhynn shrugged. "We'll see what we feel like later. I'm gonna need some more caf before I'm even coherent."

Rhynn and I had a couple cups of caf while we lounged and watched an action vid we'd all seen before. Eventually, Toni, Nori, and Dia emerged from their respective bedrooms and joined our impromptu pajama party. The other girls made plans to go to the pool later in the afternoon and spent most of the movie cajoling Rhynn and me into hanging out with them. I wasn't thrilled with the idea, but they convinced me it would be okay, and that they'd never leave me alone, and if we had security with us, it'd all be fine. Rhynn was careful not to try to sway me either way. I thought her protection of my position was sweet.

I dragged her to the infirmary to make sure her stitches were sealed with waterproof nu-skin. The doc also sealed a couple other cuts before deigning her safe to be in the water, since she really wanted to soak her aching muscles in the hot tub. Returning from the infirmary, the wonderful aroma of pizza wafted into the elevator when it opened into our hallway. Del and Mitch were both indulging at the security desk, and the door to the suite was open.

Del said, "You'd better get in there before all the good stuff is gone."

Rhynn laughed and headed down the hallway with a limping run. "Yeah! I'm starving."

By the time we headed to the pool deck, it was late afternoon. We were a motley group comprised of the whole band, plus Friday, with half a dozen of the WR security group in swimsuits and another three in uniform.

The pool area mimicked a tropical paradise decorated in deep greens with flashes of primary colors. High-intensity sunlamps flooded the room with heat and light, while misters feigned tropical humidity. Fake and real flora and palm trees in brightly painted pots created small pockets of privacy surrounded by ferns and tropical flowers. Tiki bars were tucked under palm trees hung with festive lights. Recorded sounds of birds and tropical animals played in the background.

We claimed a group of lounge chairs and a table near the hot tub. Rhynn limped in bare feet to set her towel on the chair beside mine. I touched her arm. "Is your knee okay?"

"Just a little sore."

I sighed. *Tough girls.*

She patted my shoulder. "Seriously. But the hot tub is going to feel pretty wonderful."

I tried to ignore the surrounding security and the curious interest from fans and vacationers, but I couldn't help scanning the space around us. So much had happened. I felt as though my life was spinning out of control, and I couldn't help but look around wondering what would happen next. Yesterday Celestian had left flowers at our lunch table and mail at the Purser's desk. The day before that, the light fell onto the stage and Rhynn found the note on her drum kit, and before that a note on my pillow.

Even with security surrounding us, I didn't believe Celestian could be stopped if she wanted to leave a message. I'd begun to think of her as a ghost, able to leave calling cards or make her point at will. The security staff was on alert, but I'd have felt safer hiding in our suite. Rhynn caught my hand. "Come on, the hot tub is calling."

She pulled me along with her and the rest of the band to the expansive twenty-person hot tub. One of our security team was already in the water, along with two guys and a woman drinking out of tall, unbreakable cups. I noted other security scattered through the room—the uniformed ones on the edges, others blending in with the vacationers.

I concentrated on keeping my footing as we crossed the damp tile floor. Rhynn stepped into the hot tub first and held my hand as I followed behind, stopping abruptly as the hot water hit my legs on the first step.

Rhynn tugged my fingers. "Too hot for you?"

I laughed. "Hell, no." I turned the tables and pulled her in. The heat took my breath away, but I settled into the water beside Nori.

Rhynn stretched out beside me, hooking her arms over the edge of the pool. She sighed, a blissful smile crossing her face, her eyes closed. "Damn, this feels good."

I stared at her, my breath gone. The only thoughts in my head were how good she looked and how I wished she were in my arms.

Water splashed in my face and I blinked.

Dia giggled. "Wake up, Ari!"

I splashed her back. "I'm awake."

"Hey!" Rhynn joined in the splash attacks, and in no time, it was an all-out war. We giggled like teenagers, being silly and having fun. Eventually, Rhynn and Toni got out of the hot tub to fetch us all drinks.

Dia said, "Ohhhh, someone's got it bad."

Friday watched her girlfriend with a lovesick sigh. "Yeah, I do. Toni's amazing."

Toni sauntered across the room in a black bikini. Detailed tattoos decorated her arms, legs, and back and moved with her muscles as she walked. I would have teased Friday, except that I was thinking the same thing about Rhynn. Her hair was slicked against her head, and she moved with a rolling gait and only a slight limp.

Nori nudged my shoulder. "Fri's not the only one drooling."

I sent her what I hoped was a perfectly innocent look.

Dia snickered. "You're as whipped as Friday."

"You're imagining things."

They laughed uproariously.

Rhynn and Toni returned with our drinks, and Toni asked, "What's so funny?"

Dia said, "Friday was drooling."

"I was not!"

Toni pulled a pose. "Feel free to drool any time, love."

Friday's face flushed redder, and the laughter got even more raucous. Toni and Rhynn stepped carefully into the hot tub, passing out the drinks. Toni gave Friday a kiss as she handed off her drink. I caught myself wishing I could do the same to Rhynn before I pushed the thoughts away and took a couple long sips of the sweet, icy beverage, which almost immediately gave me a brain freeze. I winced and closed my eyes. A warm hand rested on my shoulder and Rhynn's voice buzzed in my ear. "Are you okay?"

I muttered, embarrassed, "Ice headache."

She rubbed my back and I opened my eyes to see her smiling at me, her face close to mine—close enough to kiss. I swallowed. Hazel and gold flecks sparkled in her brown eyes and caught me with their intensity.

Then Rhynn sat back in the water, leaning against the wall beside me, sipping on her own drink. "Oh, that's really good!"

Nori laughed. "So you don't realize how wasted you're going to get."

After a while, Rhynn said, "I need to cool off in the regular pool."

"I'll go too."

Rhynn climbed the stairs out of the hot tub and I followed. We crossed to the bar to drop off our empty glasses and circled back toward the pool. A raucous volleyball game had taken over the shallow end while a handful of people floated aimlessly on colorful foam mats and donuts on the deep end.

We avoided the craziness and walked toward the deep end. A swarm of partiers surrounded us, jostling each other as they ran for the pool, voices raised in drunken, overexcited teasing and horseplay. Someone yelled, "Hey, it's the band!" They engulfed us in their exuberance, swept us into the group, hands slapping our backs with rejoinders to join the party. Before I had time to react or move away, I was pulled into the pool in a splashing frenzy.

As the cold water closed over my head, I heard Rhynn shout, "No, wait!"

I kicked back to the surface, searching around frantically, blinking water out of my eyes. In the midst of a group of splashing, laughing vacationers, Rhynn flailed ineffectively at the water, eyes wide with fear.

"Rhynn!" I swam toward her, pushing through the crowd. Rhynn grabbed for me as I reached her, pulling us both down.

I kicked hard, back to the surface. "I've got you!"

Rhynn fought me as she coughed and choked, struggling in panic. I locked an arm around her chest and managed to get us to the edge of the pool. "Rhynn, grab the edge!"

Using all my strength, I placed her palm against the rough rim of the pool. "You're safe. I've got you."

Finally, Rhynn calmed and her other hand joined the first. She clung to the edge of the pool and I held her tightly between me and the wall. She coughed, fighting to catch her breath.

Others gathered around us. Mitch and Rae knelt at the edge, asking if we were okay while Del, Athenon, Bagger, and Ben looked like they were going to start banging heads.

I said, "We're all right. No harm, no foul."

One of the revelers, a tallish woman, swam over. "Hey, man, sorry about that! Are you all right?"

Rhynn managed a weak nod.

I said, "We're fine. Just got surprised."

The woman looked uneasy but swam away to join her friends.

I rubbed Rhynn's back. "Take it easy. Catch your breath."

Her panic receded and she looked more flustered and embarrassed than anything. "I can't swim." Her voice was hoarse and strained. For a second I thought she was going to cry. "No pools on Moon Base. Waste of water."

I held her tighter.

She said, "Can we slide over to the shallow water?"

"Sure. There's a ladder right over there if you want to get out."

"No. I want to go in the shallow water, where I can touch the bottom." I heard determination in her voice. She pulled herself purposefully along the wall, hand over hand, and I kept close as I swam alongside. When she was able to touch bottom and walk, she moved forward with one hand on the edge of the pool until the water only reached her waist.

She stepped away from the wall. "I'm not going to be afraid."

I watched her carefully, not sure what she was thinking, trying to decide what the correct response should be.

Her expression seemed dark, determined, almost angry. "Thank you for saving my sorry ass. I'm sorry I freaked out on you."

"No problem." I thought, I'd have done anything for you. She took a deep breath, coughed again and shivered. I imagined the adrenaline of fear washing out of her and hugged her. "I'm glad you're okay."

After a beat, she returned the embrace. She trembled in my arms as she clung to me. Her head rested against my shoulder and I rubbed her back. Her breath warmed my water-cooled skin. Goddess. She felt so good. I rested my cheek against her head. Time seemed to stop, dropping a cone of silence around us.

A voice snapped, "Find a fucking room, bitches."

I looked up to see an angry woman built like a freight train. She wore a cut-off T-shirt and swim shorts. "Rhynn Knight, you're a fucking whore and a shit drummer."

Rhynn stiffened and stepped away from me to face the woman. The muscles around her jaw tightened and her shoulders straightened.

"You must be a pretty good lay to be playing in this band, because you sure as fuck don't measure up to Stacy Rowe."

I opened my mouth to object, but Rhynn laughed, a short, hard bark. "Jealous, Shallay? Get a fucking life and go sober up."

Rhynn obviously knew the angry woman who rushed forward. Rhynn stepped between us as Shallay swung wildly. Rhynn let go with a sharp right, connecting with her jaw. Shallay stumbled backward before coming at Rhynn again.

Del and Mitch jumped into the pool. After a brief struggle, the two guards subdued Shallay, each holding an arm while she struggled and swore at them.

One of the uniformed guards tossed down a set of handcuffs. Del snatched them out of the air and slapped them on Shallay's wrists. "Come on, let's go." She pushed her toward the steps out of the pool, pausing to give Rhynn a wicked grin over her shoulder. "Nice right, Knight."

They walked Shallay out of the pool area as she continued to shout insults at Rhynn until the door sealed behind them. Rhynn rubbed her knuckles, looking down.

I wasn't sure what to think of the whole confrontation, the angry woman lashing out or Rhynn punching her in the face. I'd never thought of Rhynn being violent, and I didn't understand this side of her. The fist she threw was confident—too automatic to have been new to her. Where did she learn to fight? What else didn't I know about Rhynn Knight? Who was Shallay and why did she hate Rhynn so much? "You know her?" I managed.

For a few seconds, Rhynn didn't answer. She grimaced and flexed her fingers. I was about to ask again when she looked up, her expression closed. "Yeah. Not one of my fans. We dated once. I think I've had enough water for one day. I'm going back to the room."

I blinked at her sudden change of mood. What had just happened? "I'll go with you."

"No, it's okay, you stay with the band. I'm fine. I just need some space."

I wanted to argue with her. I wanted to follow her, enfold her in my arms, bring her smile back and take the exhausted and angry expression from her face. Instead, I returned to the hot tub while Rhynn left the pool room with Ben. She walked listlessly beside him, her shoulders slumped.

Nori sat on the edge of the hot tub, feet dangling in the water. Dia floated on her back, and Friday relaxed on Toni's lap. I stepped into the hot water and eased myself down.

Nori asked, "Is Rhynn okay?"

I filled them in without sharing my more personal thoughts. Rhynn had to have been scared shitless after she'd almost drowned. Maybe that was why she reacted so uncharacteristically toward Shallay. Panic and adrenaline could make anyone lash out. I just wished Rhynn hadn't run off. I was sure she wanted to get away from the crowd, and probably away from me. Maybe it was all just too much.

She'd seemed fine, though, before Shallay showed up. I thought about how we'd been standing in the pool, the way she trembled in my arms, clinging to me. I could almost feel the smoothness of her skin under my hands. My heart felt so full. The realization of how much I wanted that feeling to continue scared me.

Toni said, "What would you say about asking Rhynn to join the band permanently?"

The sudden change of subject startled me. I pushed away my thoughts and glanced at my bandmates. "You guys already talked about this?" I wasn't angry; it was more like buying time because I wasn't sure what I thought. One voice in my head screamed yes. The other wondered if Rhynn was even interested. It was one thing to sit in with us for a little while. Being a permanent member would completely disrupt her life.

Nori said, "We did, a little bit. I like her. She's good people. She's a great drummer, and she fits in. Do you think she'd be interested?"

"Honestly, I don't know."

Dia asked, "Would you be okay with her being part of the band?"

Again, I hesitated. Would I be okay with it? Yes. To have her around all the time would be great. But was there room in the band for a relationship? Because what I was starting to feel about her…I wasn't sure that was good for the band. What if she and I didn't work out?

Toni said, "We don't need to decide right now, I just wanted to put it out there."

I dragged my hands through the water, focused on the feel of the liquid sluicing through my open fingers. "I really like her, you guys. I mean, I want to get to know her better. You know?"

Nori said, "You're falling hard."

I nodded.

Toni said, "Whether it works out or not, we'd still want her in the band."

"I need some time, to see where this goes."

"If it helps, we all think you guys make a great pair. She's as whipped as you are," Nori said.

Dia giggled. "It's so cute."

I rolled my eyes. "Thanks."

CHAPTER FORTY

Earth Date: November 2453
Cruise Ship *Star Rider*

Rhynn

The walk back to the suite was a silent one. Rhynn shuffled slowly beside Ben, wondering how badly she'd screwed up. She felt alone and frustrated. Ari had offered to go back with her, but she'd said no. Probably that was rude. Ari looked disappointed, but Rhynn needed space. Her brain was a muddle of emotions and random thoughts. She was exhausted and her body hurt.

She felt stupid and embarrassed about freaking out in the pool, nearly drowning because she was an idiot and couldn't swim. She brought everyone down because of her weakness. Ari had to save her ass. How lame was that? She was supposed to be protecting Ari, not the other way around. Then Shallay had to show up.

What the fuck had she been thinking to start fighting with the bitch? Fuck. Ari must think she was a jerk. Here she was, trying to protect Ari from a stalker, and she hauls off and smashes Shallay in the face. Fucking idiot. Not that Shallay hadn't deserved it. The bitch had used her two years ago and then blamed her for the breakup. Rhynn didn't need a girlfriend who was that angry at the world. Shallay had never turned her violence against Rhynn, but she had known it was only a matter of time. Shallay only wanted her because she wanted someone else to pay her way through life. Rhynn had a decent job, and Shallay was never able to hold one for long.

Ben let Rhynn into the suite. She locked the door behind her, showered and curled up in bed. When she woke an hour or so later, she was still alone. She got up, pulled on cargo shorts and a long-sleeved tunic and wandered into the main living area. Her knee felt looser after the heat of the hot tub and the nap had probably helped too.

She wondered when the others would be back. Restlessness ate at her. In the kitchenette, she programmed the beverage dispenser for a travel mug of strong tea. Mug in hand, she left the suite.

Ben sat watch at the security desk between the rooms.

"Hey, Rhynn. You feeling better?"

"Yeah. Is anyone around who can go with me to the observation deck?"

"Sure."

A minute later, Morgan Rahn stepped out of the security suite, looking like a typical slam-thrash fan in a cut-off black T-shirt sporting SCE's logo. "Hope I'll do."

"Works for me." Of all the security officers, Rhynn favored Morgan's relaxed energy. She needed her calmness right now.

Morgan smiled and started down the hall. "I haven't had a chance yet to see the observation deck."

"I won't be much company."

"No worries. I'm not much of a talker."

As Rhynn and Morgan stepped from the elevator onto the observation deck, Morgan said, "I'll be at the bar." She slipped away, leaving Rhynn to herself.

Rhynn felt a cold sense of loneliness grip her as she stepped further into the room. The observation deck stretched half the length of the ship. Floor-to-ceiling glassteel windows lined the entire room, including the rounded bow. A clear glassteel ceiling curved over the front two-thirds of the room, allowing a full view of the black emptiness of space strewn with countless stars.

Clusters of memory-form pillows and low tables were arranged in sunken depressions along the windows. Thin lines of inset blue lights created paths across the darkly carpeted floor between the groupings. Recessed lighting along the bar at the back provided the only other light in the room.

Rhynn chose an empty cluster of pillows in a sunken sitting area about halfway to the bow, as far away from other people as she could get.

The observation deck was surprisingly quiet compared to the rest of the ship. No background music or vids played. The thick carpeting deadened the low murmur of conversations. She settled into a memory-form pillow chair on the floor, cradling her thermal mug in her lap. Leaning back, she gazed out into the blackness. Earthers thought this was a magical and amazing view. For Rhynn, this was the familiar and comforting vista she'd known all her life.

She stargazed and let her mind wander. For what was supposed to have been a quiet, relaxing day, she felt overwrought and anxious. She remembered, viscerally, the utter terror she'd felt when the water had closed over her head. She knew she was going to die. When Ari tried to drag her to the surface, she didn't understand what was happening. All she knew was the need for air.

It took the scrape of the rough, rounded edge of the pool under her palm to break through her fear. Coughing up water, struggling to breathe, she finally became aware of the warmth of Ari's arms supporting her, heard Ari's voice murmuring in her ear over the screaming panic in her own head.

She'd felt so stupid and embarrassed and frustrated. She didn't fucking know how to swim. What damned adult didn't know how to swim?

Ari hadn't laughed at her. She'd guided her to the shallow end of the pool and held her. She whispered a promise that she'd teach her to swim. Rhynn had clung to Ari like a life preserver. The heat of Ari's skin calmed her as Ari rubbed her back, stroked her hair.

Until Shallay had shown up. Rhynn could have killed her. She didn't know the bitch was on board. The taunts had pushed her already adrenaline-fueled emotions over the edge. Putting her fist in Shallay's face hadn't been appropriate behavior, despite the fact they were riding a party barge with crazy thrash fans, and violence wasn't unheard of. What must Ari think of her? That she was a brainless thug? The whole band was probably pissed off.

She sipped her tea, but the familiar taste didn't provide any comfort.

How in the seven lunar hells was she supposed to go back and face them? What could she say? She'd had a fit of temporary insanity? She honestly wasn't sure why she'd reacted the way she had. Sure, Shallay had pissed her off, but that didn't explain the sudden flood of anger that had swept over her. Maybe it was that she'd been so vulnerable. Maybe it was the tension of constant threats to Ari and some twisted reaction to that. If she couldn't explain her behavior, she at least had to apologize.

How would the band react? Would the incident be brushed off and forgotten? Chalked up as a typical incident in the volatile world of slam-thrash bands? Would things change between her and Ari because of it?

She couldn't deny what she was beginning to feel for Ari. In any other situation, she'd ask her out to see if there was anything between them, if they might have a future. In this situation, was a relationship even possible? Technically Rhynn was an employee of the band and the record company. Maybe after the tour, when SCE found a regular drummer, or if Stacy got her shit together and rejoined the band, maybe then she could ask Ari out.

Of course, at that point she'd be back home on Moon Base, probably still looking for a job and playing in her own band. Ari would be touring and recording on Earth with SCE. Rhynn's heart ached—a painful tightening of loss that nearly took her breath away with its intensity. This tour was her fifteen minutes of fame. When her fifteen minutes ended, so did everything it encompassed, including Ari.

Two weeks ago it wouldn't have mattered. Today, the thought of this interlude ending, of not seeing Ari again, hurt like hell. Still, she couldn't act on her feelings. Goddess knew, she would love to pursue Ari, but her time with the band was limited.

She drank more tea, wishing it would make her feel better. Instead she was engulfed by exhaustion and left bereft. Aching inside, she searched for patterns in the stars and waited for the calmness and peace of space to settle her heart and mind.

CHAPTER FORTY-ONE

Earth Date: November 2453
Cruise Ship *Star Rider*

Shaine and Morgan

Shaine stood in the barely adequate space of the brig. The *Star Rider*'s security headquarters provided barely enough room for a desk, two chairs, and a locked enclosure with two cells. Garrimond, the ship's head of security, was heavyset, medium height, probably twenty years older than Shaine, with no neck and a very short, thin crew cut.

The woman who'd picked a fight with Rhynn stewed in the farthest cell, wrapped in a blanket, barefoot with wet hair.

Shaine read through the short printout Garrimond handed her. Shallay Dorr. Age twenty-six. Residence: Moon Base. Occupation: Cargo Dock Worker. A short description of the altercation. History of misdemeanor assault and public fighting going back ten years. Basic schooling, no military service.

Shaine decided Dorr probably wasn't the stalker they were looking for. A troublemaker, yes, but not a stalker.

She glanced at Garrimond. "You mind if I ask her a few questions?"

"Go ahead." He sat in the desk chair and it creaked under his weight. "Far as I'm concerned, no harm, no foul. I'll let her go when she's had time to sober up."

Shaine stood in front of Dorr's cell. "Tell me how you know Rhynn Knight."

Shallay's lip curled. "She's a whore. Can you believe I fucked her? She's a shitty lay. Arrogant bitch thinks she's something because she's playing in that fucking band of hers. Now she's sleeping her way into a new band."

Shaine asked, "What makes you say that?"

"Saw 'em in the pool. Her and the guitarist, all lovey dovey. She don't deserve to be in SCE."

"You know the members of Shattered Crystal Enigma? You've met them?"

"Just Stacy Rowe. Met her the night of the show on Moon Base. We were partying before they went on. They fucked her over, man."

Shaine kept her expression neutral, though her dislike for Shallay Dorr was growing by the second. "So, you didn't know the members of SCE before they played on Moon Base?"

"No."

"And you live on Moon Base?"

"Yeah, what of it?"

"Have you left Moon Base in the last year?"

Shallay sneered. "What's it to you, bitch?"

Shaine shrugged. "Just asking. Might be useful information."

"I ain't been off Moon Base in three years."

"I'll find out if you're lying to me." Shaine dismissed the woman, pausing at Garrimond's desk before she left. "I don't think she's related to the other matter we've been investigating, but I'd appreciate any additional information you find."

"Of course."

"Thanks, Garrimond. I'll check in later."

He grunted his reply, and Shaine sauntered from the office, frustrated that they still had no clue to who Ari's stalker could be.

CHAPTER FORTY-TWO

Earth Date: November 2453
Cruise Ship *Star Rider*

Ari

When I returned to the suite with the rest of the band, Rhynn wasn't there. A sense of foreboding settled over me as I searched our room and the bathroom. There was no sign of her and no note. I rushed out into the hall to stand impatiently before the security guard at the table. "Ben, where's Rhynn?"

"She went up to the observation deck maybe an hour ago. Morgan's with her."

"Was she okay?"

Rhynn was upset when she'd left the pool area. I'd expected to find her in our room, either sleeping or brooding, but she wasn't there. I didn't know what Rhynn was thinking, and I didn't know her well enough to know if I should go after her or not. And at the same time, I worried about Celestian and Shallay, and what unknown things could happen to Rhynn. Likely I was projecting my own fears, but I felt a very strong and immediate need to make sure Rhynn was all right.

Ben said, "She acted fine to me."

I thought, you're a guy, so she could have been absolutely freaking out and you wouldn't have noticed. I marched down the hallway toward the elevator.

"Hey, wait, where are you going? Wait a sec! Ms. Walker, wait!"

I ignored him and pressed the call button when I reached the elevator. The door slid open and I stepped in.

Ben plowed in after me, bouncing off the back wall as the door slid shut, talking frantically into his com. "Get someone in the hallway now! I'm on my way with Ms. Walker to the observation deck. No. There wasn't time. Just do it!" He shoved the com into his pocket and gave me a weak smile.

When the door opened I hurried onto the observation deck. I passed the bar and paused, scanning the room.

A hand touched my arm. I jumped about a foot.

Morgan Rahn said, "She's sitting over there."

I followed the direction she pointed. Out of the corner of my eye, I saw Morgan catch Ben by the arm and pull him toward the bar. I focused on the shock of white and magenta hair and made a beeline across the carpeted floor, stepping down into the area where Rhynn sat. She held a disposable travel mug in her hands. Her arms rested on her knees, which were pulled up to her chest as she stared through the window. Lost in her thoughts, it took her a moment to notice me, but when she did, her face lit up with the flash of a smile.

"Hey," she said.

"Hey yourself."

"Come sit down. I was just stargazing. And thinking." Her wan smile and the expression in her eyes seemed sad. I wondered what she was thinking about.

I settled myself into the chair beside hers and took in the vast view of space. So huge. Empty. Pristine. And cold. I shivered. "It's always amazing to see the stars," I said. "And a little overwhelming."

She put a hand on mine and gave it a squeeze. "What brings you up here?"

I felt heat rush to my face. "You weren't in the room. I was kind of worried." I couldn't believe how lame I sounded and I looked away. "Ben said you were up here."

"I'm glad you came."

"I am too. So, are you okay? I mean, it was a little crazy at the pool."

"I'm all right. Sorry about going after Shallay like that. I'm really not a violent person. I was already freaked out, and then she came and I just, I don't know, reacted. I hope you're not really pissed with me."

She looked so earnest and worried, I felt a bit of the weight come off my heart. I managed a wry smile. "If you hadn't punched her, I might have."

Rhynn raised a brow. "And risk those magic fingers? Naw, not worth it." She held up her right hand and flexed her fist. "She's got a damned hard jaw."

"You're such a badass. And no, I'm not angry with you. I'm just glad you're okay." I bumped her shoulder. She grinned and we sat watching the stars. I think we were okay. And Rhynn was safe. Celestian hadn't gotten to her, nor had Shallay.

I thought about asking if she wanted to be a permanent member of the band. I knew what I wanted—the best of both worlds. I wanted her in the band and I wanted to see if she and I could be together. I knew if Rhynn wasn't in the band, I'd likely lose her. Long-distance relationships were non-starters. But was now the time to bring it up? Was it too soon? I said, "When I came in, you were thinking so hard. What were you thinking about?"

She hesitated, seeming to mull over the question. She stretched her legs out and set aside her mug. The stitched gash down her knee puckered under the nu-skin covering. A half dozen short, scabbed cuts marred her bare shins. She said, "I was thinking about how fast this tour is going, and how much has happened in the last couple weeks."

My stomach sunk. She probably wished she'd never joined this tour.

"I was thinking about how much it's going to suck when it's over." She glanced at me and then away again. "And how much I'm going to miss you."

Oh, Rhynn. A wave of relief filled my heart. She would miss me. I knew I'd miss her. My mouth was way ahead of my brain. "Join the band permanently."

Her head snapped up. "What?"

"Do you want to be our drummer, for real?"

"Seriously?"

"Yeah." I loved the wonder in her expression. I wanted so badly for her to want the band for the right reasons. I hoped it felt as right to her as it did to the rest of us.

"And the others are okay with it?"

"They're the ones who brought it up. Not that we were talking behind your back. Well, I mean, not in a bad way. Anyway, they said they wanted you to join the band. I've been thinking about it too. You fit in like part of the family. Musically we all just click." I paused, took a breath, and plunged ahead. "And I really like you, Rhynn." I leaned over and dropped a quick kiss on her cheek. I could feel the heat on my face and knew I had probably blushed a radical shade of red. "A lot."

Rhynn's hand went to her cheek and a smile grew on her face. "I like you a lot too." She giggled and rolled her eyes. "That sounds like a stupid fangirl line."

My heart skipped with a mix of relief, excitement, and arousal. This time when I leaned in, she did too. Her lips were soft and warm, her fingers tentative as they slid into my hair. She tasted like sweet tea, and my brain nearly exploded with the touch of her tongue seeking entrance and then teasing against mine. Blood raced hot through my veins and straight to my groin. As we parted to breathe, I whispered her name and traced my fingertips along her jaw. I gazed into wide gold-brown eyes and the universe stilled.

Rhynn murmured, "Is this for real? Because if it's not, we need to stop."

Stopping wasn't an option. "It's for real, if you want it to be."

"I want it. You, the band, all of it."

"Good." I hadn't intended to jump into a relationship, but it felt like the right thing to do. I'd been taking musical chances all my life, shooting for my dreams. Why should this be any different? If Rhynn felt the way I did, waiting was silly. *You're a fucking rock star. Take the chance and live.*

CHAPTER FORTY-THREE

Earth Date: November 2453
Cruise Ship *Star Rider*

Rhynn

Rhynn woke tangled up in Ari, their legs entwined and Ari sprawled half over her chest, one arm thrown over her middle, her head tucked under Rhynn's chin. Rhynn had one hand tangled in Ari's long hair while the other rested on the arm wrapped around her stomach. Skin to skin.

Ari was all soft curves and defined muscle, her body perfect under Rhynn's hands. They'd spent the evening and much of the night making love. Rhynn had never felt so bowled over by emotion, swamped by happiness and contentment and excitement and lust and a little fear.

Ari shifted, and Rhynn felt the heat of Ari's mouth on her breast. She held Ari tighter and kissed the top of her head.

Ari's voice rumbled low and husky against her chest. "Morning, sweet thing."

"Isn't that supposed to be my line?"

Ari lifted herself up enough to capture Rhynn's mouth in a thorough good morning kiss.

Rhynn ran her hands up and down Ari's slender back. "Good morning."

"It is a good morning, isn't it?"

Rhynn kissed her again. Ari purposefully rubbed against Rhynn with a contented sigh. "Goddess, you feel so good."

Rhynn's libido nearly sent her into orbit. She let her hands roam, and covered Ari's shoulders and neck with playful nips and licks, appreciating how Ari pushed into her and the soft sounds of arousal coming from her throat. Grinning, she flipped their positions, leaning over Ari, and sliding a hand between her legs, wanting to hear Ari's cry of release. *Goddess, so wet and so hot.* Rhynn was on the edge of coming just touching her.

They both jumped at the loud knock on the door. "Hey, lovebirds! Get your asses out of bed! We're loading the shuttle in an hour!"

Rhynn groaned and collapsed on top of her lover. *Damn, damn, damn.*

With a pained sigh, Ari called, "We're up. Order us some breakfast!"

Rhynn reluctantly lifted herself from Ari and flopped onto her back. "Join me in the shower?"

"Only if we actually shower."

Rhynn snickered. "We can try."

An hour later, Rhynn waited with the rest of her band in the docking bay on the lowest level of the cruise ship. In that short hour, she and Ari had eaten, packed for their two-day jaunt into the Asteroid Belt and been mercilessly teased by their bandmates. They'd also finalized as a group that Rhynn was officially a member of Shattered Crystal Enigma.

Even with a severe lack of sleep, Rhynn's body hummed with excitement and exhilaration. How often did all your dreams come true overnight? Not only had she spent the night making love with the woman of her dreams, she was now a part of the band of her dreams. Tonight would be her first show as a real member of the band. Toni wanted to announce it right away. Rhynn was ready to scream it to the universe. Their road crew knew, and almost all of them had said they were glad she was part of the band. She couldn't imagine being anywhere else.

She and Ari hadn't been farther apart than about two meters since last night. They held hands as they watched the action going on around the shuttle. Rhynn wondered briefly what people would think about her relationship with Ari. Not that it mattered a whole lot; her bandmates were happy for them. The road crew was too busy doing their jobs to pay a whole lot of attention to her blossoming romance, though they'd gotten a few knowing looks and whistles.

She shifted on her feet and wished they could get on board and sit while they waited to take off. Her knee ached, probably from being a bit overused last night. The thought made her snicker and earned her a sideways look from Ari.

"What?"

Rhynn bit her lip. "Nothin', just thinking."

Ari bumped her shoulder. "Get your mind out of the gutter."

Rhynn glanced around. Morgan, Del, Mitch, Rae, and Ben, dressed in standard black WR Security uniforms, hovered around the immediate area. Morgan and Del talked quietly as they visually scanned the cargo bay, while the others had spread out around the shuttle. Shaine remained apart from the group, talking into her com.

Rhynn looked forward to the mini tour. She hadn't been to a mining facility since she'd been very young. She had vague memories of cramped apartments and a bedroom the size of a closet. She remembered playing chase with her friends, hurtling through the zero-g corridors in off-limits parts of the facility. She wanted to see those places again now that she was older, knowing she'd have an entirely different perspective.

She'd also be relieved to be away from the cruise ship and the dangers of Ari's stalker. Rhynn wasn't worried about herself, but Ari needed a break.

"I hope they didn't forget any of my guitars," Ari said.

Dia snorted. "More likely you forgot to bring your toothbrush than those guys forgot your beloved guitars."

"Hey, isn't that J'Nell Inagayl?" Morgan asked, her dark gaze focused past them, toward the back of the bay.

As a group, they turned to look.

"What's she doing here?" Nori asked.

Toni made a face. "What do you think? She's either trying to get a scoop or she wants to suck up and get on this leg of the tour."

Rhynn said, "I thought you guys liked her."

Nori shrugged. "As reporters go, she's better than most, but she can be a little persistent."

Toni coughed.

Shaine intercepted J'Nell as she swept across the docking bay in high-heel boots. Despite the extra height, Shaine towered over her. They spoke briefly and J'Nell's widely smiling visage shifted to annoyed and pissed off by the time she brushed past Shaine and made a beeline toward the band. Her smile returned as she approached. "Ladies! How are you this morning?"

Rhynn automatically started to step toward the back of the group, but Ari's grip held her in place. Ari gave an almost imperceptible shake of her head and murmured, "You're one of us now."

Rhynn wasn't sure why she felt a nervous twitch in her stomach.

Toni greeted J'Nell. "You are way too awake, J. We're anxious to board the shuttle just so we can get to the caf dispenser."

The reporter gave a knowing grin. "Did you have a late night? I didn't see any of you at the club with the other bands."

Rhynn thought, That's because we were holed up in our room fucking all night. And no, we don't kiss and tell.

Dia and Nori prattled on with J'Nell about having a quiet night and relaxing, telling her the band had spent some time at the pool during the day, and how they were a boring bunch of musicians.

J'Nell asked, "Are you excited to get out to the mining facilities, Ari?" Her gaze flashed over Ari and Rhynn. "I'm sure it'll bring back a lot of memories. I remember how much you helped me through my time out here."

Ari nodded. "I like to think we helped each other, and yes, I'm looking forward to it." Rhynn noticed a stiffness in Ari's posture that hadn't been there before. She knew Ari didn't like talking about herself. Rhynn gave her hand a reassuring squeeze. Ari hadn't shared a lot about her past, and Rhynn didn't know if her memories were good or bad, though she suspected probably a little of both. She realized she wanted badly to know all those stories, and how she had known J'Nell so long ago.

Toni said, "We have great news. We're going to announce it at the show tonight, but we may as well tell you now, since you won't be there." She glanced around the group, looking for assenting nods, before she continued. "Rhynn agreed to be our permanent drummer."

Rhynn managed an embarrassed grin. J'Nell focused a blinding smile on her. "Oh! I didn't know Stacy had officially left the group. Congratulations, Rhynn! You're such a phenomenal musician. It's a fairy-tale story how you got into the band."

"Thanks."

Ari cut a smile her way. "Rhynn's crazy talented. I can't think of anyone who'd fit in as well as she has."

"This is exciting news! I know a lot of people are going to be so thrilled. Do you want me to keep this quiet until after your show tonight?"

Nori said, "Actually, that's a great idea. It'd make the fans at the show feel good they're the first to know."

"Perfect. I'll do that. Can I get a quick shot of you waiting to get on board?"

She directed the band into a tight group with the shuttle framed behind them, chatting as she took pictures. "It's going to be different without you guys on board for a couple days. I'm sure the other bands will fill in just fine, though." She clicked another few frames. "I think Zero Hour had been hoping they'd get to join you in the 'Belt, though. Angie Moore mentioned it when I talked to her yesterday."

Ari said, "I think space in the facility auditorium is going to be an issue even with just one band."

J'Nell paused, then said, "Rhynn come in front, and the rest of you, around her. Now, look badass!" She nodded, made a squishing-in motion with both hands. "Close together, now." She clicked a few more shots before laughing and putting the camera in her bag. "Thanks, ladies! See you in a couple days! Behave!"

With a jaunty wave, she strutted back the way she'd come.

Rhynn scratched her jaw, relieved J'Nell wasn't going to be accompanying them on this part of the tour. Until now, she hadn't thought about the fans, or the attention that would be on her as the newest member of the band. Would they be happy about the personnel change? What was Celestian going to think? Her stomach twisted at that consideration. Celestian wouldn't be happy at all. Maybe this wasn't such a good idea. She frowned. Too late now. She pushed away her doubts and focused on the warmth of Ari's hand in hers. Fuck it. Life was good.

Not long afterward, the shuttle flight crew ushered the band and crew on board. Rhynn stepped into a utilitarian seating area containing about ten rows of seats, three on each side, and a sitting area in back with a couple booths and couches. Circular half-meter portals dotted the bulkheads, one for each row of seats. Built-in luggage compartments above the seats ran the length of the cabin.

The road crew sprawled in the back seats. Ari folded herself into a window seat toward the middle and Rhynn slid in beside her. Dia and Nori sat across from them, and Toni and Friday settled in front.

The shuttle may not have been luxurious, but it was still nicer than anything Rhynn had been on. One of the flight attendants stepped into the cabin, requesting they secure their safety webbing. Rhynn pulled the crash restraint across her body. The lap belt and cross-webbing secured both shoulders and clipped into place.

The engines fired up with a growling rumble Rhynn felt through her chest. The shuttle rose off its landing pads and moved slowly through the open docking bay doors. She felt the sickening drop as they left the docking bay's gravity field for open space. Ari's hand covered hers on the armrest between them.

The afterburners kicked in and the shuttle trembled as it eased away. Rhynn marveled at the size of the cruise liner as they passed her. When they were clear, the pilots poured on the power and the shuttle shot toward the Asteroid Belt.

She was relieved to release the seat restraints when they got to speed. As people shifted around, Mykal's voice boomed above the reverberation of engines and voices. He stood at the front of the seats, his head almost hitting the ceiling of the cabin, his bulk nearly filling the aisle between the rows.

"Hey, listen up! This is the schedule for the rest of the day, so pay attention. When we arrive, facility security will meet us for mandatory check-in and safety rules. Everyone gets chipped in and will get chipped out before we leave. If you don't have an ident chip embedded in your bodies, you will get one. Got it?"

He waited for general acceptance and said, "Crew and roadies, and that includes you, Friday, will be loading gear into the auditorium and starting setup. Band, you're gonna get a five-credit tour of the place before you join us. Nobody goes out on their own. If you're not accompanied by facility security, you don't leave the auditorium. This is for safety reasons. We don't need people stumbling into places they shouldn't be. Got it? You break the rules, you're outta here. Period. I am not fucking around. Okay. That's all I got. Enjoy the ride, people."

CHAPTER FORTY-FOUR

Earth Date: November 2453
Mining Facility 2137

Ari

The show we did at the first mining facility was great fun. A small venue like the cramped auditorium usually used for vid showings or company meetings is always intense. I don't know if it's because we're so much closer to the crowd, or because they were grateful for the break from the monotony of their lives. In any case, our fans were thrilled to welcome Rhynn into the fold, and the energy on stage was crazy. But the next night I knew halfway through the set that something was very wrong with Rhynn. At first I heard little things, breaks or transitions bobbling the tiniest bit. Nobody else would have noticed, but I did. And I know Rhynn did.

Every time I looked back between songs, she was gulping water from her bottle. Her face was flushed, her eyes glassy and unfocused. By the time we were down to the last few songs, I was worried she was going to collapse. She was playing at half her usual volume, barely keeping up the tempos, simplifying fills, and playing less intricate patterns.

When we finished the set, she stumbled off the drum riser, crumbling to her knees. Jax was beside her immediately.

"Rhynn!" I shoved my guitar into Gavin's hands and ran to help, looping one of her arms over my shoulders.

We lifted her to her feet, and she swayed between us, blinking furiously, obviously trying to focus. One hand flailed weakly, and I caught it in mine, nearly flipping out when I realized the wetness I felt was her palm covered with blood.

"Rhynn, what's going on?"

She shook her head and her knees caved in again.

"Fuck." Jax struggled to hold her upright.

"Her hands are bleeding!"

Toni swooped in, grabbing Rhynn from behind. "Come on, Rhynn, help us out here."

Between us, we got her backstage, mostly carrying her because though Rhynn tried a few steps, her legs wouldn't support her. As she tried to suck in air with shallow gasping breaths, I felt feverish heat pouring off her body. What the hell was happening? Security swarmed around us.

Toni snapped, "Get a medic! Hurry!"

We collapsed onto the couch with Rhynn. I patted her face, trying to get her to focus. "Rhynn, honey, talk to me."

She stared through me with no recognition or response. I reached for her hands. Both her palms were bloody, the skin raw and red and blistered. What the fuck? Her eyes rolled back in her head as her limbs trembled and jerked. Someone brought over a thin blanket and I wrapped it around her. Shaine and Morgan appeared, and Mykal, and then a couple medics with a gurney.

Rhynn's body went still.

One of the medics shouted, "I need a respirator, now!"

I stood, barely breathing, as they put a mask on her face and started oxygen flowing.

The younger of the two medics wore a concerned expression. "Her pulse is racing, Mick."

"We need to get her to the infirmary, STAT. She's breathing, heart's beating, and she's stopped seizing. Let's move her now."

The two medics loaded her onto the gurney and set it onto the back of a small air-cart. They didn't invite me, but I jumped into the passenger seat anyway. I was not leaving Rhynn. We sped down the hallways, barely missing pedestrians. The flashing lights and blaring siren echoed deafeningly in the narrow corridors.

Two medics rode in the open back of the cart with Rhynn, monitoring her vitals. The older one peppered me with questions. "This ever happen to her before? She taking any intoxicants? Has she taken any lately? She allergic to anything?"

Drugs? Rhynn? "No. She's clean. I've never seen her take anything. I don't know about allergies."

The other guy said, "BP is dropping. Drive faster, Leo!"

A very long two minutes later Leo skidded to a stop in front of the infirmary's emergency entrance. The medics unloaded the gurney and ran with it into the trauma bay. Before the doors slammed shut in front of me, I saw Rhynn's still body surrounded by medics.

Leo patted my shoulder. "They'll take care of her," he said. "Come on, there's a place to sit over here. Caf too."

He led me down a short hallway and into a waiting area with a few chairs and a beverage dispenser built into a counter against the wall. A tired-looking orderly with a mop of dark hair glanced up from a computer terminal behind the reception desk. "Hey, Leo, you got a hot one come in?"

"Yeah, drummer from the band. Keep the caf flowing. Think it's gonna be a long night for these folks." Leo patted my shoulder again. It seemed to be a thing with him, and I think, in his own gruff way, he was trying to make me feel better. "Macer will take care of ya. Your friend'll be okay."

"Thanks," I said.

Leo left and I settled into one of the hard-backed chairs to watch the door that led back to the trauma bay. I wanted to be in there. I wanted to see Rhynn. What the fuck was wrong with her? She didn't do drugs. She hadn't eaten anything we hadn't. I'd been with her the whole time. I couldn't stop thinking of her flushed face and how she stared at me without recognition. I squeezed my eyes shut, but I couldn't banish the vision of her falling off the drum riser. *Goddess, please let her be all right.*

A few minutes later Dia, Toni, and Nori rushed in, supporting Jax, the drum tech, who looked sicker than a dog, pale and feverish.

They eased him into a chair. He groaned and whispered, "Bucket."

I yelled, "Macer, we need a bucket!"

Jax leaned over and everything in his stomach splattered across the floor in front of him. Dia rubbed his back as he moaned piteously. Macer took one look at Jax and grabbed a com. "We got another one! STAT to the lobby!"

Seconds later, two medics carried Jax into the trauma room. Macer opened a closet, removed a sani-vac and dutifully cleaned up the floor.

When he finished, he studied us all dubiously. "Anyone else feel sick?"

I was sick with worry, but I didn't think I would throw up. I asked, "Have you heard if Rhynn is okay?"

"The last data I saw, they were still trying to get her stabilized." He stowed the sani-vac and took his chair behind the desk.

Nori, Dia, Toni, and I looked at each other. Mykal jogged into the lobby. "Any news?" he asked.

Toni said, "They're still working on her."

He handed Toni a com. "I need to get back to the stage and make sure our stuff gets packed up. Call if you hear anything."

As Mykal tromped away, Shaine and Morgan joined us. From the trauma bay I heard what could only have been some kind of monitor alarm going off and voices raised in earnest. It took all my willpower to stay in my chair instead of running down the hallway. Twice in the next hour and a half we heard the rapid screeching beeps of monitors and voices snapping orders.

A frazzled medic skidded through the sliding door. "I need someone to get the drummer's stick bag and bring it here as fast as they can." He held out a pair of protective gloves and a sealable clear plastic bag. "Use the gloves and don't touch the sticks; we think they may have contact poison on them. And tell anyone else who may have touched her sticks or the bag or her drums or anything else she touched, to get down here, STAT."

Morgan jumped to her feet. "I'm on it. Shaine, call ahead."

Shaine nodded sharply and Morgan flew out the door.

I wanted to ask questions, but the medic was already gone. Contact poison? Someone poisoned Rhynn? What the fuck? Was this Celestian? Or was this a coincidence? *Goddess, please let her be okay. Please, please, let her be okay.*

I looked down at my own hands, realizing that I'd touched hers, and stood slowly. "I think they need to check me too." My voice sounded far away.

Toni was at my side immediately. Macer led the way back to the trauma bay, announcing as he walked through the door, "We've got a secondary contact victim."

I found myself searching for Rhynn, but the curtains had been pulled around the area where they were working on her. One of the medics came over with a bottle. "Wash the contact area really well with this. Let it sit for a couple minutes before you rinse it off. It's a solvent." He pushed it into Macer's hands and ran back to the curtained area.

Macer pointed to a row of washtubs against the nearest wall. "This way, please."

It didn't take long to thoroughly wash my hands and arms with the solvent. To be safe, Toni also washed up, since she'd also helped to carry Rhynn backstage. I kept staring at my hands, wondering if they felt warm to the touch, or if I imagined the slight burning and itching sensation under the skin. And then I looked back at the curtained off area, where voices still spoke with quiet urgency, and anything that I felt dissipated with my worry about Rhynn.

Macer ushered us all back to the lobby.

Morgan returned five minutes later with the sealed bag and two worried roadies. Macer and another orderly ushered the roadies into the trauma bay, and Morgan passed the contaminated stick bag to a medic.

As Morgan carefully peeled off her protective gloves, a fourth round of screeching alarms and raised voices rang out into the lobby. I jerked to my feet, ready to charge into the back, but Nori's firm hand on my arm brought me back to my seat. Tears pricked my eyes, my emotions running fast and furious. It was oh-four-hundred hours. I desperately needed sleep. My stomach ached with tension. I stared at the trauma bay door, willing someone to come and tell us what was going on. Finally, another unbearable hour later, the bay door opened.

The doctor who stepped out wore a tight-fitting scrub suit. His hair was regulation military buzzed, and he held himself with a stiff bearing. "You're all here for the music people, right?"

I stood up. "Yes. How are Rhynn Knight and Jax Colter?"

"Jax is fine. He's resting comfortably. Rhynn is stable, and we're monitoring her closely. Once we figured out what the poison was, we were able to create the correct antidote." His sharp gaze scanned us closely. "Where have you been touring lately?"

Toni said, "On a cruise ship. A show on Moon Base, a few gigs on the Nor-Am continent."

He rubbed his chin. "Did you have any military bases on your tour?"

Shaine cocked her head. "Why do you ask?"

"Because the contact poison used on the drummer's sticks is something I've only ever seen on a special ops mission, over a decade ago."

Shaine said, "Someone put poison on her sticks?"

"Yes. Cyolikemite. I noticed her palms and fingers were blistering. The reaction doesn't start right away. It takes maybe an hour, sometimes as much as two hours from the point of exposure, depending on the situation. Jax's exposure was limited, so though he got sick and his skin reddened, he didn't show seizures or blisters. The other two men had even more peripheral contact, so they may feel a little off, but they'll be fine. Same with the other two women who'd helped Rhynn. Rhynn's exposure was extended, and the activity of playing and sweating moved the toxin rapidly into her system. She stopped breathing three times, and her heart stopped twice before the antidote kicked in. She's stable now, but until the toxin works its way completely out of her system, she'll be weak and the seizures may continue off and on for a few days."

"Can I see her?" I asked.

"Sure. She's sedated, so she won't be too responsive."

I didn't care. I needed to see her.

The doctor had one of the orderlies take me back into the infirmary, where five beds were cordoned off with curtains. Rhynn lay in the back corner. Jax slept in the bed next to her, with an IV running into his arm. She also had an IV and an array of monitors flashing over her bed. Her face was pale and covered with a sheen of sweat. Bandages swathed her hands.

There was no chair, so I knelt on the floor beside her bed, gently pushing damp hair from her forehead. "Oh, sweetheart."

Her golden-brown eyes blinked open and she focused on me. "Hey." Her voice sounded thin and breathy. A jerking tremor ran through her body and she groaned.

I caressed her sweat-dampened hair. "How do you feel?" I asked, and thought, yeah, that's a dumb question.

A shiver ran through her. "Cold," she whispered.

I looked around for another blanket. The med tech behind the work counter at the end of the room caught my eye. I said, "Rhynn's cold."

She said, "I'll heat up the bed and bring another blanket."

A blinking number on the monitors above Rhynn's head changed as the bed temperature rose. The tech brought a heated blanket for Rhynn and a folding chair for me. I tucked the blanket around Rhynn's shoulders.

She gasped as tremors rolled through her body again. Her muscles spasmed repeatedly before going rigid for a few seconds and releasing. Rhynn whimpered as her head fell back against the pillow. All I could do was brush the damp hair from her face and re-tuck the blanket around her. She blinked up at me and whispered hoarsely, "Can you...call my mom? Tell her...love her." Her eyes closed and she fought to catch her breath.

After several seconds, I thought she had fallen back to sleep, but she opened her eyes long enough to catch mine. "You too..." she managed in a bare whisper. Her eyes fluttered shut and she slipped into sleep.

Tears rolled down my cheeks. I needlessly tucked her in again and sat in the folding chair and cried. *You're not leaving me, Rhynn Knight. Don't you even think it.*

An hour later Rhynn still slept soundly. I desperately needed to use the restroom and get something to eat and drink. I also needed to get her mom's com code. I trudged into the lobby. The whole band was there, including Friday, Mykal, and Del. They looked expectantly at me. I held up a hand, pointed to the restroom, and did my business before returning to talk to them. Toni put a bottle of water and a protein bar in my hands and guided me to a chair.

Nori asked, "Is she doing okay? Are you?"

"She's still sleeping. I'm okay." I held up the water and bar. "Thanks for this." I drank down half the water bottle and ripped open the wrapper for a bite of the protein bar. Just that much made me feel a little better. I said, "She asked me to call her mom. Do we have her mom's com code somewhere?"

Del said, "We've got everyone's info. Part of the whole security thing. You need it now?"

I nodded. Shortly after, and with a promise that the others would take their turns sitting with Rhynn so I could sleep, I returned to Rhynn's side. I kissed her flushed forehead and used the com Del had given me to make an inter-system vid-call to Cassandra Knight.

My stomach fluttered with nerves as I waited for the call to connect. I really had no idea what I was going to say. *Hi, I'm your daughter's new girlfriend, and right now she's lying in a hospital bed because she's been poisoned, probably by my insane mystery stalker. Oh, and I also look like death warmed over because I haven't slept in a day or showered after my last show.*

I rolled my eyes at myself.

Finally the vid-call connected. The palm-sized screen cleared and a middle-aged woman with short brown hair and Rhynn's eyes peered curiously at me. "Hello?"

"Um, hi. You're Rhynn's mom, right?"

"Yes." She cocked her head and her eyes narrowed. "Oh, you're the guitar player."

I nodded. "Ari. Ari Walker."

Her expression shifted to concerned. "What happened? Where's Rhynn?"

My words tumbled over each other in a hurry to get out of my mouth. "Rhynn will be okay. We're not sure what happened, but she's in the med bay, and they think she was poisoned, and she stopped breathing, but they brought her back and she's okay, and she's sleeping right here, and I swear I won't leave her. I promise." The words stopped and I realized I was crying again. Great first impression. I sounded delirious.

Cassandra closed her eyes for a moment.

I added hopefully, "You can see, she's right here." I focused the vid cam on the bed, on Rhynn's face. I'm sure it wobbled badly because I reached over and adjusted the blanket under her chin. Her skin was still flushed, her hair damp against her head. I swallowed hard.

"Oh, Rhynn," Cassandra murmured.

I brought the com back to face me. "I'm really sorry, Ms. Knight."

"Just Cassandra. And it's not your fault. Don't cry, honey. I can feel this will be all right."

I said, "I hope so."

Cassandra opened her hand in front of the camera. She held a purple and white crystal about the size of my pointer finger. "This is Rhynn's crystal. I keep it with me so I know how she is. If the crystal is cold, she's in trouble, and something bad is happening. If the crystal is warm, then all is well. It was cold for a while earlier. I didn't give it a lot of thought, but that must have been why. It's warm now, so she'll be all right."

I frowned skeptically. "You believe that?"

Her laugh was soft, her eyes gentle. "I do. Don't worry, my daughter thinks I'm strange, too."

"She asked me to call you. She wanted me to tell you she loved you."

Cassandra smiled. "Thank you, Ari."

"She's really special."

"She is. And so are you. Take care of my little girl, okay? And call or message me with updates, because if I don't hear from one or the other of you, I'll be there to find out for myself."

After a few more words, we ended the call.

I saw some of Rhynn's traits in her mother, like her calm demeanor and her eyes. But Cassandra Knight was not what I imagined. Apparently she leaned toward paganism or mysticism. I'd expected her to be as practical and straightforward as Rhynn seemed to be. Either way, I was thankful she took the news so reasonably. I had dreaded being screamed at or blamed.

I gazed thoughtfully at my new girlfriend. But she was more than that, wasn't she? What I felt, what seemed to be growing between us, was more than a casual fling. I wasn't sure what it was, but I knew I'd never felt so strongly about anyone.

I brushed my fingertips along her cheek. It hurt my heart to see her so vulnerable and I felt sick knowing how close I'd been to losing her. Even with her face flushed and her hair matted she was beautiful to me. My strong, brave protector.

CHAPTER FORTY-FIVE

Earth Date: November 2453
Mining Facility 2137

Shaine and Morgan

In the mining facility's security office, Shaine and Morgan joined the Head of Security, Ben Lorenz, and the doctor who'd treated Rhynn. Dr. Seth leaned against the wall beside Lorenz's desk, arms folded.

Lorenz raised a doubtful brow. "You're telling me she was poisoned?"

Seth said, "I found the toxin on the drumsticks and the inside the stick bag. It had to have been put there between the last time she played and when she played tonight."

"Who had access to the stage, other than the band's tech crew?" Shaine asked.

Lorenz shrugged. "Any number of people, I imagine. It's not a fully secured area, so we didn't have login-logout restrictions in place. It's only been locked down since your people arrived this afternoon. At that point, I have a list of maintenance and security personnel who were assigned to help with the concert." He glanced toward Shaine and Morgan. "As we'd discussed, nobody other than authorized personnel were allowed in the backstage area before or after the show."

Shaine said, "This isn't the first attack on Rhynn or Ari. I thought I'd made it clear we needed you to be alert."

"I'm sure my people were doing their jobs."

"Then how the fuck did Rhynn get poisoned?" Morgan demanded.

"Maybe her equipment was contaminated before you got here," Lorenz shot back.

Seth held up a hand. "Perhaps knowing where the cyolikemite came from would help us discover who brought the toxin onto the station."

Lorenz said, "The toxin should have identifying molecular structures traceable to the lab that produced it. Let me make a call to our lab." He typed into his com console. The vid screen to the side of the desk blinked alive and a woman in a lab coat looked up distractedly.

"How can I help you, Lorenz?" she asked.

"Good evening, Doctor Lister. I need to trace the origins of a sample of cyolikemite. Is that something you can do?"

Lister sat up straight and frowned into the com. "Of course. But why?"

"We've reason to believe it was used to poison someone, and I need to know where it came from."

"Likely right here."

"What?"

"Cyolikemite is used in our metal curing process. It's mechanically injected into the raw molten metal as part of the separation process."

Shaine asked, "Who would have access to the raw chemical?"

"It's a regulated substance, so only a few personnel have access. It's secured here in the lab. On the work floor, the process supervisors can draw samples from the system if there's a problem. The sample is evaluated and the curing mix is adjusted accordingly."

"We need to know if any cyolikemite is missing from your stores," Lorenz said.

Lister rotated her chair away from the screen, typing into a terminal.

Her frustration evident, Shaine scowled darkly and balled her hands into fists. "The welfare of these women is our responsibility and so far we're failing badly. We can secure their rooms, we can make sure nobody gets to them physically, but we can't stop every random damned threat that pops up."

Lister said, "I may have found something. The logs show an additional two milligrams of cyolikemite were requested and distributed to the processing facility yesterday. Trevor, the night supervisor, signed off on it. The request indicates there was an excess of dolorite in the metal mix and additional cyolikemite was required to balance the output. The inconsistency is under investigation."

Lorenz said, "I'd like you and Trevor to come to my office. I'll track down who else was working in processing. We'll find out what's happening." He signed off the vid call and turned to Shaine and Morgan. "You can stay and be part of the meeting, or we can get back to you with our findings."

Morgan and Shaine exchanged a quick glance; an understanding passed between them. Morgan said, "I'll make sure the band and their equipment are secured. Then I'll find out if Del and Gohste have anything additional and let you know."

CHAPTER FORTY-SIX

Earth Date: November 2453
Mining Facility 2137

Rhynn

Rhynn watched nervously as Doc Seth unsealed the covering from her right hand, which burned and throbbed in time to her rapidly beating heart. Her hands had been sealed into opaque rubbery mittens filled with thick bio-gel. She felt as though she were wearing boxing gloves.

She'd only been awake for an hour after sleeping for several. Still hooked up to the rack of monitors over her bed and an intravenous drip, she felt like her brain was swimming through fog. It was hard to think. The meds kept the pain from being overwhelming, but the throbbing and burning was constant, aggravated by the churning in her stomach and a high fever from the toxin remaining in her system. Unable to keep any food down, she sipped gingerly on water, careful not to drink too much or that came up too.

Doc Seth said she'd be playing drums again in no time, but Rhynn wondered if his idea of "no time" and hers were the same thing. She was supposed to be playing tomorrow night on the cruise ship, and they were supposed to be on their way back to said ship in about three hours. The way she felt, she didn't see herself even getting out of bed any time soon.

Ari sat beside her, one hand on Rhynn's forearm while Doc Seth eased off the first gel-filled mitt. What she saw made Rhynn want to cry. Her palm and fingers were covered with weeping blisters. Raw, tattered skin seeped blood and fluid.

As the gel dried, pain screamed through her hand like a hundred knives piercing her skin and peeling it off. She squeezed her eyes shut against the agony. The intensity lessened after a few seconds and she managed to breathe again while she held her hand rigidly over a basin on her lap, afraid any movement would crack the swollen and blistered skin and intensify the pain.

Doc Seth gently rotated her wrist, studying the damage. "It could be a lot worse, believe me. The bio-gel will speed the healing process. It's already coming along. You should be able to play again in a few days, though you'll need to take it easy. Four days in the gloves, not counting today, before the doctor on the cruise ship can cover the burnt area with nu-skin so you can play. For the first couple weeks, at least, you'll have to wear gloves over the nu-skin and keep the bio-gel mitts on when you're not playing for about a week."

Rhynn nodded mutely.

Ari asked, "Will you be contacting the infirmary on the cruise ship to pass on the information?"

"Yes. I'll be in touch with Dr. Whiley and send him my notes and diagnosis. Check in with him as soon as you get on board. I'll also give you a data chip with your records."

Rhynn said, "So, for the next few days I'll have these mitts on all the time?"

"Yes. You'll have to have someone help you get dressed, eat, pretty much everything. You can probably do a few simple things, but you can't put pressure on the burned skin."

Rhynn looked at Ari. "Are you up for this?" She had never been good about asking for help. But with the mitts on, she wasn't going to be able to do a fucking thing. Talk about pathetic, embarrassing, and lame.

Ari met her pleading gaze with intensity. "I'm here for you, anything you need."

Doc Seth filled a new mitt with bio-gel and held it open. "Okay, kid, put your hand in so I can seal it up."

Kid? She tentatively eased her hand into the mitt. The icy cold gel closed over her burning and throbbing skin and she shivered. He sealed the mitt around her wrist and taped it and repeated the process with her other hand. Once she was back in mitts, he and Ari helped her get comfortable in bed again.

He said, "You may as well take a nap before you have to get on the shuttle and head back to the cruise ship. I'll be in my office if you need anything. My tech will be in shortly to remove the IV, then you can let her know when you're ready to go down to the shuttle bay and she'll call up a ride for you."

He patted her shoulder and left the infirmary. The other beds were empty now since Jax had gone back to the barracks where the road crew was staying. As the doc left, the lights in the room dimmed and Rhynn realized how tired she was.

Ari started to tuck the blanket up around her, but Rhynn lifted an awkward hand to stop her. "Lay here with me, please? I want to hold you. And I'm cold." *Did she sound whiny or what?*

Ari cocked her head. "You're sure I won't hurt you?"

"You won't. Please?" She hated to beg, but she needed to be close to Ari, to hold her and soak in her warmth.

Ari kicked off her boots and slid under the blanket beside her, carefully easing herself against Rhynn's side. Ari settled her head on Rhynn's shoulder and pulled the blanket over them. Rhynn kissed her hair and sighed. "Thank you."

"You're welcome, but you know I'm doing this for me too, right?" She snuggled in. "I always want to hold you."

CHAPTER FORTY-SEVEN

Earth Date: November 2453
Cruise Ship *Star Rider*

Ari

We made a vid call to Wayne as soon as we returned to the *Star Rider*. Of course, our intrepid manager lost his mind, because that was what Wayne Neutron did. He threw up his hands and paced back and forth. "I can't believe what's going on with this tour! What are those security people doing? I told you I should have gone along! And now your drummer can't play? What the fuck am I supposed to do with that?"

I didn't feel like dealing with Wayne being either a mother hen or a pain in our collective asses. And I *wasn't* going to put up with him berating Rhynn, especially when she wasn't in the room to defend herself. None of this was her fault. I'd tucked her into bed when we arrived and she was out cold after another dose of pain meds.

The rest of us gathered around the media center in the common room, sitting on the sofa facing the camera. I perched on the end, hoping to stay off Wayne's radar. Up to this point, the stalker's interest had been mostly aimed at me, but with Rhynn in her sights, Wayne was going to ask why. I didn't feel like discussing our budding romance with our band manager.

Toni folded her arms. "Don't get your undies in a bundle, Wayne. Shaine and Morgan are doing all they can. This stalker is playing dirty."

Nelda moved into camera range. "I'm going to set up some interviews for you while Rhynn is recovering. I'm sure J'Nell Inagayl will want to talk to you. And probably Alyson Petri and Vin Rossell. I also heard Jo Lupine is there."

I sighed. Wonderful. Exactly what I wanted to be doing.

Dia groaned. "Come on, Nelda, give us a break. Rhynn's not up for interviews right now."

Wayne pushed in front of the camera. "Also, it was so nice of you to make the decision to bring Rhynn into the band without telling me."

I surged to my feet. "The decision was ours, not yours. We didn't need your permission."

"I'm your manager. You should have told me about your plan to have her join. What about Stacy?"

Nori leaned foward. "What about her? She quit. She chose toxins and a party over the band. We chose Rhynn."

"Rhynn was a convenient temporary fill-in."

I wanted to strangle him. "Get over it. She's in the band."

"I can't manage a band when I don't know what's happening!"

Dia snapped, "Oh, for goddess' sake. Now you know. Let it go, Wayne."

"I want to talk to that security person."

"You have Shaine's com code. Call her," Toni said.

"I will. Now, when will your drummer be able to play?"

I said, "Her name is Rhynn. The ship's doctor said she should be able to play the final show on the cruise ship."

Wayne scowled. "I would rather it be sooner."

"Deal with it," I muttered and sat down, catching Nelda's raised brow look of interest. When I glanced back up at the vid screen, Nelda was studying me with a look that asked, "What aren't you telling me?"

I ignored her.

CHAPTER FORTY-EIGHT

Earth Date: November 2453
Cruise Ship *Star Rider*

Rhynn

The band, including a somewhat reluctant Rhynn, fielded three interviews the following morning. Jo Lupine and Vin Rossell wanted to talk about the cruise. Alyson Petri, who worked for a more mainstream music site, was more interested in the new recording and musical direction. Rhynn stayed in the background as much as she could. The meds made it hard to think, the toxin still in her system kept her weak and listless, and she still felt too new to the band to be part of their collective story.

She wasn't even sure the fans were happy she was a member of SCE. Dia said there were a few fanzine blogs accusing the band of dumping Stacy and insisting it wasn't the same band with Rhynn behind the drums. Rhynn expected that kind of talk. She knew she approached their music differently than Stacy but the band was happy with her playing. They wouldn't have asked her to join if they weren't. Even so, when it came to band history, Rhynn felt like an interloper.

After the third interview, Ari and Rhynn retreated to their room so Ari could change out the bio-gel in Rhynn's mittens. J'Nell was supposed to show up later in the afternoon and Rhynn really wanted to crash for a while before that.

She held her hands over the sink while Ari gently unsealed each glove and eased them from her hands. She sucked in a sharp breath as the air hit her bared skin and the gel dripped away. Stinging, burning pain engulfed her hands.

Ari whispered an apology. Rhynn forced a brave face and said, "It's okay, just takes me by surprise."

Ari nodded. "I'm going to put these in the sanitizer. Then we can rinse your hands."

"I'll just stand right here and not move," Rhynn mumbled, leaning heavily on her forearms over the narrow vanity. After the initial shock, the stinging pain subsided a bit. She turned her hands to look more closely.

The clear gel dripped slowly from her raw and blistered chemical-burned palms and fingers. In the worst places, dying yellowed tissue lined open blisters and oozed bloody fluid. She couldn't fathom how she'd be playing again in a week.

Doc Seth insisted the blisters would dry up and heal after four days in the bio-gel, when the ship's doctor could apply the nu-skin patches to further enhance the healing process. Rhynn planned to try out her hands during a band rehearsal before the final gig five days away, but it still seemed too soon.

The remaining poison in her system left her nauseous and weak. She'd woken with fever dreams last night and endured another round of muscle seizures before a dose of meds kicked in and she relaxed back into sleep. A blanket of depression settled on top of the exhaustion of recovery. Fuck. What a crappy way to start off with her new band. Would they just fire her since she couldn't play? Ari insisted nobody in the band was angry, nobody blamed her, and it wasn't her fault.

In her head, she could agree with that, but at the same time, she felt like somehow she'd brought this down on herself and on Ari too. Maybe she shouldn't have been so friendly with Ari, shouldn't have agreed to share a room, or kissed her in the observation deck and spent the night loving her.

Okay, well, she couldn't find it in herself to regret the last part. But the rest she could question. The more she considered it, the more obvious it seemed that Celestian had seen her and Ari together and decided to try to kill Rhynn because of it.

Dr. Seth had yanked her from the brink of death three times. Had it been another doctor, maybe she wouldn't have survived at all, and that thought was unsettling. She wasn't ready to leave this life, but she couldn't help thinking that almost dying had to be some kind of warning. Maybe she was wrong to have joined the band. It would probably make Celestian even angrier, and maybe the next attempt at murder would be aimed at Ari. Maybe she needed to quit SCE or at least tell the world she was quitting.

Her heart ached at the thought of leaving either the band or Ari. What the hell was she supposed to do? She didn't want to quit, and she didn't want to stay away from Ari. But for the first time in her life, she found herself feeling real fear.

Ari returned from the bedroom with the sanitized mittens and paused at the door. Rhynn met her gaze in the mirror.

Ari studied her with a concerned frown. "It'll be okay."

Rhynn looked down at her battered hands. Would it be? She didn't know anymore. "I feel like this is all my fault. Because of me, we can't play."

Ari moved behind her, reaching around to set the mittens on the vanity, and then she pulled Rhynn against her. She rested her chin on Rhynn's shoulder. Rhynn sighed as Ari's body pressed against her back, solid and comforting.

"Rhynn, it's not your fault. It's the fault of the twisted person doing this to us. Don't second-guess things. It'll work out."

"But—"

"With or without you, Celestian's threats and attacks have been escalating. I'm just so sorry you've gotten sucked into the vortex."

Rhynn swallowed. She stood in Ari's embrace without moving. In the quiet, she could hear her bandmates' voices in the common room and the low rumble of the cruise liner itself. She breathed in the musky scent of Ari's perfume and let it calm her. After a while she took a deep breath and straightened. "We'd better get the mitts back on."

Ari nodded and kissed her neck. "Okay." She reached around Rhynn and started the water, adjusting the temperature, and shifted to Rhynn's side. "Right hand first."

Rhynn gritted her teeth and put her right hand under the stream of water, quickly yanking it back as pain exploded through her nerve-endings. "Fuck!"

"Rhynn, I'm sorry!"

Rhynn took a breath, swallowed hard, and pushed back the pain. "Not your fault," she muttered. A couple more breaths, and she clamped her jaw shut and shoved her hand under the running water. Now that she was expecting it, the pain was almost manageable, and she let the water rinse the remaining gel away while Ari rubbed her back in gentle circles. When she removed her hand from the warm stream, Ari carefully pulled the bio-gel filled mitten on and sealed it around her wrist. Almost immediately, the numbing, cooling gel sucked away the worst of the pain, and Rhynn's shoulders sagged with relief.

Ari said, "You want to do the next one, or give it a minute or two?"

Rhynn's answer was to just shove her left hand under the water, grimacing at the pain, but managing not to either scream or pull her hand away. Once the water had run over the raw skin for a few seconds, the initial shock passed, and her ragged nerve endings calmed. Fuck. This was not fun. Ari got the second mitten on and was sealing it up when Nori poked her head into the bathroom.

"Hey, you guys. J'Nell is here early, so come on out when you're done, okay?"

Rhynn nodded an acknowledgment, and Ari muttered a few obscenities under her breath, ending with, "I am so sick of interviews right now."

Rhynn really wanted a nap. She met her own gaze in the mirror and saw tired eyes. Her face was blotchy and flushed from a persistent low-grade fever. Ari had tied her hair into a single pony, along with her long bangs. She needed a shower.

Nori paused at the door. "You doing okay, Rhynn?"

She sucked in a slow breath and then let it out. "Yeah." She forced a smile onto her face, shaking off the melancholy and fatigue. "I'm good. We'd better go and join the group, huh?"

Ari gently took Rhynn's hands in hers and playfully kissed the thick silicone mittens. "All better now."

The simple, silly act sent warm tendrils through Rhynn's body and soul, and this time her smile was wide and true. "Thank you."

Ari leaned in and pressed their lips together. Rhynn returned the kiss with a contented hum before she wavered a little drunkenly. Ari slid a supportive arm around her. "You sure you're all right?"

Rhynn blinked and steadied herself. "Tired. But okay."

Ari studied her for a long moment, sighed, and led her to the living room. Rhynn leaned against her for support.

The rest of the band, plus Friday, sprawled on the sofa and the floor in front of it. J'Nell faced them in the recliner, reminding Rhynn of a queen with her court. The reporter's sharp eyes flashed over Rhynn, and she felt like she was being inspected until J'Nell's face lit up in a welcoming smile.

"Hey, you two, about time." Toni waved at Rhynn and Ari from her place on the love seat with Friday curled against her.

Rhynn held up one mitten-covered hand. "We were changing out the bio-gel."

Toni's expression shifted to concern. "How are the hands?"

"Pretty rough."

Dia shifted on the couch, making room for Rhynn and Ari.

J'Nell said, "The ladies were telling me you had a horrible allergic reaction to some of the raw ore you touched touring the processing facility." She visibly shuddered. "Are you feeling okay?"

Rhynn said, "I'll be all right. Just gonna take a few days." They'd decided not to tell the real story of the poisoned drumsticks.

Ari said quietly, "The histamines are still working out of Rhynn's system. Her hands are raw with blisters from the reaction. She could have died. We almost lost her three times."

Rhynn swallowed. She heard the tremble in Ari's voice and recognized the fear in her eyes. Hell, if she thought about it for any length of time, she was scared too. And sickened to know that the most likely reason for the entire incident was because Celestian knew they were together.

J'Nell turned her concerned gaze on Rhynn. "I saw the announcement that you guys wouldn't be playing until the final show. Will you really be able to play Saturday night?"

"I'll be wearing gloves, but the doc says I should be okay." *As long as I don't have any seizures, and exhaustion doesn't take me down before the end of the show.* She didn't count on being at a hundred percent. But the show would go on, and every day she felt a little stronger.

Ari rested a hand on Rhynn's forearm, brushing the bare skin with her thumb.

J'Nell's gaze focused immediately on the touch and she said with a sly smile, "Do I detect a romance in the making?"

Rhynn glanced at Ari, who smiled happily, despite the color painting her cheeks.

"Attached at the hips," Nori said from where she lay on the floor, using a decorative pillow from the sofa to prop herself up. "About time our Ari found someone to keep her in line."

"Smartass," Ari muttered.

Nori said, "Face it, girl. You're smitten."

Dia giggled. "Ah, true loooove."

Ari made a face at Dia.

J'Nell smiled brightly. "I'm sure we'll be talking more about this," she said, winking playfully at Ari before blithely changing the subject. "Will you be doing the same set Saturday night or switching things up a bit?"

Toni said, "We haven't talked about it yet. We're going to rehearse in a couple days to see how things go, and then we'll figure out the set list."

Ari stood. "And on that note, our drummer needs a nap. J'Nell, I'm sorry to cut this short, but Rhynn had a rough night, and she's too polite to say she needs to rest."

Ari straightened to her full height, wrapped in a cape of presence, owning the room. She didn't often use her strength without a guitar in hand, but when she did, she became the group's focal point, with an air of intimidation and control.

J'Nell stood slowly. Her smile didn't quite reach her eyes. "Thank you for taking the time to do the interview, Rhynn. I know your fans will be glad to hear you're doing well and recovering. Get some rest. I'm sure I'll see all of you before the show on Saturday."

She made her goodbyes and Dia and Toni saw her to the door.

Rhynn felt a sense of relief as it shut behind her. "Thank you."

Ari said, "I think we're about done with interviews."

Nori stretched her arms high over her head, arching her back and bringing her palms to the floor with a heavy sigh. "Yeah. Totally done. J'Nell's good people, but she can be intense."

Friday spoke for the first time, with a smirk and a shake of her curly blond head. "I think she's intrigued Ari and Rhynn have a thing going."

Rhynn rolled her eyes, and Ari frowned. "Why?" Ari asked. "Seriously, we're all allowed to have lives."

Nori sighed. "Because, my beautiful friend, your romance with the drummer is going to break the many, many hearts who have fawned after you, hopelessly in love, for all these years."

Ari snorted. "You're full of shit, Nor. Besides, J'Nell's a reporter. She's always intrigued by something new. She was like that when we were kids, and she's like that when she covers other bands. She gets a piece of gossip and she starts digging at it. She may be doing entertainment reporting these days, but her background was investigative reporting for the military. That's always going to be her thing." She shook her head with a sigh and touched Rhynn's arm. "Come on, sweetheart, let's tuck you in for a while."

She took Rhynn by the wrist, and Rhynn followed her obediently back to their bedroom for a nap.

CHAPTER FORTY-NINE

Earth Date: November 2453
Cruise Ship *Star Rider*

Rhynn

In the early afternoon, the Meteor Music Hall was empty. Stools and chairs rested upside down on top of the tables and the floors were mopped. The clear glassteel walls of the zero-gravity cube were cleaned and polished, waiting for the slam-thrashers to start their wild acrobatics. SCE powered up their equipment on the quiet stage. Every sound echoed through the empty hall, bouncing wildly into the dark recesses.

Mykal and Friday turned on the stage lights and fired up the monitor PA for a rehearsal so Rhynn could find out for certain if she would be okay to play the following night. Just as the doc promised, the bio-gel had done its miracle healing, and the burned and blistered skin had healed and regrown. Of course, all her hard-earned callouses were gone. Her palms and fingers were smooth, the skin new and tender.

She felt more than a little guilty that her injuries had canceled almost a week's worth of shows, but she knew there was no help for it. Until now, there was no way she'd have been able to play. She'd been picking up sticks and working carefully for short periods on a practice pad for the past two days, but this was the first time she'd gotten behind her drum kit.

The blue chrome hardware gleamed spotlessly and the black trigger pads were a little less scuffed. Jax said he and the guys used a cleaning solution Doc Seth sent with them to make sure there was no residual poison on any surface. A new stick bag hung on her right, filled with new sticks with carefully taped grips.

Rhynn eased on a pair of thin leather gloves. The calfskin molded softly over her newly healed hands. She grabbed a pair of sticks and played through a few rudiments on the snare drum pad, getting accustomed to the restriction. The leather felt awkward and she stretched out her fingers a few times, trying to get the fit right.

As the leather warmed to her hands, the fit improved, and she played around the drum kit, testing basic rhythms, relieved to feel her hands and body fall into sync. She didn't want to push too hard, and she didn't want to over-play her tender new skin. She focused on gentle warm-ups and getting her blood moving.

As she played, she relaxed into the rhythms. She still had her speed and motion, but she had to be conscious of not hitting too hard. The gloves helped, but she could still feel the shock of her sticks hitting the drum pads. Over the course of the night, she knew, even with gloves over the nu-skin, the friction against her palms and fingers would eventually take a toll.

After a few minutes, she stopped, waiting for the others to finish tuning their instruments. Ari whipped through a set of warm-up scales, occasionally pausing to adjust the sound mods on her amps. Mykal ran the monitor board from stage left, and his gruff voice powered through the monitor speakers overhead and along the front of the stage. "When you guys are ready I'll get your feeds adjusted. Toni, your vocal's pretty hot, but let me know if you can't hear yourself."

Nori leaned into the mic on a stand in front of her and Dia. "Let's start with 'Caterwaul.' Ari, play us in."

Ari moved toward center stage, glancing around before she started the guitar intro. The soft, melodic riff, minus distortion, hung in the air, haunting and dark. Four bars in, the rest of the band jumped into the first verse.

Toni's vocal cut over the music. Rhynn played a flashy rhythm with scattered cymbal crashes, bass drums firing like machine guns in double-time. Ari's lead guitar supported Dia's scalding rhythm parts; her cleaner, edgier sound playing counterpoint to the heavy crunch of Dia's amps.

Rhynn grinned. Damn, it felt good to play. And damned if this band wasn't just fucking phenomenal. Her hands warmed up and sweat worked into the softening leather, allowing her grip to feel more natural. She rode the flow of the music, listening closely to Ari and keying off her musical lines.

They worked for almost an hour and a half, with breaks to assess how she was feeling. Her hands were aching and tender by the time they finished, and she peeled off her gloves with nervous apprehension.

Ari stood at her side, one hand on her shoulder for support. They both breathed out in relief to see that her skin, though reddened, remained intact. She would be all right.

CHAPTER FIFTY

Earth Date: November 2453
Cruise Ship *Star Rider*

Ari

After rehearsal, we gathered with the WR security team in their suite. I wasn't sure what the meeting was about, but I hoped we'd finally get some answers about Celestian. We sat around a rectangular conference table set up in one of the bedrooms with Shaine, Morgan, Del, Gohste, and the ship's head of security, Officer Garrimond. Rhynn slouched in the chair next to mine, eyes half-lidded with fatigue. I couldn't help but worry about her, even though she insisted she was fine.

The vid screen on the wall displayed a split image. One half showed Wayne and Nelda at a conference table on Earth. The second half displayed a black-uniformed Out-System Authority Investigations officer sitting behind his desk, introduced as Agent Tigri.

Wayne, as usual, attempted to take control of the meeting. "I need to know my band is safe. What good are you people if you can't protect my girls?"

"We are not girls," Toni muttered.

Agent Tigri cleared his throat. "I've been working with the mining facility people, and we've made some progress. The man who stole the cyolikemite—the contact poison—is Tikko Mallais. He works the processing production line, and part of his job is checking the balance of chemicals in the curing mix because it needs adjustment fairly often. He's ex-Earth Guard. Also did four years for assault after he left the service. Says he got a call from a buddy back on Earth who said he could make some good money on the side if he took a call for an easy job. He got a call a day later. We triangulated the call back to where the cruise ship would have been. Mallais said the contact did not give a name. The voice was garbled, so he couldn't identify it as male or female. Fifty thousand credits were deposited to his personal account. We're working to trace the deposit, but the trail is quite convoluted."

Rhynn's brows pulled together, and she squinted at Tigri on the vid screen. "But how did he get the poison? I'm not following."

Tigri said, "He noted a dip in the cyolikemite levels in the mix and over-reported it. The shift supervisor signed off without looking closely enough. When the chemical was delivered, Mallais only added half of it to the mix. He must have put the remainder into another container because the original, which was returned to the lab, was empty. When the curing mix was re-checked, it was verified because he'd only put in the correct amount, which was half of what he'd requested. It was a discrepancy that wouldn't have been caught until the end-of-month audits.

"In any case, Mallais got himself onto the stage because he's a volunteer usher, so he had clearance to be in the auditorium. All he had to do was spray the chemical on the sticks and walk off stage. We found a witness to place him at the scene, apparently looking at the drum kit setup."

Shaine said, "The key takeaway is that whoever made the call to Mallais was on the cruise ship."

Officer Garrimond pushed some papers around in front of him. "We attempted to track the call within the ship, but it originated on a disposable com so there's no record of it."

Wayne said, "So someone on the ship is the stalker who's been after Ari for months and now Rhynn Knight as well."

Toni scribbled on her comp pad and pushed it in front of me. "*Thanks, Captain Obvious.*"

Gohste lifted a remote and the split screen became three panes instead of two. "With the information we have, only a handful of people on board fit some or all of the parameters. One, they have money. Two, they were on board when the call was made to Mallais. Three, they were on board when any of the other incidents happened. Four, they have a background in the military or for assault or a history of following the slam-thrash scene."

I read the names, recognizing the three reporters on the list—J'Nell, Alyson, and Rip. But none of them struck me as the stalker type.

Jon and Rita Mall
Mick Redding
Alyson Petri
William Borland
Cleo Vishnyakova
J'Nell Inagayl
Rip Thrashman
Ammand Steele
Terrance and Steffan Orrann

Shaine said, "There's one person in particular on that list who really worries me, because she's been so close to you. Cleo Vishnyakova."

"Who the hell is that?" Toni asked.

Shaine's frown deepened. "You know her as Panther."

I felt my stomach drop into my feet. Panther?

Dia said, "No way!"

"I know. I don't like it either. Unfortunately, she ticks all the boxes. She's got the military background and contacts and skills. She's followed the music. She's got the money, though she certainly doesn't advertise it. She comes from a long line of Earth Guard veterans with a lot of stars on their collars. She's been close to you, so she's had opportunity. She's been on the inside, knew what we were doing, where we were putting our resources. And she's gone out of her way to bury her background. The security company she contracts with didn't even know she was ex-Earth Guard, let alone part of a special ops team."

Nori shook her head. "I really don't want to believe she was part of this."

Shaine nodded slowly. "I haven't interviewed her yet. But of all the people on our list, she's the most likely suspect. I've pulled her off the duty roster. I can't risk her being near you."

I groped for Rhynn's hand. She twined her fingers with mine, and though I was careful not to grip hard, the solidity of her touch grounded me while the proverbial rug was being pulled out from under my feet. Panther? She'd seemed so honest, so protective. Could we all have read her so wrong? Could I be that bad a judge of character? I reminded myself that I'd misjudged Stacy.

Wayne said, "I don't know about this Panther person, but Inagayl is an entertainment reporter. So are Thrashman and Petri. I've known all of them for years. When are you going to start questioning them?"

Garrimond said, "My people are setting up interviews. Wendt and I will talk to each of the persons on the list. Officer Tigri will also be present via vidcom."

Shaine said, "We've tightened security for the show tomorrow night. Everyone goes through weapons scanners on the way into the auditorium. My people will check all the stage equipment and the rigging with scanners and eyeballs. We'll have double the stage security, but it's a live concert, so there's always a risk."

"I'm very tired of these risks, Wendt," Wayne said.

Shaine's expression was dark. "So are we, Mr. Neutron. So are we."

CHAPTER FIFTY-ONE

Earth Date: November 2453
Cruise Ship *Star Rider*

Rhynn

The opening bands rocked the packed concert hall, hyping up the crowd. By the time Shattered Crystal Enigma took the stage for the final show of the Hammer Down Cruise, chants of "SCE! SCE!" rattled the walls.

From her vantage point on the drum riser, Rhynn could count six extra security guards posted at the sides of the stage. Besides the security contingent provided by the cruise line, she recognized several from WR—two on either side of the stage and at least four scattered through the crowd pushing each other around the dance pit down front. Panther was nowhere to be seen, her familiar presence missing from the backstage contingent. Rhynn found that more disturbing than she would have liked, in part because she felt betrayed, and in part because she didn't believe the danger was over.

While she waited for her cue to start the set, she struggled to keep her focus on the music and not over-playing her hands, rather than on possible threats.

They launched into "Victim of My Personal Hell." She glanced over her drums to her right. Ari bounced on the balls of her feet in front of her speaker stack, about halfway to the front edge of the stage. Eyes closed and her head thrown back, she wailed out the lead melody over Dia's rhythm line. Goddess, she was beautiful when she played. The music expanded out of her, lighting up her whole being.

Rhynn accented the last part of Ari's riff with a series of cymbal crashes and tom fills as they dropped back into the verse.

At center stage, Toni leaned over the crowd with one foot on a monitor at the edge of the stage, her waist-length dreads whipping around her head. She growled the lyrics into the mic, holding the fans in the palm of her hand as they shouted along with her vocal. Dia and Nori shared the stage to Rhynn's left.

Rhynn let the rhythms flow through her. Her hands felt good. The music directed her body. The syncopated bass drum pattern matched Dia's heavy guitar line while Rhynn laid out the meter on cymbal and snare.

It felt wonderful to play and to hear the crowd cheering. Rhynn sucked in the energy and pushed back more of her own. Triumph, passion, and aggression swelled in her chest. Her sticks flew across the pads with comfortable ease, and she laughed out loud.

Toni kept the crowd screaming, fists pumping in the air as they leaned against the stage.

A flurry of movement caught Rhynn's attention.

Morgan Rahn sprinted past Dia and launched herself headfirst into the crowd in front of the stage. A pulse ray shot toward the ceiling as Morgan disappeared into the bodies. An instant later other security was in the mix as well.

Rhynn kept playing. They all did. Toni, Dia, Nori, and Ari moved toward midstage.

Rhynn glanced to the side and saw J'Nell with two other reporters who'd had stage passes. J'Nell seemed focused on the action down front. Beside her, Alyson Petri was wide-eyed and gripping Rip Thrashman's arm.

Rhynn didn't have time to keep looking. They hit the bridge and she had to concentrate on getting the syncopation right. Ari walked to the edge of the drum platform, a question on her face.

Rhynn shrugged as she played. She didn't know what was going on either.

Ship security pulled a guy out of the crowd. Morgan limped behind them, supported by Athenon. Rhynn decided, judging by the lack of crowd reaction, it was likely just another fight at a slam-thrash show.

The band finished their set and twice the usual number of security rushed them off stage and down to the dressing room. Ship security officers lined the back hall, and Del Marin slammed the door behind them once they were inside. The room was empty other than the band, a handful of roadies and WR security.

Toni was the first to ask, "What the fuck was going on in the pit?"

Del pushed away from the closed door. "Morgan took out some yahoo with a one-shot disposable laser pulse pistol."

The blood drained from Ari's face and Rhynn wrapped a comforting arm around her shoulders.

Del cocked her head, listening to the com receiver in her ear. She reached behind her and opened the door.

Shaine Wendt marched in and immediately scanned the room.

"Everyone okay?" she asked.

"Sure," Nori said, "but what's going on? Is Morgan okay?"

"Morgan's fine. No encores tonight. Show's officially over."

"Someone tried to shoot us?" Dia asked. "Was that the flash of light we saw?"

Shaine said, "He said he was supposed to shoot Ari. He's all wired up on toxins. Had a chit for ten thousand credits in his pocket. He said he got the gun and the chits from a hooded guy who said the gun was a fake and it was part of a staged setup and the band knew about it."

"Who was the guy in the hood?" Toni asked.

"We don't know yet. The gunman said the voice was rough and gravelly. He didn't see a face, because the bar they met in was dark."

Rhynn said, "I thought everyone was being checked for weapons?"

"They were. Problem with those little dispo pistols is sometimes they slip through. Not enough metal in them, not enough of a charge cell to register."

"How in the hell did Morgan see him?" Nori asked.

Del muttered, "She's fucking magic."

Shaine shot Del a glare. "He wasn't acting like part of the crowd. He wasn't part of the slam circle in the pit and he wasn't paying attention to Toni. When he moved to take the gun from his jacket, she saw it as suspicious and took a stage dive at him."

Ari sat heavily on the sofa, pulling Rhynn down with her. Rhynn held Ari's trembling body close. "This is getting out of hand. I don't know if we should even be playing any more shows."

Shaine said, "We can talk about it. On the upside, this was the last show for the cruise. We dock tomorrow at Luna City. I talked to Tigri at OAI. He said they're very close to getting that deposit tracked, so hopefully we'll have definitive suspect soon."

Toni asked, "What about all those interviews you guys were doing? What about Panther?"

Shaine scowled. "She's still at the top of the list. We have suspicions, but no solid evidence. Hopefully Tigri will come through."

CHAPTER FIFTY-TWO

Earth Date: November 2453
Cruise Ship *Star Rider*

Ari

Shaine, Morgan, Del, Mitch, Rae, and Ben escorted us back to our suite, sticking to the maintenance and staff access corridors as much as possible. When we were forced to traverse the passenger hallways, I scanned the crowd looking for attackers who probably didn't exist. What I wanted to do was pull a hood over my head and run. Or hide. As it was, security kept us in a tight group, with Rhynn and me on the inside. Rhynn never let go of my hand. Even Dia, Nori, and Toni looked worried as we hurried back to our suite.

Security entered first, even though they'd left Bagger and Jorge in the hallway the whole time and nobody had been in our rooms. After a thorough scan, they ushered us in.

Rather than scattering our separate ways, we collapsed in the common room. It was late. We were exhausted but no one wanted to sleep. Security brought sandwiches and snacks from the aborted after-party. I picked half-heartedly at some chips and dried fruit. Rhynn scarfed down a couple sandwiches.

We ate and rested in silence. Dia and Nori lay on opposite ends of the sofa. Toni sprawled on an oversize recliner while Rhynn and

I shared the second recliner. I curled up on her lap, wanting to be close and glad of the protective hold she kept around me.

Finally, Toni asked, "What are we going to do?"

Nori played with a napkin, folding and unfolding it. "What *can* we do?"

"I think we need to stop playing," Dia said. "So far, Ari and Rhynn have been lucky, but it's not worth it anymore."

Rhynn rested her hand on my arm, and I could feel the heat emanating from the tender skin of her palm. She said, "I'm not worried about me. I'm worried about Ari. Dia's right. Unless they can catch this person, we need to lay low and stay safe, even if it means not leaving this room."

"I agree," Nori said. "When it was letters and roses, that's one thing, but falling lights and guns and poison are too much. It's not worth putting Ari's and Rhynn's lives on the line."

I looked around at my bandmates, insanely grateful for their support. "Are you guys sure? We'll be in breach of contract if we don't play."

Toni snorted. "Fuck it. Let Wayne worry about it. We need to be alive to play. So, we all agree, we're not playing unless they catch the stalker? All in favor, raise a hand."

Everyone raised a hand.

Nori said, "We better call Wayne. He's going to flip out."

Dia got off the sofa and walked to the media console. She poked at the controls and seconds later, the vid screen flickered to life.

Wayne looked like he'd been sleeping. He squinted at us, bare chested and bleary eyed. "Girls. What's going on?"

Dia said, "We need to talk. There was another attempt on Ari tonight."

He woke up then, sitting up straight and alert. "Is she all right?"

Dia played with the console controls, and the picture-in-picture that showed what he was seeing widened to a view of all of us.

"I'm fine. Morgan Rahn stopped him, but it could easily have gone the other way." I shuddered, as though saying it made it more real and more possible.

Toni said, "We had a vote. We're not playing again until they catch the stalker. This is ridiculous. It's not worth Ari or Rhynn getting killed."

Wayne sighed heavily. "You only have a couple more shows on this tour. If you don't play, you'll be in breach of contract, and that's going to cost a shitload of money."

"Take it out of my paycheck," Nori snapped.

He glowered at her.

Toni said, "We're not budging on this, Wayne."

He stood. It looked like he was in his bedroom, though only the dim light from his com made him visible. "We can't overreact to the situation. I need to talk to Wendt and find out what's happening."

"Overreact?" Toni stalked toward the camera over the vid screen. "Fuck you! This is serious. We're locked in our room! We have security all over the damned place and a stalker is running loose who wants Ari and Rhynn dead! We're not risking going on stage until this guy is caught. End of story!"

"I'm calling Wendt. I'll get back to you." He killed the connection and the vid screen went black.

"Stupid ass," Toni muttered.

Rhynn said, "Not much more we can do tonight. We should get some sleep."

I glanced at her. "Ever the practical one."

"Yeah, something like that. Actually, I'm just wiped."

I frowned suddenly, feeling like a jerk. "Damn, I realized, in all this crap, I never asked how your hands were feeling?"

Rhynn kissed me briefly. "They're fine. Tender, but okay. No blood." To prove the fact, she slid her hands gently under my shirt and caressed my skin. I eased away and stood up, extending a hand to her. "Let's go to bed."

"Brilliant idea." She took my hand and got stiffly to her feet. I heard her knees pop as she rose.

Dia said, "I'm sure there's going to be a lot of sleeping going on in your room."

The others laughed.

Rhynn raised a brow. "You're just jealous. We promise to be quiet."

I snorted and followed Rhynn out of the room. She was going to be so pissed when I made her put her gel-mitts back on for the night.

CHAPTER FIFTY-THREE

Earth Date: November 2453
Cruise Ship *Star Rider*

Rhynn

Rhynn jammed clothes and toiletries into her suitcase without bothering to be neat, glad she hadn't over-packed and glad she wasn't a neat freak, because packing while wearing gel-filled mittens was not an exacting process. On the other hand, the good thing about being a drummer was her clothing needs were minimal. As she packed the last of her things and checked the room to make sure she hadn't forgotten anything, it felt too final and too soon.

Despite the danger, she wasn't ready for the adventure to end. Being on the cruise ship was something new in her otherwise predictable life. Everything was exciting and different—a once-in-a-lifetime opportunity she had never even dreamed would happen. She was part of the band now, but she hadn't had time to plan or think much about what happened after the tour. She'd been too focused on the here and now to consider the logistics of moving her life from Moon Base to Earth.

The realization that the cruise was ending forced her to consider the implications. What happened when it was time to leave Luna City? Did she go back to her apartment on Moon Base? Was she supposed to go straight to Earth with the band? She and Ari had talked vaguely about Rhynn moving into the band house. They could take the room Ari now shared with Nori, and Nori would move into Stacy's old room.

But Rhynn hadn't had time to do anything other than tell her friends and her mom that she was officially part of the band. She and Leigh had an apartment. She had stuff she'd need to take with her. And what about her mom? And her band? She'd be leaving Black Plague without a drummer. At least she didn't have a job she would have to quit, but, damn. How did this all work out?

Rhynn sat on the edge of her bed, leaning her elbows on her knees.

So much change. So much to consider.

Only two things remained clear in her mind. She needed to be with Ari. And playing with SCE was a chance she had to take.

The Universe had put her in this place, in this moment. Her mom would say that Fate was Truth.

She only hoped they survived the rest of the tour.

CHAPTER FIFTY-FOUR

Earth Date: November 2453
Cruise Ship *Star Rider*

Shaine and Morgan

Gohste's fingers flitted across the keyboard. Morgan watched over his shoulder as data scrolled up the screen. She didn't understand much of what she saw, but based on the intensity of his expression, he was onto something.

"Morning." Shaine sauntered over, kissing Morgan's cheek. "What'cha got, Gohste?"

"Bank accounts. I finally found the right trail. I'm almost in."

Morgan glanced back at her partner. "What was Neutron bitching about last night before I fell asleep?"

"Demanding to know why we haven't caught the bad guy, why someone is still stalking his guitarist, and what we're going to do about it. I told him, we're security, not the System Investigation Bureau, and the authorities are working on it. Apparently the band told him they're not doing any more gigs until this is resolved, so he's losing his mind."

"Those girls have guts. They were seriously spooked last night, though. Hell, so was I."

Shaine hugged Morgan from behind. "Don't scare the piss out of me like that again. Fuck. All I saw was you diving off the stage and I had no idea what was happening."

"Sorry."

"You're very brave, love."

"Or very stupid. Either way, you're stuck with me."

"Do you hear me complaining?"

"You just did, Shaine."

Gohste muttered, "Got it."

The screen cleared, showing a flow chart of about two dozen accounts, all feeding into each other, the trail crossing back over itself and ending, finally, at a name.

"Fuck me," Morgan muttered.

Shaine blew out a long breath as Gohste leaned back. "I saved the whole trace to a data chip."

Shaine said, "We need to tell the band. And call Tigri at the OAI. And City Security and the System Investigations Bureau in Luna City."

Morgan glanced at the chron on the wall. "We need to hurry. The road crew is already loading out and we're bringing the band down to the shuttle in about half an hour."

CHAPTER FIFTY-FIVE

Earth Date: November 2453
Cruise Ship *Star Rider*

Rhynn

Rhynn hated waiting when all she wanted to do was get on with it. She lounged on the sofa with her feet up on the coffee table. Ari curled up with her head pillowed on Rhynn's lap. The whole band lay around the common room, waiting until it was time to board the shuttle to Luna City. Her bandmates seemed tired and subdued, much as she felt. She wondered if the mood was always this low at the end of a tour, or if this was just that much worse than normal.

She combed her fingers through Ari's hair, appreciating the soft texture of it between her still-healing fingertips. It reminded her yet again how the chemical burns on her hands could have ended her career. The poison had nearly ended her life. She hadn't let herself dwell on that very much. She thought about the lighting unit nearly falling on Ari and the gunman who'd missed thanks to Morgan. She smoothed the hair under her hand, traced the gentle curve of Ari's brow. A heart-stopping wave of emotion crashed over her, creating an ache in her chest that took her breath away.

Goddess, if Ari'd been killed… Having Ari ripped away would destroy her. *I love her. Oh, goddess, I love her.*

A knock on the door interrupted her thoughts.

Dia jumped up. "I'll get it." She checked the vid monitor at the side of the door and cleared the lock. Shaine and Morgan stepped into the room.

Dia asked, "Is it time to head for the shuttle?"

Shaine said, "Not yet, but we need to talk."

Nori's dark brows furrowed. "That sounds serious."

Morgan said, "It is serious. We know who the stalker is."

Ari sat up.

Toni asked, "Who?"

"Someone you know very well. J'Nell Inagayl."

Ari sucked in a breath of air. "But she's a friend."

Morgan said, "The payment came from an account in her name."

"We alerted ship security, but she already disembarked," Shaine said. "I've contacted the SIB and the local Out-System Authorities in Luna City. There's an APB out for her. She can't get far."

"Fucking hell," Toni swore. "That's insane. She's been in our rooms."

Nori frowned. "What about Panther? I thought she was your number one suspect?"

"On paper it sure looked that way, but when we talked with her we knew she wasn't the one. She had no motive, and some good reasons not to advertise her past. All legitimate. Turns out that Inagayl has lots of military contacts too. Being a reporter, knowing as many people as she does, she's good at gathering her resources. And based on some of the bank accounts she was using, she has a lot of money from some pretty sketchy places. Did she ever tell you she did undercover investigation for that military magazine she was with? She's a smart cookie."

"But why stalk me?" Ari asked. "All she has to do is call. I mean, I consider her a friend."

Nori said, "We've known her for years. Talked to her. She's been at the house. At shows. She's so normal."

Shaine said, "Stalkers tend to hide in plain sight."

Ari rubbed her hands over her face. "I knew her when we were kids. We were friends. I don't understand. If she was that in love with me, why didn't she ever say anything?" She shook her head.

Morgan said, "Maybe because she knew you'd never see her as more than just a friend. The only way she could have you was through a fantasy."

Dia added, "Think about it. Sure, you've been in touch, but it's not like you spent any real time together, you know? You never hung out, just talked from time to time, mostly at clubs."

Toni scratched her head. "And when the light fell, she pulled you out of the way because she knew where it was. Nobody ever checked her for a detonator or anything. Maybe she was trying to save the day, get your notice, because you were all focused on Rhynn. I mean, we'd told her how you guys were working together, and then she sees you guys coming out of the bedroom and finds out you're a couple."

"She was right here." Ari shuddered violently and Rhynn pulled her close, wanting to comfort her and erase the fear and horror painted on her face. Ari clung to her and burrowed against Rhynn's shoulder.

Morgan said, "We'll escort you to the shuttle bay in about five minutes."

"Has anyone let Wayne know?" Toni asked.

Shaine said, "That's next on my list. I wanted to talk to you first."

"If they catch her and we know we're going to be safe on stage," Toni said, "we'll do the gig."

"But we need to know it's safe," Nori said.

Morgan nodded. "Agreed."

CHAPTER FIFTY-SIX

Earth Date: November 2453
Cruise Ship *Star Rider*

Rhynn

The transport shuttle swooped away from the cruise ship *Star Rider* and soared through space toward Luna City, which sprawled at the edge of the dark side of the moon. Ari sat in a window seat with her forehead pressed to the portal while Rhynn leaned around her to peer down at the riot of colorful lights from the tight cluster of buildings below. Unlike Moon Base, Luna City had no dome. Instead, the individual buildings were sealed against space and connected by both underground tunnels and aboveground walkway tubes like a hamster habitat.

Modeled after the famed Las Vegas Strip of centuries past, bright lights and gaudy neon blinked and flashed, tracing skyscraping monuments of all shapes and sizes. Rhynn picked out Midas's Castle, the Golden Pyramids and the Super Space Needle, which soared well above the rest.

Rhynn had been to Luna City a couple times with her friends and her band. Shuttling out to Luna City was a rite of passage if you grew up on Moon Base. Most of the buildings were themed casino hotels, each with its own stage shows and glamour, upscale restaurants and downscale buffets, shopping centers, and clubs. Full-time residents lived in huge complexes on the outskirts of the city. In addition to the skyway tubes, elevated high-speed rail lines transformed the city into a spiderweb of connections.

Ari said, "I've never been here."

Rhynn gazed into the lights, flashes of memories ignited by signs and shapes she'd seen before. "It's an experience. Very glitzy with an undertone of sleaze. I've never stayed at the big casinos. None of us could afford those, but we'd go in and poke around, you know? Black Plague played a multi-band show at a dive club on the outskirts a couple times. It was such a dump. We weren't sure if life support was going to hold out."

"You'll have to tell me your adventures sometime."

"This whole place is made to seem larger than life."

"Why no dome?"

"They wanted a skyline that didn't limit the size and height of the buildings. I suppose it was created for theatrical effect, not a working spaceport like Moon Base."

Rhynn pointed as they banked toward two circular towers wrapped in spirals of blue neon. The taller one had a flashing electric blue crescent moon balanced on a thin spindle at its apex. "That's where we're staying. The Blue Moon. Wonder how far up the tower they put us. The higher you go, the fancier the rooms are."

Behind them, Dia snorted. "If Wayne booked it, it'll be a suite in the basement."

Rhynn watched out the window as the shuttle eased into the docking bay midway up the taller tower. Before stopping, they rumbled past a line of cargo shuttles and what looked to Rhynn like personal aircars.

The band, along with Friday, disembarked via the main boarding ramp, while their road crew unloaded equipment from the shuttle's rear cargo compartment onto hover-carts.

The WR security team stuck close to the band at the bottom of the boarding ramp. A docking crew worker brought a hover-cart for their personal luggage.

Shaine, Morgan, and Del stood a few meters apart from the rest of the security contingent, speaking to a group of uniformed personnel. Rhynn recognized the steel gray Out-System Authority uniforms and assumed the two men wearing royal blue ship suits with the Blue Moon logo on the upper arm were casino security. Del and Morgan wore street clothes, blending in with the band's road crew, while Shaine sported black fatigues with the WR logo on the arm.

After a few minutes, Shaine and Morgan approached the band with the two in-house security officers. Shaine gestured for the band to gather around her. "No sign yet of J'Nell. Out-System Authorities are actively searching for her. Blue Moon secured the concert hall."

"I wish I felt better about this," Nori muttered.

Morgan glanced at her. "Shaine and I, and Blue Moon officers Yemke and Lawrence will accompany you to your suite. The rooms have been scanned and secured. Blue Moon has handled security for all manner of politicos and entertainment stars."

A wry smile twisted Dia's lips. "In other words, we're minor players on their roster."

One of the two officers, with "Yemke" stitched on his name patch, said, "No, ma'am. Not minor at all. In fact, we're honored to be of service. We're both fans."

Lacking necks and built like tanks, Yemke and Lawrence had to be upward of two meters in height. Their muscular chests and arms bulged under the tight-fitting material of their uniforms. Rhynn decided she felt somewhat reassured. It didn't hurt that both men carried stun guns in thigh holsters.

Shaine said, "Everyone stay close."

Lawrence and Shaine led the group toward a service elevator. Nori and Dia guided the hover-cart stacked with the band's luggage and Ari's favorite guitar. Toni, Friday, Rhynn, and Ari followed while Morgan and Officer Yemke brought up the rear.

Lawrence said, "You're staying in the second tower, so we'll go down to the fiftieth floor and take the skyway across."

Dia said, "I told you Wayne wouldn't spring for the good rooms."

"The suites for you and your road crew and the security detachment are very nice. They have in-room hot tubs."

Toni laughed. "Good to know."

They were immediately assaulted by a crowded cacophony as the elevator opened onto a wide, brightly lit, blue-tiled corridor lined with tourist trap convenience shops and food vendors. People wandered almost shoulder-to-shoulder between the shops, with music piped in over a hidden sound system. At the far end, almost a city block away, a clear glassteel walkway crossed to the next tower. Breaking up the center of the corridor, clusters of gambling kiosks clanged and pinged and flashed while people laughed and cheered or stood seriously making their bets.

Rhynn held Ari's hand in a loose grip, feeling more overwhelmed than she'd expected as she took in her surroundings. The last time she'd been in Luna City, she'd been a nameless face in the crowd, one of any number of anonymous tourists seeing the sights with her friends. She hadn't been in the Blue Moon towers, but she'd wandered a few of the other casinos.

If you saw one casino, you'd seen them all—the bright lights, the loud jangling of the gambling machines, the rumble of the crowd, the clashing odors of exotic foods, the sharp odor of too many people in an enclosed space. The smaller casinos and the dives that she'd played were like that, their life support systems barely able to keep up with the needs of too many people and the exhaust from illicit smoking dens tucked into the outskirts.

To Rhynn, the wide corridors through the Blue Moon Casino felt only vaguely familiar. On edge, she felt hyper-aware of people assessing her and her bandmates, perhaps wondering why they were surrounded by armed security officers. Rhynn was pretty sure she and her friends didn't look like they deserved security.

More likely, tourists probably thought the crowd was being protected from the rough-looking musicians, rather than the other way around. Even Dia and Nori, with their black leggings and colorful cut-off shirts had a dangerous edge of attitude. Toni's leather pants and tight white tank showed off tattoos and muscle. Her wildly colored dreads hung down her back and swung as she moved confidently.

Still, there didn't seem to be any recognition in the looks they got. Slam-thrash bands didn't rate very high in the mainstream entertainment echelon. They had their fans, but they weren't part of mainstream culture.

Dia slowed as they passed a flashy gift shop filled with Blue Moon Casino souvenirs. "Hey, can we stop for a T-shirt?"

Shaine glanced over her shoulder. "I don't think this is a good time."

Dia pouted and Nori elbowed her with a grin. "You're such a kid, Dee."

"Shut up. I know you want one too."

Morgan said, "You'll have time to play tourist after the show."

"We can get ya a good deal. I know a few of the sellers," Yemke said.

Dia twirled and walked backward, giving him a flirty smile, "I'm gonna hold you to that, big boy."

Yemke blushed like a sixteen-year-old. "Sure."

Shaine put a hand to her ear, probably listening to her in-ear com, then flashed back a quick hand signal.

Morgan dropped back from the group.

Toni asked, "You guys think Wayne is going to make it for the show?"

"He'll be here," Ari said. "If for no other reason than to make sure we don't bail on him."

Nori said, "We should put Toni's song into the lineup."

Rhynn asked, "Which one?"

Ari laughed. "'Disposable.' Wayne hates it."

Rhynn had to think to place the song, then smiled. The lyrics were angry anti-corporate, anti-management, the guitar riff dark and heavy and lightning fast.

At the end of the corridor, they entered the clear glassteel skyway between the two towers. Rhynn felt a slight rush of vertigo as she stepped into the tube. The clear blue glassteel tiles made it seem like the floor dropped from under her feet. She almost stumbled before regaining her sense of balance.

The lights of Luna City illuminated the skyline—flashing neon designs and LEDs, full color video billboards selling products and promising entertainment and riches. The light and color glared wildly against the black of space.

"Holy shit," Dia muttered, stopping to turn in place, wide-eyed.

"You are such a tourist," Toni teased her. "Keep moving, keep moving, we're holding up traffic."

"You are such a bitch."

"There's a 360-degree view on top of the space needle at the Seven Wonders Casino," Rhynn said. "We could—"

A deafening explosion cut off her words as the floor dropped out from under her.

CHAPTER FIFTY-SEVEN

Earth Date: November 2453
Luna City

Morgan

Morgan saw Shaine's flashed hand signal and dropped back from the group before they reached the skyway entrance.

Gohste's voice buzzed urgently in her earpiece. "Morgan, behind you, seven o'clock, Moonie Gifts shop."

Morgan slowed to look at some T-shirts and tunics at a kiosk, casually easing around, scanning for J'Nell Inagayl. She strolled behind a gambling kiosk and weaved through the crowd, stopping at the store next to Moonie Gifts. They'd planned well, having her in street clothes, allowing her to blend in as she worked her way to the display in front of Moonie Gifts. Gohste said, "She's in the back of the store. Two undercover security coming in on your left."

Morgan grunted an acknowledgment under her breath. She glanced past the rack of travel bags with Blue Moon logos. Two not-so-under-cover security loitered on the other side of the entrance. Big, muscular guys. She almost rolled her eyes. What was it about security companies that made them think size was more important than brains? She was glad Shaine didn't operate that way.

She pretended to peruse a rack of wildly printed tunics at the edge of the store. Out of the corner of her eye, she watched Inagayl pass between the aisles, picking up trinkets, putting them down, moving toward the entrance.

Inagayl stepped out of the store. Her white-blond hair shone in the glaring hallway lighting. Morgan kept her head down and watched out of the corner of her eye. Her instinct was to tackle the bitch, but she waited. Her muscles tensed as she stepped around the rack of shirts and took a step toward Inagayl.

Gohste reported, "Band is in the skyway. Security is moving in."

J'Nell's pale eyes tracked toward the skyway tunnel with a cold, hard expression. Morgan stepped within arm's reach of her. Inagayl reached into her pocket and muttered something under her breath.

Morgan launched herself forward.

A shockwave of sound and energy slammed her face down into the floor just as her fingertips touched Inagayl's arm.

CHAPTER FIFTY-EIGHT

Earth Date: November 2453
Luna City

Ari

I laughed at Dia as she stared wide-eyed at the flashing lights and glitter of Luna City. I would have been right there with her, but I was still too uptight about the situation with J'Nell to be able to feel her sense of wonder. I leaned into Rhynn, giving her hand a gentle squeeze, glad to have her beside me.

I didn't understand why in the hell J'Nell was doing this to me. I'd always been a friend to her. I'd stood up for her when we were kids. I'd been her friend when she had none. I'd been thinking hard about those times. When she'd left, she'd been so heartbroken. I'd missed her, but thinking back, her messages had been so sad, so much more distressed, while I had moved on with my life. When she popped back into my life as a music reporter, the band gladly did interviews with her. I tried to remember what our early interactions had been like, but so much of that time was a blur of gigs and the drama of being a young musician sowing my wild oats.

I'd never flirted with J'Nell. Dia had. Hell, Dia flirted with everyone. There was no sexual tension between J'Nell and me. She never gave any clue she was interested, let alone obsessed with me.

I don't remember her ever asking me out. Still, she always seemed to know where we were playing, and what we were up to. She never seemed surprised to run into me in clubs when I was out seeing other bands. I suppose she'd been following me even back then. Maybe the fact that I wasn't interested is what spurred her interest.

Even with all the security around us, I assessed the people around me and Rhynn. Who had a gun? Who might J'Nell have hired to attack us? I was more afraid for Rhynn than myself. It was my fault Rhynn was in J'Nell's sights. It was my fault, but I couldn't stop being with Rhynn. I wanted to be near her, to touch her, to feel her presence. Rhynn had so much confidence and strength. I loved the way she held herself, the way she simply did her thing, not pretending to be anyone other than who she was.

When she played, I felt her passion. I heard the brilliance and the force of her personality. I fell in love with her drumming as quickly as I fell in love with her. I loved the physicality of her energy as she played, seeing how much she enjoyed the act of playing and lost herself in the music. I loved her graceful power and intensity. She had a tough, practical, and laid-back exterior. But I knew instinctively that she hid so much more under the surface.

Toni teased Dia about being a tourist and Rhynn said, "There's a 360-degree view on top of the space needle at the Seven Wonders Casino. We could—"

The explosion was deafening. The shockwave threw me forward even as the floor dropped out from under us. I grabbed for Rhynn.

We hit the slick tile, sliding downward. Sharp pain slashed into my back, but I only had a second to wonder what hit me before my head slammed against the floor, shattering my vision with stars.

CHAPTER FIFTY-NINE

Earth Date: November 2453
Luna City

Morgan

"Morgan! Morgan, can you hear me? Morgan!"

Shaine's voice finally broke into Morgan's consciousness.

Fuck. Morgan lay on her stomach, letting the pain roll over and through her. Her whole body felt bruised.

The screech of alarms sounded over people screaming and shouts of panicked voices. She tried to shift and realized something heavy lay across her back.

Explosion.

She had a moment of heart-stopping panic before she realized she was breathing. There was air, and it wasn't being sucked away from her. No atmosphere breach, then.

"Morgan! Answer me! Are you there?"

Shaine! She tried to push to her feet. Table, she thought. Table fell on me.

Swallowing, clearing her throat, she forced strangled words into the mic. "Shaine? Are you okay? Is Friday okay?"

"We're in the skyway. It's holding for now. Are you all right?"

Morgan gritted her teeth and wriggled from under the broken table.

Red and blue emergency lights flashed through the smoky haze. The entrance to the tunnel was sealed, though the airlock door hadn't completely closed. White instant sealant puffed like a solid, deformed marshmallow along the bottom of the door, maybe a meter up from the floor.

To Morgan's left someone groaned. A man lay with a piece of ceiling lighting trapping his legs. She looked toward where J'Nell Inagayl had been. A shock of white-blond hair was visible in the rubble half a body length away.

If you're not already dead, I'm gonna beat the shit out of you, you dumb-ass bitch.

Stiffly, Morgan climbed to her feet. She muttered into her mic, "Inagayl's here." Shoving through the debris in front of the shattered storefront, aware of the shouting and confusion around her, she focused on the white hair.

Inagayl struggled to disengage from a clothing rack that had toppled on her. Morgan grabbed it and threw it aside. Inagayl blinked blearily for a second before her expression hardened and she lurched to her feet.

Morgan slammed her shoulder into Inagayl's gut, knocking them both back to the floor with a painful thud. "Fucking bitch."

Inagayl twisted wildly, freeing her arms. Morgan ducked away from a wild fist coming at her face, then jabbed a solid right to Inagayl's jaw, bouncing her head off the floor, and her eyes rolled back in her head.

Morgan shook out her fist, relieved to see the two hulking security guards coming toward her. Other uniformed security personnel filtered into the area. She made sure Inagayl was still out and said, "Shaine, I've got Inagayl. Security is on its way."

"Great job, hon. Now we need to figure out how to get us out of here before we run out of heat and air."

"Is anyone hurt?"

"Nothing life-threatening."

Gohste's voice crackled in Morgan's earpiece. "An evac team is on the way to the skyway airlock near you. ETA two minutes."

Morgan peered through the clinging haze toward the skyway entrance ten meters away. Even at this distance and through the eddying smoke, it was obvious the explosion had left the airlock controls a charred mess of plastic and metal. "I don't think you're going to get out of the skyway from this side, Shaine. The airlock is toast."

"And the skyway tube broke away and slid down from the hatch. Just auto-sealant and prayers between us and vacuum, Morg."

Fear twisted Morgan's stomach into wicked knots, her heart aching as images of her wife and her foster daughter flashed behind her eyes. She needed to do something. Now.

CHAPTER SIXTY

Earth Date: November 2453
Luna City

Rhynn

The violence of the explosion hurled Rhynn forward. The tunnel scraped down the outside of the building wall with a piercing shriek of stressed metal and the wild popping of power leads being ripped apart. Rhynn scrabbled desperately to stop or slow her slide down the sloping floor but landed hard in a pile of people and luggage. As she reoriented her brain and her senses, she heard people shouting and moaning over the uneasy creak of metal and plastic. The air smelled of burnt plastic, electrons, and smoke.

She sucked in a breath and coughed from the sharp tang of smoke. Air. They had air. But the smoke was not a good thing.

Rhynn assessed her situation. Hands and feet wriggled without eliciting any jarring pains. The soft surface under her middle was Ari, sprawled beneath her, eyes closed, but at least she could feel the slight rise and fall of her chest. She lifted herself off Ari, pushing to hands and knees with a sharp jab of pain from the pressure to her palms and still-healing knee stitches.

Ari groaned.

"Ari? You okay?" Rhynn lifted a hand to gently caress her cheek, grimacing when she left a bloody mark along Ari's smooth skin.

"I think so."

Ari sat up gingerly, blinking and looking around. A trickle of blood rolled down from her hairline.

"You're hurt," Rhynn said.

Ari shook her head. "I'm okay." She locked her fingers around Rhynn's wrists with a concerned frown. "You're bleeding."

Rhynn shrugged. She picked out her bandmates, all moving now. Ignoring the pain in her hands, she crawled to Dia, lifting a couple of suitcases off her. Barely a meter to her right, the hover-cart lay on its side, their luggage strewn around them. Through the dim red glow of emergency lighting and the flashing neon lights of the city, she identified the rest of their group, starting to shift and dazedly look around.

The force of the explosion had canted the skyway to a forty-five-degree angle. On the higher side, the tube was bent, the glassteel stretched and warped. Auto-sealant covered the skyway's connection to the closed air-lock hatch leading to the smaller tower. The lower end of the skyway where Rhynn and the others landed had blown loose and slid down almost two meters, blocking the top of the airlock hatch which was mostly covered by solidified foam sealant filled in around the edges of the skyway.

A man bolted to his feet, scrambling up the tilted walkway. "We gotta get out of here!" he shouted, his voice high with panic. Two other men started to follow.

A sharp snap-bang of metal cracked into the quiet and the floor abruptly dropped another few centimeters with a squeal of stressed metal and the weak hiss of whatever sealant remained to fill in the space. A scream of fear echoed off the glassteel. The three men froze, and everyone seemed to hold their breath. Rhynn's heart slammed against her ribs.

The emergency lighting flickered and went out, leaving only the shadowy flashing light from the city's neon.

Shaine Wendt's authoritative voice sounded confidently in the dark. "Everybody stay put and relax! They're sending a rescue team!"

"We're trapped! We'll run out of air and die!" The man started scrambling up toward the door again, lost his footing and skated backward. He fell into the hover-cart, bumping it against the foam-covered outside wall.

The skyway creaked and settled again.

Shaine yelled, “Everyone calm down! Stay still. We’re going to get out.”

Rhynn counted a dozen people in the shifted walkway with no running life support. Would the walkway hold in place until they could be rescued? If it continued to drop, when would the glassteel or the sealant finally give? Even a tiny crack would suck out what little air remained. Icy fear shuddered through her.

CHAPTER SIXTY-ONE

Earth Date: November 2453
Luna City

Morgan

"Thanks, guys," Morgan said as the two undercover officers pulled a securely handcuffed J'Nell Inagayl to her feet. Morgan flexed her sore knuckles.

Inagayl glowered at her, wild hatred burning in her eyes. "They're going to die," she hissed. "All of them. She thinks she's too good for me. She's not good enough. And the other bitch can die with her."

A shudder of fear ran through Morgan, but it wasn't fear of J'Nell Inagayl. It was fear for her wife and Friday and everyone else trapped in the skyway.

The guards led Inagayl away. Morgan was pleased to note that she was barely walking on her own. Good. Fucking bitch.

"Rahn!"

Del Marin scrambled through the chaos with two burly Out-System Authority officers in her wake.

Morgan lifted an arm, glad to see a familiar face. As they approached, she pointed to a black box, smaller than the size of her palm, resting on the floor. "Pretty sure that's the detonator," she said. "I don't have anything to grab it with and I didn't want to get any prints on it."

Del pulled a plastic bag from a pocket and retrieved the small component. She passed the bag to one of the security officers.

"Thanks, ma'am. We'll take care of it."

Morgan and Del picked a path through the debris-littered corridor toward a group of emergency personnel huddled around the damaged airlock hatch. Morgan looked through the dust-hazed portals on either side of the hatch to see a small emergency air-car hovering above the skyway.

As she and Del approached the emergency crew, one of the men spoke into a com unit. "Try to keep everyone quiet in there. The sealant is holding, but it's not made to support a lot of movement."

Shaine's voice crackled over the tiny speaker hooked on his shoulder epaulet. "Roger that. We've got minor injuries only. The danger is the increasing cold and lack of life support."

Morgan felt a wash of relief hearing the calm, controlled tone of Shaine's voice. She barged her way through the men, stopping in front of the big man with a mop of blond hair. She noted that he wore commander's bars, but that didn't stop her from saying, "We need a plan to get them out."

He blinked down at her. "Who the hell are you?"

Shaine's voice came over the com. "Morgan?"

The commander frowned, sharp eyes flicking over Morgan. She looked him up and down in return. The name-patch on his chest read "BENTON."

Morgan said, "Yeah, it's Morgan."

"She's my second, Benton, so keep her looped in."

Shaking his head, Benton said, "Sure. We're trying to decide how to stabilize the walkway."

Morgan asked, "Can you shut down the local gravity well, or even lower the power closer to zero-g? That would take the pressure off the seals."

Benton snorted. "And have everything within a half kilometer floating all over the place? I don't think so."

Morgan wanted to smack him. "They do it on Moon Base, out at the docks complex. They manipulate the surrounding wells and minimize the area of zero-g."

"Hell of a lot less people there than here."

Shaine broke in. "Air is okay right now. My comp says maybe another forty minutes before we start having real issues. But the temperature is dropping, which will be a problem a lot sooner."

Morgan swallowed. The clock had officially started.

CHAPTER SIXTY-TWO

Earth Date: November 2453
Luna City

Ari

A growing blanket of frost crystallized over the skyway's clear glassteel, dimming the gaudy neon and the pulsing red and blue lights from the emergency vehicles circling above. The faded colors reminded me of being in a dance cube with a fog machine running.

Minus the sound.

The quiet was nerve-racking. The comforting hum of life support was completely missing. I could hear the ringing in my ears. The glassteel creaked ominously, probably both because of the explosive damage and because the metal cooled quickly without heat from the life-support system.

To my left, Shaine spoke quietly into her com, frowning as she worked on her comp pad.

Rhynn and I ended up half sitting, half laying on the cold tile, steadying ourselves on the angled surface with our feet braced against the foam sealant rising a meter or so from the floor and covering the blue-tinted glassteel that was the outside of the building. The skyway had dropped a good two meters. Thank the Goddess the sealant had halted the skyway's movement, but it left only a bare meter of the hatch visible and no way to open the sealed airlock unless there was a way to cut through it.

I shivered. The temperature had already dropped sharply. Cut off from heat and life-support, our time was severely limited.

I held Rhynn as she sat between my longer legs. Her hands rested palm up in her lap. I nuzzled her hair and kissed the base of her neck. She relaxed against me and I pulled her closer, trying to keep some heat between us. I murmured, “How’s the hands?”

“They’ll be fine.”

I didn’t bother arguing with her. The reddened skin on her palms wept droplets of clear fluid and blood. I was sure she was in pain, but there was nothing either of us could do about it.

I squinted through the skyway ceiling as an emergency vehicle eased closer. A blinding searchlight traveled the length of the skyway, lingering first where the glassteel tube bent down from the hatch above us and then focusing on the damage where the skyway was sealed against the outside wall at our feet.

The vehicle dropped lower. I felt as much as heard the force of its engines as it came closer, then pushed up and away. The skyway shuddered and groaned with the pressure from the hover-jets.

A chorus of screams broke the silence. I froze in place and held my breath.

Shaine barked, “Benton, keep those assholes at a distance!”

“What the fuck are those idiots thinking?” Rhynn muttered.

I asked, “How are they going to get us out of this?” My voice sounded pathetically weak and whiny.

Rhynn pressed her wrists against my arms, making contact without using her hands. “I wish I knew.”

CHAPTER SIXTY-THREE

Earth Date: November 2453
Luna City

Morgan

Benton watched scrolling text on his comp pad as he listened to the voices on the external com speaker on his shoulder. He said, "We'll have to get to you from the outside."

Shaine's voice cracked from the speaker. "What if you dropped a rescue tube from one of the skiffs?"

"Risky. Have to be long enough to keep the skiff's thrusters from putting pressure on the skyway."

Morgan said, "You can seal two tubes together to give you the length. Probably need at least fifteen meters, preferably twenty. Send someone down in a suit, tied off to the skiff so they're not putting any weight on the skyway. Seal the tube to the skyway. You'd have to back-fill atmosphere into the tube with enough air pressure to push air into the skyway too. Then cut a hole in the skyway ceiling. Hang a cord ladder down and pull everyone up and out."

Benton looked at her like she was crazy. "The skiffs are weight limited, you know. You'd need to use a narrow rescue tube. Guy like me in a suit would barely fit with room to work."

Morgan rolled her eyes. These guys were slow. She'd already worked out the logistics. "Then send me. I'm half your damn size. I know my way around a laser cutter, sealant, and working in space."

Benton stared at her.

Del Marin sad, "Morgan's a fully trained systems maintenance tech. She's not shitting you."

Morgan growled impatiently. They were wasting time. "Let's do this, now, before my wife and kid are dead because you're wasting time fucking around."

Fifteen minutes later, in the Blue Moon landing bay, Morgan waited at the base of the boarding ramp to a med-evac skiff. The hover-jet engines idled as techs called out last-minute checks. She wore a full vacuum suit for space, the helmet on the floor at her feet. She flipped through the diagnostic screens on the built-in control readout on the back of her left wrist. The diagnostics were similar to those on the specialized work suit she'd used on Moon Base. Her old suit was a lot more technical, but the minimal rig the evac team provided was lighter and more flexible, which worked for what she needed to do.

Benton and Del jogged across the docking bay with an evac tech wearing a vac suit and a personal thruster harness.

As they reached her, Benton was talking into his com. "Wendt, you guys still hanging on in there?"

Shaine's voice sounded thin over his external speaker. "Temperature just below freezing and dropping fast. Nominal oxygen, no breaches."

Morgan heard the tension in her wife's tone.

Benton said, "We're about to load out. Sit tight."

"Right. Out."

Benton glanced around the group. "Let's go."

As Morgan picked up her helmet, Del laid a hand on the arm of her suit. "You be careful, girl. Get them out safe."

"Will do. See you in a bit." She followed Benton and the tech up the ramp, settling and sealing her helmet as she did. She perched on the bench along the skiff's outer wall, facing the rest of the evac team while she focused on the helmet's minimal heads-up display. Telemetry, including basic life support readings and suit diagnostics, scrolled across the upper part of the faceplate when she focused there. Her suit showed no breaches. Internal life-support nominal. The suit's canned air tasted slightly metallic and smelled faintly of sweat and stale cologne.

She used the wrist controls to flip through the com frequencies. "Shaine? You copy?"

A quick burst of static before Shaine's voice was in her ear. "I copy. You okay, Morg?"

"All good. Pulling away now, all suited up. Wanted to tell you I love you without the rest of the universe listening in."

"Love you too, sweetheart."

"Gonna get you and Fri out of there."

"I know. Getting damned cold. Temp is falling about a degree a minute. Running out of time, babe."

"I'm not going to let anything happen to you or Friday."

"I know. Love you, Morg."

"Love you too, Shaine."

Morgan blinked away tears, glad the tinted helmet glass hid her face, and flipped off the private channel, letting the voices of the evac team distract her from the anxiety building in her chest. The pilot talked to air traffic control, Benton and the others muttered quietly as they strapped in.

She noted the accordioned rescue tube sealed to the emergency hatch in the center of the skiff's floor. Morgan would drop with the rescue tube down to the skyway, controlling its fall using a safety wire connected to the winch at her waist. Her job was to connect the tubing to the skyway and cut a hole in the glassteel to get everyone out.

The other suited tech, Rich, would exit the skiff from the main airlock and use his thruster pack to fly down, monitor the rescue tubing and spray external foam sealant around its connection to the skyway. Once the tube was sealed, they could pump fresh air and heat into the skyway from the skiff.

They had to work fast. But they'd do it. They had to.

CHAPTER SIXTY-FOUR

Earth Date: November 2453
Luna City

Rhynn

Rhynn couldn't control the constant shivers running through her body. She sat between Ari's legs and they faced the outside wall of the Blue Moon tower with their feet braced against the frozen auto-sealant. Ari pressed her trembling body against Rhynn's back. She covered Ari's arms with her own, trying in vain to hold their heat in. Their breath puffed vapor clouds into the icy air.

Toni, Friday, Dia, and Nori, sitting in similar positions, crowded in beside them. Three men sat on the other side of Dia and Nori, awkwardly propped against the tipped luggage cart. Lawrence, Yemke, and Shaine huddled together and continued to communicate quietly with the evac team.

Even without hearing Shaine's report of the temperature, Rhynn felt it dropping. Her fingers and toes were numb. Her butt was numb. She clenched her jaw to try to keep her teeth from chattering.

An emergency vehicle passed over and momentarily bathed them in flashing red and blue light. Rhynn squinted through the frosted glassteel, barely able to see the shadow of the rescue skiff hovering well above them.

Ari whispered, "What are they doing?"

Rhynn shook her head. "Not sure."

The skyway echoed with an ominous creaking of metal.

Dia choked, "*Dios mio*!"

One of the men muttered, "Whatever they do, they better do it fast."

Shaine stood, slowly and carefully. "Everyone relax. They're going to seal a rescue tube to the skyway. They'll cut a hole and bring us up. Sit tight, okay?"

Rhynn swallowed, pulling Ari's arms tighter around herself. Her hands were so cold they had stopped bleeding and no longer hurt because they were mostly numb. After a lifetime living on Moon Base, freezing to death in space was not the way Rhynn wanted to go. Not when they were so close to safety. And not now. Not with the feather touch of Ari's breath on her neck. No. Rhynn was not ready to die.

She yawned and realized the air was getting saturated with carbon dioxide. If she was yawning, she was either not getting enough oxygen or succumbing to hypothermia. Or both.

She silently willed their rescuers to hurry.

CHAPTER SIXTY-FIVE

Earth Date: November 2453
Luna City

Morgan

Morgan halted the winch at her waist when she was within arm's reach of the skyway. She held the end of the rescue tube away from the glassteel.

"I'm in position, Benton. I'm going to lay the tube on the glassteel. When I say go, switch the magnets on for a seal."

"Roger that."

"Shaine, did you hear that?"

There was a pause and Morgan's heart raced with panic.

Finally, Shaine said, "Copy." Another pause. Shaine's voice sounded shaky and strained. "Hurry. Frostbite. Air stale."

"Hang on, almost there, baby." Morgan adjusted her grip on the edge of the rescue tube. With one boot hooked into a rung of the ladder built into the inside of the tube, she hung face down. Straightening her arms, she stretched the tube to the frosted glassteel of the walkway until it connected.

"Benton, magnets on."

"Copy. Magnets powered."

The indicator lights around the collar of the tube flashed from red to green as the electromagnets connected the tube to the glassteel. "The tube is secured. Rich?"

"Spraying sealant."

Morgan squinted through the frosted surface, searching for any sign of movement. "Benton, are you pumping air and heat down the tube?"

"Heat and O2 on full."

"Keep me updated. This suit has shit for external diagnostics, so I can't tell."

"It's an emergency suit, Rahn, not a working suit."

"Yeah, well, it sucks."

Benton snorted.

Morgan unclipped the laser cutter from her toolbelt. "Shaine, I'm going to start cutting through."

The silence was deafening as she waited for the reply. "Shaine? Shaine! Do you copy?"

No response.

Fuck.

She fired up the cutter and pressed the barrel against the glassteel. As her gloved fingers closed on the trigger, a thin blade of super-heated light melted into the clear twelve-centimeter thick metal until she felt the vibration that told her she was through.

Fighting to keep her hands from shaking with nervous tension, she guided the cutter carefully along the inside of the tube's collar, making the opening as large as she could without touching the emergency tube. Red-hot glassteel sparked against the blade. She tried not to look directly at the light and hoped the metal wasn't dripping on or spraying anyone below. She wished Shaine could tell her what the effects were on the other side.

The arc of her circle grew slowly.

She checked in as she worked. "Benton?"

"I read you, Rahn. Nominal atmosphere in the rescue tube. Temperature is minus two and coming up."

Morgan's heart pounded. Not warm enough. Not fast enough. "Shaine! Baby, talk to me!"

She got no reply and continued to guide the cutter as fast as she could. *Too slow. Too slow.* Were they already dead? Probably unconscious from cold or loss of oxygen. The thought of losing Shaine and Friday created a painful hole in her chest and made it hard to breathe.

Halfway around the circle her hands and her arms ached from pushing the cutter. She needed one of the larger construction blades that chewed through the metal like a bit. She fought for leverage, struggling to brace herself against the tubing.

Benton said, "I'm reading mostly CO2 and a little O2 coming up from the skyway."

Morgan pushed the cutter harder, willing it to move faster. She yelled again to Shaine, knowing she'd get no response.

With two centimeters of glassteel left to cut, she unhooked a length of cable from her waist. She clipped one end to a ladder rung and secured the magnetic contact to the center of the circle she'd nearly cut free. Then she shoved the laser through the last bit of glassteel.

The circle dropped free and swung away. Morgan clipped the cutter to her belt and panned the flashlight built into her helmet across the dark space below her.

"Send down med-evac! Now!"

She eased herself into the skyway with the winch-line attached to her suit, landing in her own personal version of hell. Everyone in the skyway lay or sat hunched over, silent and still, eyes closed. Frost dusted their bodies and their hair. Too late.

She hissed a string of curses, carefully treading between the bodies until she dropped to her knees beside Shaine. Heedless of the barely habitable atmosphere, she ripped off her gloves and unclipped the seals to remove her helmet. She gasped as the icy air hit her skin and burned her lungs. Pressing her fingers against Shaine's skin, she prayed for a pulse at her neck, leaning close to try to feel her breath.

Oh, Goddess, please, please.

Barely there, the faint throb of a pulse, a feathering of breath against her cheek. Alive. Barely. She laid a soft kiss on Shaine's bluish lips, then sat up on her knees. Where was Friday?

Three med-evac techs wearing bright yellow suits dropped cautiously out of the rescue tube. The lights on their helmets swung brilliant beams through the skyway as they guided collapsible gurneys through the opening.

The extra weight caused the skyway to shift sharply, the metal shrieking its implied threat. A wisp of heat warmed Morgan's face when she looked up.

She ran her fingers through Shaine's short red hair and took the self-heating blanket from one of the med-techs, tucking it around Shaine's body. She watched a medic fold blankets around Friday and her new girlfriend before strapping them into gurneys, which were immediately pulled up into the rescue tube. She was aware of the chatter coming through the speakers in the helmet at her side. So far, she hadn't heard anyone note any deaths as they moved among the injured, covering them with blankets and getting them ready to transport. She felt Shaine's breath against her cheek when she put her head down again. It gave her hope.

CHAPTER SIXTY-SIX

Earth Date: November 2453
Moon Base - Aldrin Hotel

Ari

Even after three days, I couldn't shake the chill from my bones. I pulled the thick comforter higher around me and Rhynn. We snuggled on the king-size sofa-sleeper in the living room of our suite in the Aldrin Hotel on Moon Base. Toni and Friday huddled in their own comforter beside us. Nori and Dia had taken up the recliners on the other side of the room. Between our body heat and the ambient room temperature turned up to tropical, it felt almost as good as being submerged in heated bio-gel in the trauma center at Luna City.

My memories of being trapped in the skyway remained vague. Numb from the cold and past the burning pain of frostbite, all I wanted was to sleep. My thoughts rambled aimlessly through images of my life. I remember feeling a resigned contentment knowing that at least I'd found Rhynn before the end. I had no memory of the rescue. None of us did. By the time they reached us, we were unconscious from hypothermia and lack of oxygen.

My first memory was waking in a clear, sealed, coffin-sized container, panicked and disoriented and submerged in heated bio-gel. I flailed weakly in the viscous, bluish-green-tinged fluid. It took several terrified moments before realizing I'd been fitted with a full-face breathing mask.

Reassuring voices penetrated my consciousness, sounding far away through the earplug speakers. Gloved arms reached into the container, calming me, guiding my hands from the mask, assuring me that I could breathe, and telling me to relax, heal, and sleep.

I spent a full day in the bio-gel to heal the frostbite and bring my body temperature to normal, and another two days in the hospital under observation. The whole band remained on enforced rest in the hotel in the Moon Base Dome. I wasn't complaining. I felt cold and stiff and generally crappy. The doctors said our bodies were working overtime repairing the cell and tissue damage from the cold and the oxygen deprivation we'd experienced.

There'd been a constant stream of people in and out of both the hospital and the hotel suite. Wayne and Nelda, several Out-System Authority officers and System Investigations Bureau Agents, our road crew, Del Marin, Morgan Rahn, Rhynn's mom, and a few of Rhynn's friends.

On the upside, I still had all my fingers and toes and ears. My ears and nose were currently smeared with healing cream. I'd lost my callouses to frostbite and damaged tissue, fingertips reddened and tender. Nori and Dia dealt with similar damage that would keep us all from playing our guitars until our digits were healed.

Poor Rhynn wore bio-gel mittens over her hands again. Because of her already injured palms and fingers, the frostbite had done more damage, and it would be a couple weeks before she'd be using her hands without mittens.

Wayne paced our hotel suite, wearing a path in the carpeting in front of the windows. His fingers flew on an oversized comp pad as he muttered incessantly under his breath. At one point he stopped short and said, "We can jump start the tour in five weeks, with a special on-demand performance at the Blue Moon, and then head back Earthside."

I bit my tongue on a rude reply. Touring was last on my priority list right now. I couldn't even think past the current day. And how in the hell were we supposed to play a full show when all our callouses were gone? It was going to take two months just to get back into decent playing form. Rhynn couldn't even hold a damn fork, let alone drumsticks.

Toni said, "Make it three months." She didn't open her eyes. Friday curled against her, only the very top of her curly blond head visible above the blankets covering them.

Wayne's brows shot up. "Three months? Rhynn should be able to play again in a couple weeks, right? That's what the doctors said."

Rhynn's voice was rough and weary. "No, Wayne. In two weeks I can ditch the gel-mitts. When I can actually play will depend on how my hands heal. It could be at least three months before I can play through a show. The tissue damage goes almost bone deep."

She closed her eyes with a pained sigh.

"I can't put the record label off forever."

"Don't be an ass," Dia snapped. She pulled her blanket closer and curled into a tighter ball on the recliner.

Cassandra Knight carried a tray of mugs filled with hot tea into the room. Her resemblance to Rhynn still made me do a double-take. They had the same intense eyes, and currently aimed identical expressions of annoyance at Wayne.

"Mr. Neutron, I think making plans at this juncture seems rather premature, given all these young women have been through. I'm sure you can make the record company understand." Cassandra set a mug near each of us. Rhynn's mug had a straw.

Wayne was nothing if not persistent. "We can find someone to sub for Rhynn while she heals."

Anger coursed through me. "Absolutely not."

Nori said, "Fuck that."

"Just get us the three months," Toni growled. "Then you can work us to the bone."

From the breakfast bar between the kitchenette and the living room, Nelda looked over her shoulder. "I'm sure we can convince the label it's in the band's best interest to be well healed before they go back on tour." She lifted a hand to press a lock of hair into place behind her ear.

Wayne glowered. "They're going to bitch about the cost of rescheduling."

"Of course they will. And you and I will simply have to bitch back."

"This is coming out of your monthly income," Wayne growled at us.

"Seriously?" Nori untangled herself from her blanket to reach for her mug. She turned a grateful gaze toward Cassandra. "Thanks, Mama Knight."

"You're welcome, dear." Cassandra shot Wayne a glare. "And if you girls ever find yourself short of funds, you let me know. I've got money stashed away for emergencies."

I looked to see if Cassandra was joking. She locked eyes with me. "You're all my daughters now," she announced, as though it was the most obvious thing in the world.

Rhynn mumbled, "Don't argue with her. Pointless."

Warm comfort suffused my chilled body.

Toni said, "Thanks, Cassandra. You're good people. Seriously. It's sweet you're here taking care of a bunch of women who should be able to take care of ourselves."

"You're more than welcome. Besides, it's nice to be a mom once in a while."

Nelda stood, snatching up her comp pad. "Come on, Wayne. Let's go find something to eat."

Wayne stopped his pacing and stared blankly at her, as though it never occurred to him to either eat or leave us alone. Then he followed her out of the room.

Watching the door close behind them, I thought, Shaine's guys will talk to them in the hallway. Then I remembered we were no longer under security protection. J'Nell was in lockup. The bombing alone was going to put her away for life. From the law's point of view, the stalking was secondary and minor.

We hadn't gotten much out of the OAI or the SIB agents on the case, but the net news said J'Nell had learned a lot of her bomb-making skills from her father when she was younger, apparently to help her with a terrorism story she was working on. He'd shown her how to make bombs as an example of what could be done with basic tools. He was quick to protest that it was innocent and that he'd never imagined that a decade later she'd actually use that knowledge to harm anyone. It didn't surprise me that she'd fooled him too.

It was a relief to know J'Nell was safely locked away, though I knew it would be a long time before I didn't constantly look over my shoulder, or feel uncomfortable in a crowd, or not feel a wave of fear every time the mail came.

Rhynn shifted to rest her head against my shoulder and I smiled reflexively. Just knowing Rhynn was at my side gave me the courage to plunge ahead with my life.

CHAPTER SIXTY-SEVEN

Earth Date: May 2454
Nor-Am Continent, Central Los Angeles Megalopolis

Rhynn

Rhynn floated on her back in the swimming pool with her arms wrapped around a flexible float tube. Music blared through the open patio doors. Nori, Dia, Toni, and Friday lay on lounges in the shade on the patio. Just another day in the SCE band house.

She sucked in the thick, humid air that tasted like smog and chlorine. She still wasn't sure if the sensation was better or worse than the flat, metallic-tasting air on Moon Base. But the cool water lapping her naked body was the most sensual thing she'd ever experienced. Ari swam beside her, and she openly appreciated the whole of her lover's lithe, muscled form.

Warmth flushed Rhynn's skin, knowing what Ari's body felt like under her hands. Ari caught Rhynn ogling her and smirked before she ducked underwater. Rhynn appreciated the glimpse of Ari's bare ass. Ari's hair brushed tantalizingly against Rhynn's back as she swam beneath her. Smooth skin and heat displaced the cool water as Ari slithered her arms around Rhynn's shoulders and wrapped her legs around Rhynn's waist. She placed a light kiss on her neck.

Rhynn wanted to hold Ari, but knew if she did, she'd sink, so she clung to her float and turned her head to lick droplets of water from the tip of Ari's nose.

Ari grinned. "I think I like you trapped in the water like this."

Rhynn was dizzy with joy. "I like being trapped by you."

Ari laughed. "I am so glad you're here with me."

"Me too. I've never been so happy."

"Me either." Ari kissed her again and leaned back, her expression more serious, her eyes distant. Emotions played across Ari's face, a mix of dark and thoughtful shadows behind her eyes.

"What's wrong?"

"Not a thing, babe. Not a thing. Was thinking back to when this all started with a bouquet of bloody roses. Never thought it would end this well."

Rhynn released the float with one hand and caressed the soft curve of Ari's cheek. "Never in my wildest dreams could I have imagined this. Love you, Ari."

"Love you too, Rhynn."

Bella Books, Inc.

Women. Books. Even Better Together.

P.O. Box 10543
Tallahassee, FL 32302

Phone: 800-729-4992
www.bellabooks.com